LIE WITH ME

TAYLOR HOLLOWAY

TAYLOR HOLLOWAY
ROMANCE

I couldn't resist Lucas.
One sidelong glance, one sexy smirk and I was his. But
before I even knew what was happening, I was in way
over my head...

My perfect new relationship isn't what it seems.
It's a big, elaborate, insane lie we're selling to his friends.
A quid pro quo designed to get us both what we want.
All we have to do is pretend.

So why does my heart hurt every time I look at Lucas?
Why does my pulse pound when we touch?
Why can't I go a single night without dreaming about him?

Sometimes when he looks at me, I think he knows I'm
falling.
Sometimes I think he feels the same.
I worry that he can see straight through me almost as badly
as I hope he does.

Pretending that Lucas is mine isn't hard. Remembering that
he isn't will be.

Lie with Me is a fake-relationship romance featuring a bold alpha hero who's about to meet his match in a feisty, smart-mouthed heroine. It can be read as a standalone or as part of a series.

1

RAE

"I don't feel so good."

Cliff didn't look good, either. In fact, he looked awful. My boss's round face was always ruddy, but right now he was puffy, beet red, and his ordinarily beady eyes were bulging out of his swollen eye sockets. Throughout the short drive downtown from the Austin airport, he'd only been getting puffier, itchier, redder, and grumpier. I was starting to get genuinely worried about him.

"I think you're having an allergic reaction to that bee sting," Annie said from the backseat. This was the third time she'd said it, and I was fairly sure she was right.

Cliff dug his thick fingers beneath his collar, scratching at the hives that were spreading over every inch of visible skin. He loosened the tie that had grown too tight around his neck and groaned.

"I wonder if I might be having an allergic reaction," he

mumbled as if he'd just had some kind of spontaneous insight. "What kind of rental car company lets their cars be infested with fucking bees?"

Infested was probably a stretch. There was a bee. One. It probably flew in the open window looking for a sugary taste of Cliff's soda. Cliff just happened to be unlucky enough to swallow it—or attempt to swallow it—and then spit the front half of the bee out, getting stung on the inside of his mouth in the process.

Cliff wiggled in his seat uncomfortably. "Rae, do you think you could drive any slower? I swear, this is why I usually don't let you *girls* drive. You drive like my grandma. And she's been dead for just about thirty years."

I made eye contact with Annie through the rearview mirror. Her expression was more uncertain than offended by Cliff's blatant, casual misogyny. For once, I was willing to excuse it, too. Although the joke in the office among my female coworkers was that Cliff was so named because his mother took one look at him when he was born and wanted to jump off one, I'd never seen him like this. He was often obnoxious, sexist, and generally dismissive of women's ideas, but not usually *totally unreasonable when we were obviously right.*

"I think we should get you to an emergency room just to rule out anything serious," I said, attempting a reasonable tone.

Cliff harrumphed. "Don't be hysterical, Rae," he

snapped at me. "I'll be fine in a second. We can't be late to this meeting."

Hysterical? You ate a damn bee!

"Cliff—" I tried again, but he cut me off with a rude noise.

"Hush! Now why is it so hot in here? You *girls* always want it to be so damn hot."

Annie and I exchanged another glance through the mirror. Somehow everything was always our fault. Soon he'd probably be blaming us for the bee.

"I'm not hot, Cliff," Kyle volunteered from the backseat. The poor guy always tried to be decent, despite being naturally more of a quiet person. His kindness earned him a glare from Cliff.

Kyle wasn't hot because the car wasn't hot. If anything, it was cooler than comfortable. Cliff cranked up the air conditioner anyway. He was sweating profusely, and he'd begun wheezing a bit with every breath.

I was driving us to a preliminary meeting with a new target company. Usually I didn't get to drive, and we were all subjected to Cliff's hatred of safety norms, but today just kept getting weirder. Not only were we in Austin, a town I'd just moved from a few months before, but now the engagement was already spiraling off track. We all needed to get back on track.

This was a crucial meeting, and the first of many in which we would try to convince our target that he wanted to sell his business to us after letting us investigate every square inch of it. Since I was the second most senior person here, Kyle and Annie, the technical members of our evaluation team, were looking to me to do something about Cliff. Annie was painfully shy, and Kyle had just joined our team six weeks ago; if something was going to get done, it was up to me to do it.

In the handful of months that I'd been working for the Azure Group, I'd never led an onsite acquisition team before. I'd worked my way up to second in command in record time, however, and I was well aware that my only chance of moving up further was by replacing Cliff or someone like him. As hard as Cliff was to work with, I had no desire to take his place because *he'd died from a simple bee sting*. Still, I sensed that a battlefield promotion might be near.

And that wasn't the only thing near. "We're here," I told the group. I shifted the car to park in front of The Lone Star Lounge and turned to Cliff. "You need to go to the emergency room," I ordered him. "You're not well. You can't meet with the client like this."

Cliff, who was fighting a coughing spell, shook his head furiously. His mouth framed an obvious "no," but no sound escaped, even after his coughing sputtered to an end. When he finally did manage to make a noise, it was a small panicked wheeze. He clutched at his throat in a panic.

Shit.

I'd seen *My Girl*. I knew how this ended. Not willing to waste another second, I threw my door open and prepared to sprint across the parking lot. It was dumb luck we were scheduled to meet our client at a bar I was familiar with— my old roommate, Emma, was engaged to the owner. I was about to impose on her hospitality in a fairly big way.

God dammit, Cliff. Don't you fucking die at my friend's bar, you pompous, chauvinistic pig. Not before you recommend me for a promotion.

"Kyle, call 911!" I shouted over my shoulder. "Annie, get his jacket and tie off."

"On it," came the in-unison reply.

I'd run track in high school. Even in the three-inch heels and pencil skirt I was wearing, I was fast. I dashed across the asphalt, garnering stares from other patrons who were making their way to happy hour. I threw open the door to the bar and marched into the middle of the room.

"Does anyone have an EpiPen? There's a man in the parking lot going into anaphylactic shock. He was stung by a bee. It's an emergency."

I wasn't using my inside voice, and when I want to be loud, *I am LOUD*. It comes from being a born New Yorker, telling off catcallers in a big city, and working in a heavily male-dominated business. I was no shy, retiring flower at the best of times. When I needed to be scary and pushy, I could be terrifying. As expected, the room fell instantly silent. People stared at me like I'd just announced the rapture.

Lucas Stevenson was somewhere in this bar, but I couldn't spare more than a passing thought about this possibly being our first interaction. The tech wunderkind had created what was probably another brilliant innovation, one that the Azure Group desperately wanted to acquire. I would focus on that later. Right now, my annoying boss was potentially going to die if I didn't make a scene. So, I would make a scene.

"Please! Anyone! I need an EpiPen right now! Please!" I repeated. I stared around me at the faces of strangers, entreating them to listen. In New York, people are good at ignoring strangers, but when there's a crisis, a real emergency, strangers will help. I prayed it would be the same here in Austin, Texas.

"I have one." My friend Emma, an extremely petite blonde, was thankfully behind the bar tonight. She extended the slim injector to me.

My breath slid out in a relieved rush and I flew over to grasp it. "Thank you," I managed. "Thank you so much." I looked at the device in confusion. I'd just realized that I didn't know how to administer it. Emma was already rounding the bar.

"I can show you how to use it, if you need me to," she was saying. "Did you call 911?"

I nodded. "Yes, and yes. Follow me."

Thank God for Emma.

We ran back outside to where Kyle and Annie were desperately trying to assist Cliff. My trip back to the Four Runner was a lot slower than my trip from it. My tiny blonde friend had very short legs by comparison.

"I'm sorry for showing up like this," I told her as we ran. "Thanks for your help. Seriously."

"No problem, Rae," she panted, "It's great to see you." She shook her head at me. "Although when you texted me and Kate that you were going to be in town for a few days, I didn't expect it to be so, um, exciting."

Despite the circumstances, I felt myself smiling. "Me either. My job isn't usually this crazy, I swear."

"Okay, so what do I do?" I asked when we got near to Cliff. He was still in the passenger seat, clutching at his throat and obviously struggling to get enough air. His reddish color had turned a deep, ugly purple. He was still making noises though; that had to be a good sign.

"Pull off the blue cap and then hold the orange end against his thigh," Emma explained as I unwrapped the injector. She was shaking slightly, and her voice was tremulous, but I tried to ignore it. Emma knew what she was doing. She had a PhD. "Keep the injector there until it clicks and then count to five."

"I'm going to inject you with this," I told Cliff, in a loud, clear voice. I shook the EpiPen in front of his purple, swollen face. "Your airway is closing up. We have to stop your reaction from getting worse."

He shook his head furiously as soon as I said the word 'inject.' What a baby. Did he want to suffocate? Too bad. He wasn't allowed to die.

"This is happening," I told him. "Don't test me."

Cliff tried to bat my hand away when I did as Emma

directed, but Kyle and Annie helped me hold him still. The click of the needle was tiny, but I felt it. Cliff definitely felt it. He made a noise somewhere between a whine and a moan, jerked a bit, and then glared at me like I'd just poisoned him. Then, as I removed the needle from his skin, he started to shake violently. I blanched.

"What's he doing?" I squeaked.

"That's normal," Emma said when my gaze snapped to her delicate features. She looked nervous. "It's good, actually. It means the medicine got in him. He'll shake for a while, and may feel frightened, cold, or paranoid. But he won't die, and he'll be able to breathe better soon." She paused. "I've, um, I've never done this before, but that's what the instructions said." Her expression was sheepish.

I'm glad she didn't tell me this was her first time before I injected him.

All four of us stared at Cliff anxiously while he shook like a leaf. He shook and jerked, but just like she said, he *was* starting to breathe more normally. He took deep, grateful gulps of air. His plum color began lightening into a healthier, but still unnatural pink. He wasn't able to speak, but over the next ten minutes he became increasingly responsive, though he was also clearly confused and dizzy.

"I—I just don't know how to thank you," I stuttered at Emma, and she patted my arm comfortingly with her little hand. I jumped at the contact, which served to remind me how long it had been since anyone had touched me. I found myself appreciating her contact more than I probably should. I managed a small smile and she returned it.

"Welcome back to Austin," Emma told me. I laughed weakly at her. Whether she knew it or not, my ex-roommate, Emma, was my angel this afternoon. I could not imagine what I would have done without her help. I wasn't sure how long Cliff would have been able to wait for help.

I relaxed a little bit at her words, and then relaxed a lot more when the high, familiar squeal of an ambulance began to grow closer. The white and red vehicle peeled into view around the corner with the squeal of brakes, bringing with it flashing lights, lots of questions, and professional help. The next hour was a bizarre, dizzy whirlwind.

"No, no. You stop that," the paramedic, Vanessa, told Cliff when he tried to rip the IV out of his arm. Both her tone and the way she grabbed his hand and held it was just like one would do with a kid, not a fifty-something-year-old who just acted like a child. "Be still now," she chided. He continued to mumble something, and she pushed a syringe into his tube and depressed the plunger. "There you go," she told him. "That'll help you relax."

A moment later, Cliff nodded incoherently, and his eyes slipped closed.

"Is he going to be okay?" Kyle asked for all three of us.

Vanessa and her hunky partner, Sam, exchanged a glance at one another. Then they both shrugged.

"He needs to be seen by a doctor," Vanessa said after a moment. She'd clearly been trained to dispense the minimum amount of information necessary. I knew she couldn't make us any promises. "He's stable now and that's what's most important. We do need to take him to a hospital though. I know they will want to run some tests on him."

The two of them had instantly taken over when they arrived. I'd never been so glad to suddenly *not be in charge*. The truth is, I had no idea how to treat Cliff. Other than the EpiPen, I knew next to nothing about allergies, especially the dangerous, life-threatening kind. Vanessa and Sam clearly saw it every day. They knew exactly what to do, and, even more impressively, they knew how to comfort and contain us at the same time.

"One of you is welcome to ride with us," Sam offered as they finished getting Cliff ready to transport. "But only one. For insurance reasons."

"I'll do it!" Annie volunteered instantly. She was looking at his impressive biceps and big green eyes longingly. There was no denying that the paramedic was easy on the eyes. Unfortunately for Annie, I was pretty sure that Vanessa and Sam were partners in more ways than one. I usually have pretty good instincts for knowing when a man is taken. The way Vanessa eyed buxom Annie with thinly veiled suspicion told me it was true.

"Kyle, you follow the ambulance. I'll go meet with Stevenson and explain things," I told him. "I'll meet up with you later."

I expected Kyle to argue, but he didn't. "Okay." He seemed really shaken by the entire experience and kept looking around at everything with worried eyes. He usually spent his time poring over financial records, so this was way out of his wheelhouse. I patted his arm comfortingly. Vanessa and Sam loaded Cliff's gurney into the back of the ambulance, and Kyle slid into the driver's seat of the rental SUV to follow.

"See you soon," he said. "I'll call you if anything important happens."

I nodded.

"Thank you so much!" I cried to the ambulance, waving goodbye to the paramedics and letting them take my entire team away. Vanessa gave me a thumbs-up through the open driver's side window. She had confirmed that we'd done the right thing injecting Cliff with the EpiPen, possibly even saving his life. Getting an airway open during an allergic reaction apparently becomes exponentially harder the longer you wait. Even Cliff, although he was in and out of consciousness and whose tongue was several times larger than normal, admitted that he appreciated what I'd done. Annie and Kyle called me a hero.

I didn't feel like much of a hero. I felt utterly exhausted and drained. More than anything, I felt like I'd just been in a fistfight. I slumped down on the curb and put my head against my knees, thoroughly depleted of energy. Now I had to meet with our client alone, and there was nothing that I wanted to do less. Meeting with Lucas Stevenson in my current rumpled state was not ideal, and I was already horribly late. I figured taking a moment to collect myself while sitting on the curb was allowable. I wondered if I could slip inside and make it into the bathroom to touch up my makeup first. It had been hours since I looked in a mirror, but I had a feeling my hair was doing bad things atop my head. It had been in a sleek bun, but that was hours ago.

My phone beeped in my purse, and I checked it wearily. There were a number of things waiting on my attention. Fourteen new emails, dozens of texts and, interestingly, the app belonging to our client. The app that we were here to acquire. It chirped that it had a notification for me.

Curious, I pressed a button and the minimalistic interface of Notable Match popped up. I'd installed it on my phone during the flight from New York, but I hadn't had a chance to really mess around with it yet. The new notification had come in about the time we arrived at the bar, but I was just now seeing it.

You have a new match, the app informed me in cartoonish text. *Lucas Stevenson is within two hundred feet of you.* A man's face, square jawed, hazel-eyed and devastatingly handsome, blinked on my screen. The man in the photo looked a lot more like a model than a tech guru. *That's Lucas Stevenson?* I doubted it. He probably used a fake photo. A small heart icon spun, grew and exploded into dozens of smaller hearts.

His app had matched us as a couple? I was still staring at my phone while sitting on a curb, dumbfounded, when someone cleared their throat behind me. I twisted around, looking up and into the face of Lucas Stevenson. He looked just like his picture. I closed the app as quickly as I could, but I could tell he'd already seen it.

"Can I buy you a drink?" he asked with a smile.

2

RAE

"So, is Cliff going to be okay?" Lucas asked me a few minutes later. We'd snagged a table out on the patio of the Lone Star Lounge, and I'd been explaining why our meeting was an hour late.

"I think so," I told him, sipping at the beer he'd recommended. It was a Hefeweizen from a local brewery—Live Oak. I liked it. I liked it even more with the orange slice he'd insisted I add. "I apologize. This isn't at all how our initial client meetings usually go. I can't even show you the PowerPoint, since my coworkers took the rental and all my stuff to the hospital."

I could already tell that this meeting wasn't going to get more normal, either. He wasn't a normal client. About the only similarity between Lucas and our average client was the thick-rimmed glasses he wore. He was young, at least thirty years younger than usual—possibly only a handful of years older than me. He was also wearing a Metallica T-shirt and beat-up jeans rather than a suit. Lucas was well built, too, broad shouldered and with defined muscles visible beneath his clothes. Most of our clients were potbellied, middle aged CEO's. Honestly, I had to do my best not to stare. The man was gorgeous.

"Well, I would hope not," he laughed, drawing me back from ogling him. It was a good-natured, pleasant laugh that made the corners of my mouth turn up. "I'm glad your boss is gonna' be okay. I'll take a rain check on the PowerPoint." His sandy brown hair was tousled in a way that was either totally unintentionally sexy or carefully coiffed to look unintentionally sexy. Either way, I wanted to touch him. It. I wanted to touch it.

Get it together, I told myself firmly. *You're in a business meeting, not on a date.*

"So," Lucas continued, "tell me about yourself, Rae."

I blinked at him. *Me?* No. That couldn't be what he meant. He meant the firm.

I launched into the canned answer: "The Azure Group was established in 1996 at the beginning of the tech boom. Our portfolio is in excess of sixty billion dollars and we specialize in acquiring the best in emerging software. We've got a full service—"

"Management and consultancy team, as well as an in-house evaluation and due diligence operation," Lucas interrupted with a smirk. *He knew my pitch as well as I did.* "I read all about the Azure Group before accepting this meeting," he admitted. Clearly, he had a photographic memory, too. The consensus in the office was that he was a genius, and I had a feeling that I was about to find out if it was true. "Of course, I'm familiar with your firm. *I was asking about you, Rae.*"

My lips parted in surprise. "I'm part of the evaluation team. I help investigate new prospective portfolio companies, like yours."

Lucas smirked at me and arched an eyebrow. "And?"

I fought the urge to shift uncomfortably in my seat. Why did this feel like a date? "And I work with a technical and financial subject matter team to determine whether we should make an offer to acquire those companies."

If Lucas already knew all about the Azure Group, he probably already knew all about the team that had been sent to meet with him. Actually, I was certain that he did. I wrote him an email myself explaining about each of us, although Cliff had been the one to attach his name and send it. He loved to take credit for another's work. He called it 'delegating.'

"What about you, Rae? I want to know about you." His hazel eyes were an incredible color, green on the inside near the pupil, and golden brown on the outside. I couldn't help staring deeply into them.

"Me?" I was feeling very out of my depth. I thought I was ready to conduct one of these meetings by myself. I'd seen Cliff do it dozens of times. But none of those meetings had been anything like this. I took another nervous sip of my beer. "Okay. What do you want to know?"

"Where are you from?"

"Um, I'm from Flushings." Then I remembered we were in Texas, and that Lucas probably didn't know where that was. "It's a neighborhood in Queens. I've lived in New York my whole life, except for the two years I worked on my MBA here in Austin. How about you?" It seemed only fair to turn the tables on him. After all, he was asking me personal questions.

He smiled. "I'm from the west coast. I was born in LA and moved to Texas for school and just... stayed. I like it here. So, how'd you get into the private equity business?"

That was easy enough. "I went to NYU and double majored in business and economics. I worked at a hedge fund for a year after college and the pay was good, but I hated every second of it. So, when a former classmate of mine told me about an opening at Azure Group, I jumped. I've been portfolio building ever since."

"Do you like working for Azure Group?"

What sort of a question was that? That wasn't what this meeting was about. And how could I answer it honestly while still being professional? I tried. "I enjoy puzzles. Deciding whether to acquire a company and pricing our offer fairly and appropriately requires a lot of the same skills that I enjoy."

"That's not an answer. If I say that I like water, and then say that sharks also like water, that doesn't mean I also like sharks." His tone was challenging. My heart fluttered. I loved a good challenge.

"Cum hoc ergo propter hoc," I answered. I took logic in college too. In Latin, the fallacy translated to 'with this, therefore because of this.' It was also known as the correlation-causation fallacy.

His incredible hazel eyes widened, as did his smile. He was clever. Probably much cleverer than me. "So, you don't like it?" His question was teasing.

"Assuming that conclusion would be a logical fallacy, too," I told him, still feeling like I was being evaluated.

"That's a fair point. Post hoc ergo propter hoc." Lucas grinned. I'd clearly just won a point. The Latin translated to 'after this, therefore because of this,' and it was also called the questionable cause fallacy. "Do you like your job, Rae?"

What I really enjoyed most about my job, and what was still incredibly rare, were conversations like this one. Times when I was able to match wits against someone who was my equal or better. I lived for negotiations and the chance to be challenged. But I didn't say that to Lucas. It would reveal too much.

"I like a lot of things about my job," I told Lucas, deciding to be halfway honest. He was quick to display his intellectual ability, but he was a genius. I could hardly blame him for acting like one. "I like the challenge and the pace. I like learning about companies and distilling what makes them profitable. I like making the argument for or against their acquisition. And then, once I've learned everything I can, I like moving on to the next one. Obviously, there are some things that I dislike about my job, too. But on the whole, I can't complain."

That answer didn't seem to satisfy him. "Why do I get the feeling you're only telling me the positives?"

I smirked. "Because you're a client, of course."

"And if I wasn't?"

I didn't know what he was getting at, but if he had reservations about the company, I could maybe do something about that.

"If you weren't a client, I'd tell you that Azure Group is a gigantic faceless corporation that has more yearly profit than some countries have GDP. Employees like me are cogs in wheels within wheels. Our lives don't matter much to the machine's operation. It can be hard to work for a big bureaucracy sometimes, especially if you're like me." I shrugged.

"What do you mean, like you?" He seemed genuinely interested.

I shook my head. This was getting too personal. How could I tell him I was dissatisfied with my new job but too afraid to ever complain? That wasn't professional.

He was looking at me carefully, as if weighing two alternatives. We sat in silence for a moment.

"I have a proposition for you, Rae."

"Isn't that my line? And a bit premature?" I arched an eyebrow at him for a change. We were nowhere near the negotiation phase of this process. There were weeks of investigation and due diligence that needed to happen first. I wasn't authorized to make an offer, and I definitely wasn't authorized to accept one.

"It's a proposition for you, Rae. *Personally*. Not for the Azure Group. I find myself far less interested in them than I am in you."

My lips parted in surprise. This conversation was wildly out of control. Still, I couldn't help but wonder where it would go. This was fun. "What's your proposition?"

"Are you single?" His hazel eyes were bright.

I blinked at him. "What... um, I mean yes, I am. Single, that is." I felt another hot blush on my cheeks.

He likes me? He must like me!

"I want you to pretend to be my girlfriend."

Oh.

3

RAE

"Excuse me?" I must have misheard him. I set down my beer and stared at it slack-jawed, worried that I'd somehow gotten myself incredibly drunk from just a half pint of beer. What was in this glass?

"I want you to pretend to be my girlfriend," Lucas repeated. His gaze was direct, and when I met his eyes, I felt a blush heating my cheeks. I hardly ever blushed. Now, it felt like my body was betraying me. His smile widened when he saw it.

"Why?"

He was no longer looking directly at me. Instead, he was staring at the table between us. "It's a complicated thing to explain." All of a sudden, he sounded a million miles away, although he was as confident as ever. "The why is unimportant."

"Not to me. I have faith in your rhetorical skills. Why

don't you try to explain?" My voice was dry. If he was going to make such a wildly inappropriate request, he had better be willing to explain it. Private equity deal or no, I don't let business associates treat me like a piece of ass, although men had tried before. *I'm not in that kind of business.*

Lucas took a very long time to reply. "I've got a hunch about you, Rae. I might be wrong, and if I am, I apologize, but I think you're an ambitious, talented, intelligent person who is frustrated by where you are right now in your career. I think I know a way for you to get the edge you want, and it involves pretending to be my girlfriend."

He could see all that about me just from our conversation?

"That wasn't the question I asked," I stuttered.

Lucas smiled at me, just a quick flash of white teeth that faded a second later. It was a totally humorless smile. "Right again." His voice was unexpectedly sad. Wherever he'd gone emotionally, it was dark there. The light had gone out of his hazel eyes, and somehow it tugged at my heartstrings despite the weirdness of the situation.

"I should get up and walk out of here right now." I said it as much to myself as to him. But it was true. He'd just overstepped the boundary of a professional relationship in a fairly mammoth way.

"Why haven't you?" He seemed genuinely interested. He took a sip of his drink afterward and regarded me over the rim.

You want him, my traitorous libido suggested, *and you're excited that he just made you an indecent proposal.* I ignored it.

"I don't know," I admitted. "Maybe it's curiosity? It might be pity."

Lucas grimaced and looked like he wanted to spit out his mouthful of beer. He swallowed hard before answering. *"Don't stay here and listen to me out of pity. Anything but that. Stay here out of curiosity, or ambition, or even anger. But not pity. I don't want your pity."*

I smirked. "Well, that's just too bad for you, because you have it. If there's something in this for me, you're going to need to get to the point. Because if I can't pity you for seriously suggesting something as ridiculous as me—a perfect stranger—pretending to be your girlfriend, I'm running out of curiosity very quickly. You don't get to say something like that and then not explain it."

My anger seemed to encourage him or at least snap him out of his funk. "Fair enough," he said. "Then let me try to explain it. I've got a situation of my own that would benefit from me having the appearance of a serious girlfriend. You've got a situation of your own that would benefit from cinching this deal on your own. I'm willing to trade my app or, rather, the agreement that I will sell the app to the Azure Group at a favorable price in exchange for your companionship. We will both end up getting what we want."

"I'm not a call girl. I don't sell my *companionship*. Not ever." This was non-negotiable. I squared my shoulders and stared down my nose at him.

His eyes got huge. "I wasn't suggesting that. I swear."

Then he smirked at me with an easy confidence. "You're a very attractive woman, Rae, but look at me. I've never needed to purchase that sort of female companionship. I'm not about to start now."

He was extraordinarily handsome, ridiculously smart, and phenomenally successful. And he clearly knew it. I decided to accept his answer. If he made half an effort, he could probably get any woman in this bar to go home with him tonight. Including me.

"Alright, then what were you suggesting?" My next question was softer and less angry.

"That I will guarantee to you that I'll sell Notable Match at ten percent below whatever we determine is fair market value in exchange for you pretending to be my girlfriend."

"I'm *not* going to sleep with you." It needed repeating. It just did.

"I know. Again, I swear I wasn't asking that." He spread his hands wide. I believed him. I nodded.

"Why do you want me to do this? Why me?"

Lucas's smile was smoldering, and his words were slow. "You're my type. People will believe that we're a real couple. People I need to convince."

I felt hot and squirmed in my seat. I was his type? What did that mean? Curiosity was driving me crazy. Thankfully, he decided to explain.

"Notable Match put us together, and I've got faith in my

creation. Besides, you look and behave very much like the type of woman I date."

That almost made it worse. "You exclusively date tall, twenty-seven-year-old strawberry blondes from New York who work in high-powered corporate jobs and like to argue?"

He smirked again. "Something like that, yeah."

"And you want me to *pretend* to date you."

"Yes." Behind his glasses, his gaze was incredibly direct. "That's what I want."

"I can think of only two reasons you would do something like this, and neither of them are particularly flattering." In my mind, he was either trying to win back the love of his life or too ashamed to admit he was gay and needed a beard.

"As long as it won't get in the way of our arrangement, I won't hold your opinion of me against you." His response was dry. Was he always so sarcastic?

I chewed on my lip for a second. "If you're gay or something, you should just tell people. I won't knowingly help you live a lie." Lucas' eyes went wide, and I continued in a rush. Was I onto something? "My brother's trans, and he's my best friend. If he knew I did something that tacitly supported the idea that people should have to hide who they are and who they love, he'd be furious with me. And I'd be furious with myself. There are plenty of valid reasons that some people can't or won't come out, but I don't have to help contribute to the lies." I felt a bit embarrassed when I fell silent. I felt very strongly about this, and it showed.

Lucas was quiet for a second. "It's not that. Really. I'm sure you probably don't trust me, but I hope you can give me the benefit of the doubt and believe that I wouldn't ask you to violate any deeply held principles. Especially ones I share. I'm not hiding anything about my sexuality. That isn't what this is about." We exchanged a long look. Eventually, I nodded.

"Okay. Then the only answer is that you're majorly hung up on an ex-girlfriend. Are you trying to win someone back through jealousy?" I asked it rudely, and it was a guess, but it was really the only possible reason that a man like Lucas would do something so ridiculous.

He went stiller-than-still. *Bingo*. Lucas had an ex that he wanted back.

"I'm not a great liar," I told him. "I don't like lying as a general rule, so I've never really practiced it enough to get good."

He smiled. "That's okay. I'm just asking you to pretend that you like me for a few weeks. Hopefully, you don't find me too horrible to make that act convincing." Lucas looked at me like *he knew I was attracted to him*. I swallowed hard. I must be such a terrible liar that I'd already made my crush crystal clear.

Lucas' smile widened when I didn't immediately reply, and I frowned at him. I needed to get my feelings on lockdown. That kind of arrogant smugness made Lucas simultaneously more and less attractive to me. I hated that he thought I was so easy to read and manipulate.

"I'll have to brush up on my acting skills," I told him with as much of a poker face as I could muster. His smile faltered after a moment. Good. There was no reason I needed to broadcast everything.

"I'm not asking you to make up your mind about this right now," Lucas told me, changing the subject. He clearly didn't want to talk about feelings, either—neither mine nor his nor his ex's, whoever she was. I pushed thoughts of her to the side. She was really irrelevant. Lucas' plan was probably doomed to fail, but I could still get what I wanted: my promotion.

"I'm in." The words were out of my mouth in an instant. This was too good an opportunity to pass up. "I'll do it."

He sat up abruptly. "What? You will?"

"Yes," I told him with a smile. My mind was already running through the terms of the arrangement. This was a business deal like any other. And I may not be a genius, but I knew how to make a good deal, and I knew an opportunity when I saw one. "But first I think there are several details we need to work out."

4

LUCAS

RAE—MICHELLE Rachel Lewis—according to her LinkedIn and Facebook, had thrown me totally off my guard. She pushed her shiny hair behind her shoulders and pursed her ruby-red lips at me. Her blue eyes sparkled mischievously beneath long, long eyelashes.

"Details?" I echoed. I still couldn't believe she'd said yes.

"Yes, the terms of our agreement to, um, date," she said, pulling out a pad of paper from her purse and staring at me across the patio table like it was her own personal boardroom. "I think we need to work them out immediately, don't you? Transparency of expectations is essential to any good deal." Her subtle New York accent was unexpectedly exotic. I'd never found it to be a sexy accent before, but she made it that way.

"Alright." If I kept my answers to a minimum, maybe

she wouldn't realize how utterly out of my depth I suddenly was. I hadn't thoroughly thought any of this through yet. I was being impulsive when I made the proposition and had fully expected her to tell me to fuck off and die.

The truth was that Rae made me feel weirdly tongue-tied, and that wasn't something I could remember ever dealing with before. She was phenomenally attractive, with a perfect, hourglass shaped body, long limbs, and a delicately beautiful, lightly freckled face. But it wasn't just the way she looked that had me distracted. She was quick and witty and clearly a strategic thinker. And now, she was about to be my fake girlfriend. If I could make it through this negotiation, that is.

"How long are we talking about for this whole fake girlfriend thing?" she asked, scribbling nonstop on her notepad.

Good question. "Until the deal closes, if absolutely necessary. Hopefully not that long." I was flying by the seat of my pants here, so I made my voice sound as confident as possible. I smiled at her like I had everything figured out. Maybe she bought it. It was hard to tell.

"We've already established that I won't be providing any of the physical girlfriend stuff, like sex, but I also want to make it clear that I won't be doing your laundry, cooking, or even living with you or giving the appearance of living with you. I have my own life and will only be in town as needed before the closing. You already know the schedule of when I'll be here. I'll also be in town to attend a friend's wedding soon, and I can give you the dates."

"I understand." I felt myself smiling. Laundry? Good Lord, I would never ask this beautiful, brilliant creature to do my laundry. Also, she'd probably demand my soul as payment if I did. I had a bad feeling I'd just entered into a negotiation that I was in no way prepared to have.

"What expectations do you have of me as your fake girlfriend?"

I took a sip of my drink before answering to buy myself some time.

"I feel like it would be better to keep the agreement open ended and not enclosed by a set of defined objectives and activities, but I recognize that wouldn't give you enough of an idea of what I'm wanting. I would want you to help me create a believable record of our 'relationship' on social media, accompany me to social events when your schedule allows, and otherwise pretend to be in a relationship with me when you're in town and not working."

"I don't want my coworkers to know about any of this."

"Of course not."

"And I would expect that you would keep the truth about this arrangement to yourself as well."

"That's fine."

"I'm okay with the rest of what you suggested, but I'm not going to make out with you in public or anything like that."

A vivid, adolescent fantasy of kissing Rae, crushing her

curves against me and teasing her mouth until she was breathless shot through me. The thought was made all the more visceral by the fact that she was staring at me, pouting those lips in my direction. Blood rushed below my belt, making me glad we were sitting down. It had been so long since I'd felt this sort of sexual attraction to anyone that I was surprised by it.

This isn't about Rae, I informed my suddenly reawakened body. *This is about getting Victoria back.* My cock disagreed, and I tried to ignore it.

"I'm not asking you to do anything beyond your comfort zone, but we will need to be... convincing. Some posed pictures should do the trick. And I might need you to dance with me."

"Dance with you?" She looked suddenly nervous. I seized on the shift in her mood. The power imbalance slid my way again.

"You don't like dancing?" I smiled encouragingly at her, although my voice was teasing. I bet she looked incredible on the dance floor. Her body was full and curvy in all the places I liked to see moving when a woman dances. The way her pencil skirt nipped in at her waist and then gripped her full, round ass was not something I could miss.

"You ought to know upfront. I'm a fucking terrible dancer." She bit her full bottom lip with her pearly white teeth.

God, that little mouth on her. And I wasn't referring to naughty language.

I gave a little strangled laugh at her expression. "Neither am I. Trust me. I'm just talking about the middle school slow dance thing. We'll need to attend a wedding together in a couple of weeks."

"A wedding?"

"My friends who own this bar, Ward and Emma, are getting married."

She blinked. "Emma Greene?"

My jaw dropped open. "You know her?"

Her eyes were wide. "Yes. We're good friends. She was my roommate while I was getting my MBA at UT. I'm already invited to their wedding."

She was?

"Do you know Ward, too?" I questioned. This could really complicate things.

She shook her head. "Not very well. We've met, obviously, because they started dating while Emma and I lived together. I know his sister, Kate, pretty well, too." Her expression was curious. "So, you're Ward's friend?"

"Yeah. We went to college together."

It was a small world.

Rae's expression became doubtful. "I don't think I would feel good about lying to Kate or Emma. Besides, *I seriously owe Emma right now*. She's the one who gave me the EpiPen to save Clint."

"Oh. Yeah, that makes sense. I think Wendy, one of the waitresses, keeps one around for her peanut allergy." Wendy was the Lounge's newest waitress, and granddaughter of the bar's founder and original owner, Willie Paxton. Ward and Emma were under strict instructions from Willie to keep her out of trouble. And away from peanuts.

We both paused to consider the complexity of our overlapping friend group. "I think we can work around Kate and Emma. I won't ask you to mislead them, but maybe if you could just... not share all the details right away?" I was seriously making this up as I went along, but my voice sounded confident enough.

"You mean lie by omission?" She didn't look happy about the prospect.

I frowned. "No. But you don't tell them all the details of your dates, do you?"

She frowned. "No. I guess not."

"So maybe just don't tell them all the details about us right away. Besides, how would you even explain this to them?"

Her face was conflicted. "I don't know. But I'll just tell them the truth and ask them to keep it a secret. Is that okay? I don't feel comfortable keeping it from them, and they're going to ask." She trailed off, looking concerned.

I nodded. Kate and Emma were trustworthy, and it wasn't like either of them would tip off Victoria. They despised her. "I can handle all of that. I won't ask you to risk your friendships, but, if anything, your relationships with Kate and Emma will add to the believability of our relationship," I ventured. I was already considering how to use this detail to my advantage.

"Really?" Rae didn't look quite as convinced.

"Yes. I'm sure of it." It would drive Victoria crazy to know that I was dating one of Emma and Kate's friends, and provide a very plausible explanation for how I met Rae. It could definitely work, although I'd have to be careful.

"So, you want me to attend Ward and Emma's wedding with you? I can do that, since I don't have a date anyway." Rae nodded and then frowned. "I'll dance if I have to, but just understand that I will look stupid if I dance. What else?"

Fuck if I know. I shrugged, and then a stray thought occurred to me.

"There's one other thing," I ventured, "and it's not a deal breaker if you don't want to do it. I guess it's just more of a request..." I trailed off uncertainly. I looked at her, already feeling guilty.

"What is it?" She looked curious, if not a bit wary.

My words spilled out in a rush. "Will you dye your hair a different color red? More red?"

Her hands flew to the strands flying free around her ears, and her face fell. "You don't like my hair?" Her voice was suddenly very soft and small. I saw hurt flickering in her expressive green eyes.

I swallowed hard. "I didn't say... I do like... it's just...

look, you don't have to do it. I'm sorry I asked." I wished I could go back in time and kick myself.

Unlike my two best friends, I was a good liar and a great bullshit-er. Cole was too genuine and reasonable of a person to ever mislead someone convincingly. Ward was too blunt—his methods were always direct, sometimes even rude. Usually, I would have come up with a better way of telling Rae that I thought I just wasn't able to handle her hair color being so similar to Victoria's, but I wasn't up to it at the moment. And now my words had backfired.

She shook her head. The vulnerability that I'd seen disappeared in an instant. Walls went up behind her eyes and her next smile was confident. "I'm happy to dye my hair whatever color you'd like. You can pick out the shade yourself if you want."

The sudden shift in her mood made me nervous. I'd clearly offended her, and although that hadn't been my intention, there was no walking it back. The damage was done and now she was on her guard. I was an idiot. "I don't need to pick the color. I was going to suggest a shade that's more red than blonde but just... never mind. It's not important. Don't feel pressured if you don't want to change it." My response sounded more like an apology than anything else.

"Don't be silly," she told me, still wearing that fake smile. "It's just hair. I'll have it dyed by the next time you see me. Anything else?"

I shook my head guiltily. She must have seen my weakness, because she sat up straighter and set her hands on the table in front of her. She leaned forward and pounced on the opportunity to change the subject. She was in control once more.

Rae smiled sweetly when I tensed. "Now that we've worked out what I'll do for you, we can talk about what you'll do for me. I'll need you to give me some kind of assurance that you'll keep your word to me about the sale. And you need to make it clear to Azure Group that you're only going to work with them if you get to work with me."

"I'll have my lawyer draft some sort of an agreement."

"There's no way to make a fake relationship legally enforceable," Rae told me. "I'm not a lawyer, but I work with a lot of them and I do know that."

I blinked. She was right. "Well, you're closer to being a lawyer than me. What do you recommend?"

She shrugged her shoulders. "This is a question of trust."

"How about a handshake?"

Her eyes narrowed and then she rolled them. "That might be how you do things in Texas, but I wasn't born yesterday. I'm not going to just believe you. Right now, there's nothing to make you keep up your end of the bargain to me. I could go through all this trouble and then you might choose not to sell."

Clever. She was right again. Not that I would lie to her, but she didn't know that. I nodded.

We sat in silence for a second while we both puzzled over it.

Suddenly inspiration struck. "How about I give you five percent of the stock ownership certificates right now. Then, when the deal is signed with Azure Group, you can give them back to me and I'll give them to Azure group. If it seems like I'm going to go back on my word to you, you can just walk and keep the stock. Then you'll personally own a stake in the company and can do whatever you want."

She looked at me in obvious disbelief. "You'd do that? I'd have the power to completely fuck you over at any point. Even minority shareholders can stop a deal."

"I'm going to just believe you. I will demand a handshake, but that's how we do things in Texas." I knew I was wearing a confident face, but inside, I knew this was a risky move. But somehow, I trusted Rae. She wasn't the type to fuck someone over just because. I could tell that she didn't have it in her.

You've been wrong before, a negative voice reminded me. I squashed it. I wasn't wrong about Rae.

She stared at me for a long moment. "You must really want her back, whoever this woman is."

Victoria. Just an offhand remark about her made me feel lightheaded and weak.

"Yeah, I do." It's not like I could lie about it. I saw her face every time I closed my eyes.

"Alright, I agree to your terms." Rae seemed full of emotions, but I didn't know what they meant. She was so beautiful, and that could be dangerous. I would need to be careful around her. I couldn't afford the distraction. I did my best to be businesslike.

"Great. I'll have the stock certificates sent to your hotel room." I smiled at her. "I'll take my handshake now."

Rae extended her small, pale hand over the table to me, and I shook it. Her hand was dwarfed by mine, but I knew better than to underestimate her. Her strength was evident to me, and she would soon have the power to make or break my entire life. I prayed that I wasn't making a huge mistake. I had a good feeling about this though. I was smart enough to pull this whole thing off. Wasn't I?

5

RAE

"How do I feel? I feel like dog shit, Rae," Cliff grumbled. "I probably look like dog shit, too." He was wearing one of those horrible, backless hospital gowns and looked uncomfortable atop the lumpy, industrial-looking hospital bed. Wires and tubes extended from his arms and hooked into machines, turning him into a reluctant, foul-tempered cyborg.

God, I hate hospitals. Just being in the room reminded me of when my dad was sick.

"I'm sorry, Cliff," I told him. He huffed dismissively in response. His mop of gray hair shook aggressively, free of its usual oiled style. I'd long thought he was wearing a toupee, but now, I wasn't so sure. Nobody would have a toupee that ugly. No way. That hair was real.

As obnoxious and painfully hard to take as Cliff was, there was no dignity or comfort with being in a hospital. I'd spent more than enough time in hospitals when I was a kid. The smell was exactly the same as I remembered; it was the scent of strong chemicals mingled with sadness, sickness, and death. I couldn't wait to get out of there. I imagined Cliff felt the same way.

"When are they going to let you out?" I asked, and he shrugged.

"Ask that heifer of a nurse they gave me." He dropped his voice conspiratorially. "None of the nurses here are even remotely attractive. That used to be the one upside to being sick! Now they just let anyone be a nurse. Even men. *It's disgraceful.*"

It took some effort on my part, but I managed to avoid lecturing Cliff that nurses were medical professionals and not around for his entertainment or sexual titillation. To Cliff's right, Annie and Kyle exchanged a disgusted glance. Usually I tried my best to insulate them from the worst of Cliff's opinions. Tonight, there was no way to do that. They were getting the full Cliff treatment.

"The doctor said that as soon as his echocardiogram came back, they would consider discharging him," Annie explained since Cliff seemed unduly fixated on the nursing situation.

"I didn't need an echocardiogram," he groused. Annie rolled her eyes.

"Just like you didn't need an injection of epinephrine to open up your airway so you wouldn't choke to death?" she challenged.

"Did I ask your opinion?" he snapped back at her. "How about you keep your commentary limited to the job."

"That's—" Annie started.

"Excuse me—" Kyle tried.

"Why don't you and Kyle both wait outside?" Cliff interrupted, speaking over them. "I didn't realize until tonight how annoying you both were. At least Rae is *rational*."

I knew it was pointless to try and defend them. It would only make Cliff turn on me. The best way to help them was to get them out of his line of sight. Neither seemed particularly put out to be banished to the hallway. "I'll tell you guys everything later," I said in a low voice as I shut the door. They looked relieved to be away from Cliff. I could hardly blame them.

"Alright, how'd it go?" Cliff asked me now that we were alone. "Is he as much of a genius as they say?"

"It's hard to say whether he's a genius, but he's interested in selling," I told Cliff. "The meeting went well. I think we're in business. We can start due diligence tomorrow."

"I hope you unbuttoned a few of those buttons like we talked about," Cliff told me, staring unabashedly at my chest. He was really laying it on thick today. I tried to chalk it up to his experience with the allergic reaction and some kind of mind-altering drugs he might be on, but it was hard not to take offense. Besides, this wasn't all that much different than his usual behavior.

I didn't rise to his bait. "Once we get you discharged,

we'll need to talk about the management agreements," I told him, trying to steer the conversation back towards business. "I'm not sure that Stevenson will like our standard terms. He seems very independent."

Cliff shook his meaty head. "Azure Group won't budge on that. I've tried before, but unless you've got something on McKenzie, Stevenson will be signing the same deal as everyone else." He shrugged. "They fuck everybody over equally, at least. So, you can't say it's unfair."

A light knock on the door interrupted us. A man wearing a stethoscope stuck his head in. He evaluated the situation in an instant and recoiled.

"May I come in?"

Cliff nodded at the man reluctantly. "I suppose. I hope you've got my discharge papers in that folder." He eyed the folder in the doctor's hands.

The doctor, a forty-something-year-old with a shaved head and bright, caramel brown eyes shook his head. "I'm afraid not, Mr. Monroe. You're going to have to suffer through our hospitality for a few more hours. My name is Dr. Alvarez. Do you mind me discussing your health information in front of your..." he looked at me curiously, "daughter?"

I bit back a smirk. Thank God, no. "Coworker," I corrected. "I'm his coworker. I'll step out if you like, Cliff." I started to make towards the door.

"Nah, stick around," he suggested. "I don't care if you hear. This'll only take a moment. I'm as healthy as a horse." He looked at the doctor like he was daring him to disagree.

The doctor didn't seem the least bit concerned with Cliff's feelings on the matter. "If you mean a horse with a defective pacemaker, then yes," he told Cliff. "I'm afraid your echocardiogram revealed some serious issues that we need to discuss."

"You'd better be shitting me, son." Cliff's tone was the same one he'd use to scold a dog.

"Mr. Monroe, I assure you that I am not shitting you." The doctor smiled a thin, very cold smile.

I liked this doctor. He gave zero fucks about whether or not Cliff liked what he was telling him. He'd probably just finished stitching a stabbing victim back together or delivering a baby or something. It was obvious that Cliff's feelings were just not high on his priority list. He pulled out the results of the test and began explaining them in terms as simple as I think he was able. I didn't really understand what he was talking about at all, though it sounded serious. Cliff looked entirely blank.

Cliff interrupted after a few seconds. "I don't know where you're from, doctor, but I don't speak that language."

"I'm from Houston, Mr. Monroe." Dr. Alvarez's response to Cliff's casual racism was equal parts displeasure and sarcasm.

"Well, can you break it down for me? Give me the bottom line? I don't know what you're babbling on about." Cliff was still talking a good game, but I could tell that he was starting to become concerned. His pink skin had turned pale and he clutched his hands together across his middle.

"Certainly. You have heart disease, Mr. Monroe."

"I knew that already." My boss frowned. "It runs in my family. Everybody has it. My dad died of it. Uncle too."

The doctor nodded. "And that genetic predisposition likely contributed to your development of the disease. It has also been exacerbated by your obesity, heavy drinking, sedentary but high-stress lifestyle, and use of tobacco."

Damn. Dr. Alvarez was really sassy. I guess he'd seen one too many patients with attitude today.

Even Cliff didn't seem to have a snappy comeback for that. "Fine. I guess, um, I guess I need to go on Nutrisystem and scale back on the booze. But why does that mean I need to stay in the hospital? Just up my blood thinners and send me on my merry way."

"I will be upping your blood thinners, but before we can, as you say, send you on your merry way, we're going to need to address your pacemaker."

"What's wrong with it?"

"It's off."

Cliff frowned deeply. "What do you mean, off? They aren't supposed to turn off."

Dr. Alvarez smirked. "And they say I'm the doctor around here."

"What do you mean it's off?"

Dr. Alvarez looked at Cliff like he wasn't sure if he was

being messed with and then seemed to conclude that Cliff genuinely didn't understand what he was being told. "Your pacemaker has malfunctioned. It's no longer working as intended."

Cliff frowned. "That's... that's bad."

"Yes, Mr. Monroe." Dr. Alvarez looked relieved that he'd finally gotten through to Cliff. "I'm afraid it's very bad, but entirely correctible. We need to get you home to New York and scheduled for surgery. Your cardiothoracic surgeon will need to remove the defective device and implant a new, functioning pacemaker. These malfunctions are extremely rare; yours is the first I've ever seen. We probably never would have caught the problem if you hadn't been stung by a bee, had a reaction, and put so much stress on your heart." He shook his head. "You're actually a very lucky man."

I had to wonder whether or not Dr. Alvarez thought that Cliff was undeserving of his luck. I'm sure he saw plenty of people in this emergency room who had bad luck. People that were just going about their daily lives when something horrible happened to them. A terrible accident or an act of violence, for example. Dr. Alvarez probably saw lots of innocent, nice people that had done nothing to contribute to the issues that brought them to his ER.

Then there was Cliff. He'd been doing his level best to kill himself through poor lifestyle choices for the past thirty years. But even swallowing a bee couldn't kill Cliff. He just kept on ticking. Like a fat cockroach.

"Well," Cliff said to me after the doctor departed, "I guess you'll be on your own for this deal with Stevenson."

"I guess so." I tried not to sound too excited.

"I hope you don't screw this up too bad."

His faith in me was always so inspiring.

I smiled at him. "I'll be fine. You should focus on getting better."

Cliff shook his head at me. "Do you know what you're getting yourself into?"

"Sure," I told him. "I got this."

6

RAE

WHEN I GOT to my hotel hours later, after spending much more time with Cliff at the hospital than I anticipated, the stock certificates were waiting for me. I stared at them in silent dismay. *What the hell had I been thinking?*

And what the hell had Lucas been thinking? Assuming these certificates were real, and I would verify with the Texas Secretary of State's Corporation Division that they were as soon as they opened the next morning, I was in possession of five percent of a company worth—potentially—several million dollars. They felt almost weightless in my hands, but I knew they were the most valuable things I'd ever touched.

The stock wasn't even the tip of the iceberg. What was much more valuable to me in the long run was the boost to my career. This stock was just temporary collateral for my peace of mind. The real win would be sealing this deal. And all I had to do was pretend to be Lucas Stevenson's girlfriend.

I flopped down on the cushy hotel bed and stared at the ceiling. This was not how I'd expected this day to go. Not even close. When I woke up in my Brooklyn apartment this morning, I could never have foreseen the day turning out the way it had.

Usually these acquisition trips followed a fairly unremarkable pattern. Our team—usually four people—showed up to meet with the client. Cliff always did most of the talking in these initial meetings. I stood there and answered technical questions, but mostly it was the Cliff show. He would do his song and dance, the client would nod nervously, and then the next day, we would start the real work of valuation.

The process ordinarily took between two and five weeks of short visits but revolved almost exclusively around meetings and discussions on technical and financial specs. Then, a tense negotiation would end in either a huge celebration because we bought the business or a crushing defeat because either the company proved to be worthless, wasn't a good investment, or we couldn't make a deal.

This time, it wasn't going to be like that. I held the key to the deal right in my trembling hands. *Actually, I was the key.*

All I had to do was pretend to be the client's girlfriend for a while.

My head hurt.

I'd never been a great liar. In fact, truth and facts were my forte. But I was going to need to learn quickly if I was going to deliver.

Lucas was already on top of his end of the bargain. In my inbox, a message from him to my boss's boss, the formidable and terrifying CEO of Azure Group, Carla McKenzie, outlined in no uncertain terms that Lucas only wanted to work with me on the deal going forward. According to Lucas' email, he felt that I had 'a unique understanding of his priorities and aspirations' as well as 'impressive intellectual and negotiation ability' overall. Although the wording was professional, something about the verbiage felt like a double entendre and left a strange, unpleasant taste in my mouth.

Meanwhile, Cliff was clearly down for the count. He would need to return immediately to New York for more treatment and might be out of the office for several weeks.

The net result was that I was now running this engagement myself. Our CFO wrote me personally to congratulate me on my handling of the crisis with Cliff. She clearly indicated that success on this acquisition would mean a permanent promotion for me, complete with a raise, bonus, new title, and corner office. I'd be skipping over the next five years as second-in-command and moving straight into senior management. The thought was as exciting as it was scary.

Lastly, Michelle—her email to me concluded, and yes, she was using my legal name because she probably had no idea who I was—*I want to reiterate how impressed I am with your handling of the unfortunate events with Cliff this afternoon. The ability to find an opportunity within a crisis is very rare indeed. I look forward to seeing how the next few weeks play out.*

You and me both, McKenzie. I read and reread her email until the words were seared into my memory. Just receiving an email from her was a huge step forward in my career. People like me were like drones to her—interchangeable and disposable workers who would never ascend to her level. Even Cliff was a drone, although a slightly higher ranked drone than I was. McKenzie was the queen bee.

A group text from Annie shook me out of my email hypnosis.

Annie: What time are we meeting the client tomorrow?
Rae: Noon. I spoke with Stevenson about the schedule. He's not an early riser.
Kyle: I like this guy already. What's your impression of him?
Rae: He's young and independent. Seems very sharp. You know, just your average tech genius turned millionaire entrepreneur.
Kyle: Never mind. He sounds like an asshole.

Annie: He sounds very impressive to me. How are his algorithms? As good as they looked in the prospectus?

Kyle: Lol. Are we still talking about this deal? Or is that girl code for something else?

Annie: Haha. I meant the matchmaking algorithms for Notable Match.

Rae: I didn't get a good look at his algorithms. Not yet. I forwarded you a few things he sent over though.

Annie: Awesome! Thanks Rae. I'll check it out.

Kyle: Do you have a present for me too? Some new financials perhaps?

Rae: I sent you first quarter numbers this evening. Get some rest guys, it's going to be a long day tomorrow. If we start at noon, we may not end until eight or nine p.m.

Annie: Good night!

Kyle: Thanks for the financials Rae. See you guys tomorrow in the lobby. Eleven thirty?

Rae: Let's make it eleven forty-five. His building is only four blocks away.

Although my texts to the team were confident, and I hoped they sounded competent, I secretly worried that I was anything but. I changed into my pajamas, curled up under the covers, and couldn't sleep a wink. Every time I closed my eyes, I saw Lucas Stevenson's smiling face and heard his cool, teasing voice. He was basically a stranger to me, but he'd taken up residence in my brain like he owned it.

I couldn't stop thinking about him, and if I was really, truly honest with myself, I didn't want to. In my mind's eye, I could see him clearly: his height, his strength, his humor, the heat in his eyes when he looked at me. Even though he probably only wanted me because I looked like his ex, I knew exactly what I'd dream about that night. And it wasn't his algorithms.

7

LUCAS

I ENDED up staying at the Lone Star Lounge a lot longer than I intended that evening. After my adrenaline filled meeting with Rae, I just didn't want to be alone. The activity and light of the bar were a welcome distraction.

"Was that Rae I saw you with? I knew she was coming to town, but I didn't realize she was here to evaluate your app." Emma zeroed in on me when the patio emptied out and I moved inside to sit at the bar. Her curiosity was obvious. My buddy, Ward, was at her side cleaning glasses, and he looked over with interest of his own. The evening rush was over, and the room was almost empty at this point, so we could actually talk.

"Yes, she's part of the valuation team for my app." My reply was factual and succinct. I prayed she'd let it drop and change the subject.

Emma nodded. "Did she say if her coworker is doing

better? I think the other two people that were with them went to the hospital."

"Apparently he's gonna be okay, yeah," I answered. The fact that Rae's boss had unexpectedly become ill had been a real stroke of luck for me. I probably would have never had an opportunity to speak to Rae alone like that if he hadn't. Still, I didn't want the guy to die or anything.

"I'm just glad all that went down outside the bar," Ward chimed in. "The last thing I need is somebody dying in here. Poltergeists are bad for business."

"Rae probably saved that guy's life," Emma said. "You should have seen her, Ward. She rolled up in here like something out of a Western. Or Terminator."

"Since when do you watch Westerns or Terminator movies?" I teased Emma. She was basically the epitome of Ivy League snobbishness. I couldn't imagine her enjoying Spaghetti Westerns or action thrillers. She'd probably think both Clint Eastwood and Arnold Schwarzenegger were low-brow Teutonic trash.

"I watch *Westworld*," she said innocently. "Same thing."

Ward and I exchanged a glance. With effort, I let it slide. She technically wasn't wrong, and that was progress for Emma. When I met her, she only watched documentaries and news programming.

"So, is it normal for you to meet *members of your acquisition team* for an evening drink?" Ward asked. "Because that sounds more like a date than a business meeting to me."

I shrugged, forcing myself to look casual. "Well, it's not like I have an office."

That, at least, was true. I worked with a handful of independent contractors, one who helped with graphics, and one who did the books, and one who helped me with the routine programming I didn't have time for. When we did work as a team, which wasn't often, we met up in the coworking space in my building, the Lone Star Lounge, or my loft.

"The Lounge is your office," Ward said. "I ought to start charging you rent."

He wouldn't dare. "I pay rent," I replied. "In beers."

"When was the last time you paid for a beer here?" Ward asked, rolling his eyes so hard he ought to worry they might pop out.

Come to think of it... "It might've been a while," I admitted. "But you've been keeping track of my tab, haven't you?"

Ward treated me to another eye roll. "I'm gonna start. And I'm gonna start charging you rent."

"Uh huh. Send me an invoice."

"Don't tempt me."

"I'm good for it."

"You had better be. Otherwise I might come collect." He cracked his knuckles in fake threat. I smirked.

"I'm sooo scared." In all honesty, if the threat were serious, I would be. Ward was a former NFL player whose second career owning a bar involved occasional stints as a reluctant, but effective, bouncer. If motivated, he could probably be a real threat. But he wouldn't hit me. We were friends. Plus, I'm too smart to get in a fight with Ward. I'd distract him and then run away.

"I outweigh you by like thirty pounds. I could knock you into next week." He tried for menacing and swung wide.

I made a dismissive noise. "And um how many of those thirty pounds are muscle?" Ward was so easy to tease, it almost wasn't even fun. Almost.

"All of them. I'm four inches taller than you— I have to weigh more."

"Two and a half inches when we're both barefoot if I recall correctly." We'd measured before, back in college. I didn't care what his Wikipedia page said about him, Ward was six three and not a centimeter more.

"Your elaborate hairdo doesn't count as height." He laughed at me and attempted to reach across the bar to pat my head. I leaned back, out of his grasp, and frowned at him. That was just rude, and not just the part where he tried to pat me like a dog. I didn't have a hairdo. This was just my regular hair. It didn't like to lie flat. I'd surrendered that fight long ago.

"It's irrelevant anyway, because I can outrun you."

"Is that a challenge?" Ward talked a good game, but he'd absolutely destroyed one of his knees playing football, prompting his early retirement. After multiple surgeries, extensive physical therapy, and lots of time, he was mostly healed up from the injury, but he'd never be able to run very well again. He was lucky he could even walk. In the early days after his injury, we'd thought he'd be in a wheelchair for life.

"More like a fact." I gave him a pitying look. Like me, Ward hated to be pitied. It was an easy way to push his buttons.

"You can outrun me, but you can't outrun the collections agency." He sneered.

"I don't need to. I'm about to sell my app."

"To Rae? I'm still not sure I believe that you weren't on a date."

"To Rae's firm, Azure Group. And that was a business meeting." Mostly. Sort of.

"Looked like a date to me." He raised his eyebrows condescendingly.

I shook my head. It wasn't. I don't date. Not anymore. But all that needed to change, at least, as far as the outside world was concerned.

"What if it was? What, were you spying or something?" I asked.

"Dude, I work here." Ward laughed at me.

"So, why weren't you working instead of spying on me?"

"I wasn't!"

"You were too."

"I was not."

Emma set down a pint glass with a loud thump. She sighed dramatically. "Jesus Christ! Stop bickering!"

We looked over in surprise at her unexpected outburst. I don't think I'd ever seen her snap like that before. Usually all the snapping at this bar was done by Ward's sister, Kate.

Ward looked at his fiancée, affecting innocence. "We weren't bickering. This is just how we talk."

She shook her head. "Sorry." Just as quickly as it had appeared, her anger vanished. "I know you two bond by being mean to each other. I'm just really tired. It's been a long night. Watching Rae's boss nearly die took a lot out of me. I feel like I could sleep for a week."

Ward wrapped an arm around her waist affectionately and she snuggled into him. They were adorable. It was gross. And yeah, I was jealous.

Victoria and I used to be like that.

Ward was oblivious to my inner heartbreak. He was dealing with his own. "I know. It's hard without Kate and Willie here." His voice had turned wistful.

Ward's sister had managed the business side of the bar as well as bartending and waitressing as needed. She'd opened up a business of her own and quit a few weeks ago. Willie, the bar's founder and former owner, had also retired recently. That left Ward to pick up all the slack, without two of his best friends. That was probably why Emma, a college professor, was pulling shifts to help in the first place.

"At least we've got Wendy working nights for the rest of the week," Emma said, nodding. "She's getting the hang of everything pretty well."

"It's in her blood," Ward joked.

"Speaking of things that are in Wendy's blood, we need to get another EpiPen," Emma said. "I gave the one we had to Rae's boss."

Ward nodded.

"I'll talk to Rae about it tomorrow if you want," I suggested. "She mentioned she wants to pay you back. Something about billing it as a corporate expense?"

"She's one tough cookie," Emma said approvingly. "I'm so glad she did the injection. Wendy explained how to do it, but I'm not sure I could have actually stuck somebody who was literally dying like she did. She stayed calm the whole time, too."

I could fully imagine Rae taking charge of a situation like that. I smiled at the thought. She was really something.

"I know that look," Ward said, interrupting my daydream. "You've got a little bit of a thing for her." His tone was shocked. "Don't you?"

"Actually, I've got a huge thing for the pile of money her company is gonna give me, but I'm not blind either," I replied with a grin. "See you two later."

I got out of there as fast as I could (without paying, as usual). The last thing I needed was Ward figuring me out before I had time to thoroughly strategize for myself and figure out what I was going to do with the whole Rae situation.

Was she hot? God yes. Did I like her? Sure. But she wasn't Victoria.

Yet somehow, and even though it made me feel guilty and bizarrely like I was being unfaithful to a woman who said she didn't love me anymore, I still couldn't stop thinking about Rae. My dreams that night were filled with confusing images of fierce, beautiful redheads. I wasn't sure if it was Rae or Victoria's name that was on my lips when I awoke. But for the first time in a long time, I was smiling.

8

RAE

THE COLOR on the box said 'true red' and it wasn't lying. I stared at myself in the mirror, astounded by how much a little change in color could change my looks.

Bye bye demure strawberry blonde. Hello sexy fire engine red.

"Do you like it?" Annie asked anxiously. She'd been kind enough to help me this morning. Her head was cocked to the side.

"Yeah, I think I do?" I stared in the mirror like the woman reflected back might disappear any second. She was the sexier, more vivacious version of me.

"Good. Because I absolutely love it."

We grinned at each other and then laughed like teenagers. Although Annie and Kyle were usually my coworkers, I was now temporarily their boss. What that meant for Annie and me, I didn't know. We'd always been friends first and had grown pretty close over the months on the road. There aren't many women at Azure Group. We tended to stick together for safety. And happy hour commiseration.

"So, what made you want to go sex bomb all of a sudden?" Annie asked.

I shrugged. "I just felt like it was time for a change," I lied.

The funny thing was, even though I probably wouldn't have had the guts to dye it without Lucas' 'encouragement,' I'd always been curious about what I'd look like with bright red hair. Truth be told, I wasn't the biggest fan of my natural reddish blonde hair color. I thought it looked a bit dull and boring. This new color, in my humble opinion, was freakin' awesome. I ran my fingers through the fiery strands excitedly and giggled like an idiot.

I loved my new hair.

I also loved the fact that the Texas Secretary of State verified that my stock certificates were legit. This deal and this day were off to a good start. Hopefully, this afternoon we could begin the more normal aspects of the acquisition process, including getting Kyle and Annie to work on the investigation. And maybe, I could figure out exactly what this whole 'pretend girlfriend' thing was going to require (besides the hair).

When Annie and I met Kyle in the lobby at noon, his reaction to my new look was appropriately surprised and professionally complimentary. But it was nothing compared to the way Lucas reacted. He was literally open-mouthed and mute when he saw me. His eyes widened appreciatively, and his pupils became huge. A few awkward moments passed at the door to his loft as he stared.

"Lucas, these are my coworkers, Annie Washington and Kyle Chen." I told him, trying to pull us back on track. Lucas snapped his mouth shut and ripped his gaze away from me with obvious effort to shake hands with them. "Annie is our technical specialist. She'll be reviewing your algorithms and app infrastructure. Kyle is our financial analyst. He'll be reviewing your financial statements, tax statements, et cetera."

We generally didn't conduct our due diligence efforts within the homes of our targets' CEO, but this was no ordinary acquisition. Lucas led us forward into his loft and pointed at what I assumed was his dining table. Arrayed before us were several laptops, a small server, and a number of stacked reams of paper.

"Okay. Have at it," Lucas said with a grin. "Everything's right there."

Kyle and Annie exchanged a stunned look with one another. This was not usually how it went. This level of immediate transparency was unusual, to say the least. Usually our target companies would make us sit through at least two days of boring meetings before they ever let us near real information. Cliff liked to call the preliminary few meetings the 'turd polishing' stage. I preferred not to think about that visual, but I preferred skipping the advertising and grandstanding even more. This whole process would go so much more smoothly if all clients would just show us to the records and let us work.

So, I shrugged when they turned to me in confusion. "At least we don't have to go digging through file rooms this time, right?"

Since we'd all spent our fair share of time in file rooms and drafty basements, they nodded with matching bemused smiles and got to work. Lucas and I were left standing awkwardly at the door. I could feel Lucas' eyes on me, even before I turned to meet his gaze.

"I'm going to be honest with you," I told him after a few minutes of very stilted small talk. "You just did about ninety percent of my job by putting everything out for us to work on. Usually I have to pry information out of executives like a guard at Guantanamo going for terrorist toenails."

He smirked but looked confused. "Well, we signed a non-disclosure agreement, and you agreed not to take anything out of this room," Lucas said, shrugging. "So why wouldn't I show you what you came for?"

"Beats me. I've never understood all the cagey weirdness either. I think most executives just don't want us to see their dirty laundry."

"My dirty laundry is in the bedroom over there," he said, pointing. "You can see it if you really want to. It's not that exciting. I promise not to ask you to clean it or anything."

I smiled at his sarcasm. "That's an extremely generous offer, but no thanks."

"Are you sure?" His voice had dropped a half-octave and was just above a whisper.

"If I didn't know better, I'd think you were just trying to get me into your bedroom." I winked.

Oops. Did I seriously just say that out loud?

God, Lucas was easy to flirt with. It was so easy to forget that we were just business associates. I looked over in shock, but Lucas just laughed. Thankfully Kyle and Angela didn't notice. Those two had gone straight into nerd heaven as soon as they sat down. It would be hours before either came up for air.

"Do you want to go grab a cup of coffee downstairs while they work?" Lucas asked, accurately interpreting my glance at my coworkers for the worry it was. I did not want them figuring out my side arrangement with Lucas.

I nodded. "Sure. We've got business of our own to discuss anyway."

One latte order later and we faced one another across a narrow booth.

"I checked your stock certificates," I told him. "They're real." My voice was matter of fact.

He arched an eyebrow and hid a smile behind a sip of his espresso. "Yes, I know they are."

"Do you like my new hair?"

I already knew he did, I was just fishing for compliments. Yes, I'm shallow sometimes. Sue me.

"I liked it before too, but yes," he replied. "I like it." His eyes lingered on the long, red strands.

"Do I look like her now?" I asked boldly. I just really needed to know. For some reason, it was important for me to know if I looked like his mysterious ex-girlfriend that he was willing to go to such great lengths to get back.

He stared at me for a moment and cocked his head to the side as he considered it. "Not really, no." His voice was soft.

I blinked. "Really?" I touched my hair, suddenly wondering if he thought I wasn't attractive now or something. Or not as attractive as *her*. "I would have thought that's why you wanted me to pretend to be your girlfriend."

He shook his head. "You're beautiful, Rae," he said, smiling mischievously at me. "I'm fairly sure you know that already, or you wouldn't be asking."

"Beauty is in the eye of the beholder," I replied. "I didn't ask about that though, I asked if I looked like *her*."

"Victoria." He said her name like each letter cost him. Like her name was a prayer.

"I don't look more like her now? *Victoria*? I thought that was why you wanted me to dye my hair..." I trailed off uncertainly.

He shook his head again. "It's not that. I mean, you both have red hair, but that's about it."

"Wrong color?" I pushed. Maybe she was more auburn red than fire engine red or something.

His smirk widened into a smile. "It's really not about the hair color, Rae."

"I don't understand." I bet her nose was smaller than mine. I'd always thought my nose was a bit too big. And it had a little bump in it. I resisted the urge to touch it.

He took another sip of espresso. "I don't know that I understand either. It's... it's not an easy thing to explain. You and Victoria aren't really the same. You don't look the same, you don't act the same. But on a certain level, you are the same. I guess it's an attitude thing?" He shrugged.

An attitude thing? I hoped that was good. He was looking at me like it was a good thing.

"Will you tell me about her?"

He blinked. "Why?"

"Because I'm curious. And maybe it will be helpful to me when I'm pretending to be in love with you if I know what you like." I smiled my most winning smile. "Maybe it will help her be jealous if I seem like a bad version of her, too."

Tell me, dammit. Tell me about this mysterious Victoria creature that's got you so thoroughly under her spell.

A humorless smile played across his features and vanished. "I'll tell you about her some other time. There's more important things to talk about right now."

I bit back my disappointment and curiosity. Why was *Victoria* so great? I wasn't sure when I'd become jealous of her. It wasn't really that I wanted Lucas so badly. He was hot, yes, but it wasn't that. It was more about the way Lucas looked when he talked about her. Like she was the only woman in the world. I was sure that no one had ever talked about me that way. The thought ate at me.

"What do you want to talk about?" I asked, forcing myself to sound pleasant and not petulant. I'd find out about her eventually, whether he told me or not. I've got good investigative skills.

"Our date tonight."

"What?"

"Oh, do you already have plans?"

"No, but—"

He interrupted. "Do you have any dietary restrictions? Meat? Seafood?"

My anger rose. "No, but Lucas, I would appreciate it if you could keep in mind that I don't like being *told* that we're going on a date. Even if it's a fake date. At least do me the courtesy of asking first. I'll do the best I can to fulfill my end of the bargain here, but I've still got feelings and I don't take orders from you."

His full lips parted, and he sighed. "You're right. I apologize." He dragged a hand through his tousled hair. "I have less than no idea about what I'm doing here. You're my first fake girlfriend."

I giggled, remembering something. "You're not my first fake boyfriend."

His eyebrows rose high on his forehead. "I'm not?" He blinked. "Really?"

I shook my head at him. "Nope. In eighth grade I

pretended to date my friend, Thomas, because a mean girl in another class had a crush on him and he was scared she'd kill him if he turned her down. I was his protector."

"And did you save him from the mean girl?"

"I sure did. She didn't want to mess with me." I was still proud of that, all these years later.

"Well, if we're going back to middle school, I guess you aren't technically my first fake girlfriend either," Lucas told me. "I 'dated' a girl in sixth grade for two weeks before she broke up with me. She was going to a concert and was sure John Mayer would see her and fall in love with her. She didn't want to be a cheater, you see, but she'd wanted some 'experience' before she met her true love. So, she was really doing me a favor when she called it off."

I smirked. "Oh definitely. Did she try to get back with you after the concert?"

"Yeah. But by then I'd already moved on. To her best friend."

"Harsh."

"My middle school was a pretty cutthroat place romantically speaking," Lucas told me.

"Mine too." Cutthroat was right. It was a blood bath. Children are cruel. Teenagers are worse.

"I bet you broke a lot of hearts in high school."

"I was actually quite nerdy. But I still managed to do okay." I had a few dates. One semiserious boyfriend. Nothing major. I was a late bloomer.

"You? Nerdy? I don't believe it."

I cringed. "Believe it. I wear contacts now, but I was a mess back then. I had braces, glasses, baby fat, an emo haircut, and an attitude the size of Texas."

"So, you were an ugly duckling?"

"I don't know if I was water fowl, but I was definitely foul tempered enough to send most boys running for the hills."

"Some guys like a challenge." His grin said he was one of them.

"Are you speaking from personal experience?"

His sexy smirk was back. "Nowadays, yes. But dating in high school was not really a challenge for me."

"Self-confidence clearly isn't much of a challenge for you either." My voice was dry, but I liked a man who knew his worth. Lucas' confidence was one of the things that attracted me most.

"I played football in high school," he explained. "I was the quarterback. I was popular." He said it without pride or modesty. It was just a fact.

I nodded. Even if he wasn't brilliant and gorgeous, being a talented athlete would have put Lucas in the middle of the in-crowd. When you added up everything, he must have been the king of his school. "I see. So, were you going to ask me on a fake-date tonight or something?" I found that I was eager to return to the subject of spending more time with him.

"Yes," Lucas said with a smile. He cleared his throat and

sat up straight. "Rae, will you go on a fake date with me tonight?"

I fluttered my eyelashes at him. "Why yes. I'd be delighted to go on a fake date with you tonight, Lucas."

* * *

"So, on the technical front I've got good news and bad news," Annie said to Kyle and me over lunch. "Which one do you want first?"

I was busy picking all the peppers off the hamburger on my plate. Why on earth would anyone want to ruin a perfectly good hamburger with gigantic chunks of spicy sadness? Texas was weird. I shrugged at Annie's question. "The good news?"

To be honest, I'd been hoping we could just eat lunch and not talk about work. But I could tell that both Annie and Kyle were brimming with new insights from their morning research. It wasn't that I didn't want to hear them, I did, it was just that I liked occasionally taking a break from work. But that wasn't the Azure Group way.

"The good news is that it looks like Stevenson gave us everything we need to perform a thorough audit of both his intellectual property and his basic code."

I smiled. "That is good news. I'll never forget that auxiliary server room in Detroit." That place still gave me nightmares. At the reference, Kyle shivered.

"Me either. Those raccoons had a really good thing

going," Annie replied with a shake of her head. "You gotta hand it to them for resourcefulness. They made a mess, but it was nice and warm in their nest."

Flashbacks of many pairs of gleaming eyes peering out of dark cabinets pinged through me. Lucas' fancy, tasteful loft was a hell of a lot better than that had been. Cliff had to get a rabies shot after that trip.

"I still can't believe we bought that piece of shit company," Kyle added. "They were way over-leveraged." His tone was disbelieving. Privately, I knew the reason we purchased the failing Detroit telecommunications company was because one of Azure Group's executives was an investor and he didn't want it to fail. I kept it to myself. There were a lot of not-so-great things that went on behind the scenes of Azure Group. Part of my job was to protect Kyle and Annie from it as much as I could, so they could actually do their jobs. Speaking of which...

"So, what was the bad news?" I asked. The idea that Lucas was hiding something serious was concerning.

Annie frowned. "The bad news is that I don't understand his matchmaking algorithms yet. I was expecting something that was halfway like our other portfolio companies, but he's on a whole other level. The math is incredibly complex, and the variables are just ridiculously numerous. I guess I should have known that it would be really tricky to use musical preference for matchmaking, but damn."

"Will you be able to figure them out?" Being able to

thoroughly evaluate why something like a matchmaking algorithm was unique and valuable was kind of her job.

"Eventually." She shrugged. Her expression was both intrigued and annoyed. I had total faith in Annie's ability to figure out the algorithms. She'd never met a puzzle she couldn't solve before. I smiled at her encouragingly and received an eyeroll in reply. "Don't worry. I'll figure it out," she insisted. "I always do."

"How about the financials?" I asked Kyle.

He lit up like a golden retriever who'd just heard the word 'walk.' He swallowed down a bite of french fry as quickly as he could to answer. Kyle was a couple of months straight out of business school and eager to prove himself. His ambition, energy, and drive made him fit right in on our team.

"I'll be done with my preliminary report by the end of the week. He doesn't have a lot to report on since his company is so young. Obviously, he's operating at a loss right now since he has no advertising. It's not a complicated job for me." He grinned at Annie, who stuck her tongue out at him. He stole a fry off her plate in reply.

One of the reasons that Lucas was looking for a private equity investor in the first place was to do all the things that he didn't know how to do. Like marketing. In order to make his app truly successful, he'd need to monetize the concept. That meant advertising. One of Azure Group's strengths was in providing the expert advice and connections to our portfolio companies that would allow them to grow.

The other reason was capital. Scaling up his app beyond a successful prototype would require money. A great deal of money. Unless he wanted to take on a lot of individual investors or sink his own money into Notable Match, Lucas would need to sell the majority stake to someone like Azure Group. Unfortunately, his desire for assistance would come with a considerable loss of power.

"Have you discussed the CEO considerations with him yet?" Annie asked. Sometimes I wondered if she could read my mind.

I shook my head at her. "I'm waiting for the right moment," I admitted. Azure Group was willing to accept the idea of Lucas remaining the CEO, but they would be able to remove him at any time and for any reason. Whether he understood that they would become his bosses, I wasn't entirely sure. I had a bad feeling that he imagined some sort of strategic partnership between him and Azure Group. That wasn't how this worked.

"He's going to hate our management agreements," Kyle asserted. "I can tell this is a guy that dances to his own beat. You should see his bookkeeping. Its immaculate but... eccentric. He included a spreadsheet along with his P&L sheet of the music I should listen to while reviewing it as well as a recommended list of accompanying snacks. He doesn't strike me as somebody that's used to answering for himself or how he spends his time."

"He gave you a personalized playlist for reviewing financial records?" I asked Kyle.

He nodded, grinning. "It's a lot of New Wave. Some early punk stuff and grunge."

"I got a playlist for the code, too," Annie said. "All electronica. I'm not gonna' lie. I really, really like it. I forgot how good Radiohead's electronic stuff was."

Yeah, he might have a problem adapting to a more traditional corporate approach. Lucas would either have to give up all of his control of Notable Match in exchange for a higher price or keep the illusion of it for a lower price. I hoped that he chose the former over the latter. My time at the company had proved to me how rarely the original leadership enjoyed being subject to new corporate overlords. I couldn't see Lucas enjoying the idea of flying up to New York and putting on a suit to justify himself to a board of directors every quarter. He was too independent for that.

"We'll cross the CEO bridge when we get to it," I told Kyle and Annie. I put on a professional smile. "First we have to get through our due diligence. Just because it looks good right now doesn't mean there's anything here that we want to invest in. Lucas may be leading us on. Keep at it. Find out all his secrets. We need to know if he's hiding anything."

If only I could convince myself to follow my own advice.

9

RAE

ONE PROBLEM with going on a fake date while on a business trip was that even if I knew what I wanted to wear, I hadn't packed it. As it was, I had to improvise. I ended up wearing a sapphire colored wool sheath dress that I usually wore with a matching blazer and my highest heels. A side benefit of my new hair color was that my blue eyes popped more than they had before, so a little mascara and blush was all the makeup I needed.

Lucas snapped a couple of photos of us before going into the restaurant. They were cute. Convincing. We looked like a real, happy couple in them. He carefully posted them to social media before we went inside. I knew Emma and Kate would see it and ask me questions, but I'd cross the bridge when I came to it.

"Taking a New Yorker to a seafood place in a landlocked

city is a very ambitious move," I told him as we sat down. "We're notorious snobs, you know."

"Good," Lucas replied, grinning. "I told you I like a challenge. Prepare to be wowed."

His confidence and good humor were contagious. I wanted to be skeptical and snobby, but he was right. This place was amazing. I ordered a bouillabaisse, fully intending to criticize every bite, but it was heavenly. I found myself relaxing and enjoying myself. I drank a glass of buttery white wine, ate my fish soup, and talked to Lucas. This was a hell of a lot better than room service and pay-per-view in my hotel room.

"So, what made you choose this restaurant?" I asked between bites of my soup. "Do you come here a lot?"

He shook his head. "No, I've actually never been here before. I've always wanted to come though."

"You didn't bring Victoria here?"

Just hearing her name made him wince. After a moment he shook his head again. His sandy hair danced around his ears. "No, we never came here. She doesn't eat seafood."

"Allergic?"

"No."

"Vegan?"

"No."

"Religious thing?"

"No."

Each question sounded a bit more desperate, and each 'no' sounded a bit sadder.

"She just... doesn't like it? Any of it?"

He shrugged. "She has a lot of foods she doesn't like." I thought I detected a tinge of annoyance, but I might have imagined it.

Or maybe it was my own. The thought of never eating seafood again was anathema to me. "Do you really mean *any seafood*? No shrimp? No oysters? Lobster? Calamari? Sushi? Not even fish sticks?"

"None of it." His expression was bemused.

"Why?"

"She's just picky and not very adventurous."

Picky and not very adventurous? She sounds like she'd be a bore in bed. Or anywhere, actually.

"Well, more bouillabaisse for me." I thought about making a joke about there being 'other fish in the sea' but thought better of it. Too corny. I happily ate another bite. It seemed to melt in my mouth.

"So, you aren't disappointed in my selection?" He seemed genuinely curious. I wondered if he really wanted to please me or just didn't want me to be difficult. I decided it didn't matter.

"I'm not the least bit disappointed. Feel free to subject me to all the seafood Victoria hates until you two get back together."

"Duly noted. I'm glad you like it." His smile was wide, and it looked very real. I thought it was possible that he honestly wanted to make me happy, and that thought in itself made me happy, too.

Lucas didn't have to be nice to me. Our 'relationship' was fake. But he was being very nice, in addition to being funny, clever, and interesting. I found myself really enjoying his company much more than I'd hoped or intended. Too much.

He took more pictures of us at our table. The entire evening was exceptionally well documented. The waitstaff clearly thought we must be going out for our anniversary. They sent us a free dessert to 'celebrate.' That was a bit awkward, but I'm not one to turn down a dessert.

"You want to hear something sad?" I asked Lucas as we ate the cake.

He raised an eyebrow since his mouth was full of chocolate.

"This is the best date I've been on in a while, and it's not even real." I shook my head. "Dating in New York is the worst."

"Really? I would have thought the singles scene there would be pretty good."

I groaned. "No. *It's horrible*. At least for women. It's fantastic for men. The ratio of single, straight women to single, straight men is almost three to one."

"Maybe my app will help."

I smirked. "It certainly can't hurt. But if I end up going out with one more popped collar, boat-shoes-wearing guy who just wants to talk about his parent's Hamptons house, or is perfect aside from being secretly married, you're gonna get an angry text and a one-star review."

"I can't take any responsibility for the *quality* of who you match with. That's up to your taste in music and the magic of the algorithms."

"It matched me up with you."

His smirk turned into a real smile. "There's no accounting for taste."

"So, what's the magic? How does it really make the matches?" I hadn't had a chance to talk to Annie about it again yet.

Lucas smiled at me mischievously. "It's a secret."

"You know I'm here to figure it out and decide if it's worth buying, right?"

"You wouldn't be here if you didn't already think it was worth buying. And if you can't figure it out, that's on you. I've given you all the information." As always, his confidence was rock solid. It made me respect him more that he knew what he was worth.

Fair point. However... "Why won't you tell me?" My eyes narrowed. "You must have a reason not to be transparent about it, since you've been totally transparent about everything else."

He shook his head. Lucas clearly wasn't going to tell me.

Fine, keep your secrets.

"Will you tell me about Victoria now?" I asked, remembering his promise from earlier to tell me about her.

As always, he flinched at her name. "I guess so. Clearly, you aren't going to let it go."

"I'm just curious," I said, feeling weirdly guilty. I didn't like seeing him sad. "Never mind. You're right. There's really no need for me to know. I'll let it go."

He blinked in shock and stared at me in silence.

"What?" I asked after a moment when he continued to look at me with a mixture of surprise and suspicion.

"You're just going to let it go?" He looked at me like he was trying to figure out if I was being passive-aggressive. That wasn't really my style. If the situation merited it, I preferred aggressive-aggressive to passive-aggressive.

"Yeah." I could be reasonable when I wanted to.

"Really?" He clearly thought I was messing with him.

I shrugged. "We're not really dating, and even if we were, it doesn't matter. It's none of my business. If you don't want to share, that's your choice. I'm a big believer in respecting other people's choices. Especially if they don't affect me one way or the other." I paused for a second to gather my thoughts. "Besides," I told him, "talking about her clearly makes you sad. I don't want to make you sad. I'd rather have you happy."

After a moment, he smiled at me and it was a different sort of smile than I'd seen before. It tugged at my heart in a way that made me feel weak and lightheaded. There was heat in that smile, and pain, and hope. All of a sudden, my own heart was hammering against my ribs. My eyes lingered on his lips, his hands, and his beautiful, expressive eyes. I could sit here all night, just looking at him. But touching would be better.

Just what had I gotten myself into?

If this scheme didn't end up mending Lucas' heart, there was an increasing chance it might break mine.

* * *

ALTHOUGH THE FOOD was long gone, we lingered at the table over coffee. The differences between a real date and a fake date, as least as far as I could tell, were few. Even the fact that Lucas *didn't really like me* seemed distant as we talked. I was shocked to find how much we had in common, and because I didn't need to impress him for a second date, I felt like I could really be myself.

"So, Lucas, do you have, like, a thing for redheads?" I asked him, setting my cup down into my saucer with a little clink. I'd never be this brazen on a real first date, but I was honestly just curious. He'd said that he had a type. I assumed it was my hair that had attracted him in the first place.

Lucas looked a bit uncomfortable, but his tone was not defensive. "It's not a thing. It's just a preference." He shrugged. "Lots of people have preferences."

I smirked at him. "Do you remember your first redhead?"

His big hazel eyes blinked. "Huh?"

He probably thought I was talking about sex with his

first redhaired partner. I rephrased. "The first redhead that you liked. There must have been some formative female in your past that created your preference. A celebrity maybe? Or a redheaded babysitter?"

"That's a very personal question, Rae." His words were serious, but his tone was teasing. There was a mischievous smile on his handsome face, and it invited me to keep digging.

"Well, we are on a date," I countered.

"A fake date."

"You're no fun," I pouted.

"I'll answer your very personal question if you'll answer one of mine."

A challenge? Oh, sweetie, you don't even know what you're getting yourself into.

I smiled innocently. "Well, let's up the stakes then. We both get three extremely personal questions."

He smiled right back at me. "Okay. I'll play. But we both get one pass. Deal?"

"Deal."

I extended my hand over the table formally and he shook it. Then he sighed.

"Okay. Why do I prefer redheads, was that your question?"

Nice try.

I shook my head. "My question was, *who* caused your preference for redheads?"

He shifted in his seat. I could tell that he knew he'd

been caught. Finally, he sighed. "Okay. Fine." He shook his head and then took a deep breath to prepare himself. "I'm the middle child in my family. I have an older sister and a younger brother. When my sister was sixteen or seventeen and I was eight or nine, she made a new friend. Her name was Jodie. Jodie had red hair. Jodie was *gorgeous*. Legs for days. She, uh, caused an awakening in my eight-year-old mind. All of a sudden, I realized that girls were not gross after all. Let's just say that I spent a lot of time around my sister that summer, and that one time, I might have *accidentally* walked in the room while Jodie was changing into her bathing suit." Lucas looked totally and completely mortified.

I giggled and his embarrassment visibly deepened. The tips of his ears turned adorably red. That was such a benign, ordinary story. What normal, healthy, eight-year-old boy wouldn't try to get a look at a pretty, naked teenage girl? Still, I could tell that Lucas was worried that I would judge him.

"That's so cute," I told him. "Thanks for telling me."

He didn't seem to know quite what to do with the pronouncement that I found his story cute. After a moment he straightened, going businesslike and confident again. "My turn," he told me. "Are you ready?"

"Bring it on. Do your worst," I challenged. My past was a pretty open book. I didn't have a lot of secrets, and those that I did have, he wouldn't have a chance in hell of guessing.

84

"Why did you agree to be my fake girlfriend?"

That was his first question? I frowned at him. Coming up with an answer that didn't sound insipid was a bit difficult.

"A couple of reasons," I told him. "One, this is my first and probably only chance to leapfrog over my boss, Cliff. You know, the one that swallowed the bee the other day. Clenching this deal will let me do that." I smiled at him. "The second reason is a bit less practical. I was curious. I'm going to be honest with you, Lucas. I don't think this will help you get your girlfriend back. But everyone says you're a genius. So maybe I'm wrong. I want to see how this plays out."

Lucas listened to my reasoning with a bemused expression on his face. He shook his head when I was finished. "Well, that wasn't the answer I was hoping for, but I did ask. Your turn."

"What was the answer you were hoping for?" I asked, curiously.

Lucas arched an eyebrow at me. "Is that your second question?"

I bit my lip. *Crap.* Did I want to use my second question to know the answer? I nodded reluctantly.

Lucas' smirked widened to a grin. "I hoped you were a born romantic and were one hundred percent sure it would work."

I frowned. Lame. That wasn't a good answer at all. My secret heart had wanted him to admit that he wanted me to tell him that I was dying to spend time with him because he was equally into me. I should have known better. I rolled my eyes. "Your turn."

Lucas looked at me for a long time. Long enough that I started to feel self-conscious. "Why are you so ambitious?"

I blinked. "What?"

"I looked you up," he told me. "Your resume is on the Azure Group website. You graduated from high school at sixteen, from college at twenty, and were valedictorian of both. You were a track star in high school and college. You're not tall enough to ever run super competitively, but you did very well. It seems like you've gone your entire life looking for challenges and then moving on. You even said that was part of the reason you liked your job. You got to learn what there was to learn, but then you move on. You say I'm a genius, but you're more successful than most people with my IQ. When did you realize enough wasn't going to be enough?"

He looked me up? Should I be surprised and flattered? I was, but I should have known that he would. Maybe he'd looked me up before we'd even met. Answering his question was easy.

"Why am I so driven to succeed?" I frowned. "I guess I realized that I was better at schoolwork than most of my peers when I was really young. Probably kindergarten. But my parents always made it clear to me that being smart isn't enough. You have to *achieve and succeed*. Stupid is as stupid does. Just sitting around being smart and doing nothing is wasting all the gifts you've been given. Considering my childhood, I internalized that message probably more than most kids." I shrugged. "I just like solving problems and puzzles. I guess that's all it comes down to. I know I can solve the hard problems, so I do."

Lucas merely nodded at me. His expression was neutral. I had no idea if my answer pleased him or not. "Your turn," he said.

This was my last question. I thought it over carefully. "Can I save my last question for another time?"

Lucas shrugged. "I'll probably regret this, but sure."

"Okay. I'll do that. Do you want to ask me your last one?"

"What did you mean before when you said 'considering your childhood'?"

Fuck. I shouldn't have mentioned that.

Lucas must have seen the change on my face, because his fell. "You can pass if you want."

"No, it's fine." I sighed. "My dad died when I was a kid. He was diagnosed with brain cancer about the time my younger brother was born. So, I guess I would have been around four. He finally passed away when I was eight. That's what I meant about internalizing the things he said to me. Because I was so young when he died, all the things I do remember him saying meant a lot to me."

Lucas' eyes had gone huge. "Rae, I'm so sorry. If I made you remember anything painful, that wasn't my intention at all." He looked stricken.

"It's really okay." I smiled at him encouragingly. "It was a long time ago. I'm okay talking about him."

It was true, mostly. I didn't mind talking about my dad, but I still rarely did so with strangers. Usually I would only talk to friends the way I was talking with Lucas. I needed to make sure I remembered the realities of our situation. We weren't friends. We weren't on a date. We were temporary business partners, and that was all we'd ever be. Maybe if I kept reminding myself that, I could keep myself from getting emotionally invested.

10

LUCAS

VICTORIA 'LIKED' the photos of me and Rae on Instagram *and* Facebook. All of them. Which meant she looked at all of them, one by one. The thought that she even cared enough to look at them kept me awake all night. I knew her well enough to know that they probably kept her up too. She wouldn't like the idea of anyone else having me, even if she thought she didn't love me anymore.

Hope was something I'd kept alive for eighteen months by feeding it a little bit of my soul on a daily basis. But now, at last, I had something else to feed it. Evidence. Those 'likes' on social media fed my hope and it swelled in my chest and bloomed.

At the same time, another unfamiliar hope had begun to take root in me. I refused to acknowledge the traitorous feeling, not yet, but my night with Rae had sparked something. It had been a long, long time since I'd enjoyed a night out with a charming, attractive woman. Even if she was just pretending to enjoy my company, I had forgotten how much I liked it.

And she'd been so beautiful in her little dress and high heels, with her hair pulled back from her face in a high bun. I couldn't ever remember meeting anyone so effortlessly elegant. Rae had a gorgeous, long, graceful neck. I'd never been much of an admirer of women's necks, but Rae had an incredible one. I could easily imagine kissing the curve of her neck with lazy, light kisses, smelling her perfume and holding her close against me. I could imagine nipping her neck, panting against her neck, moaning desperately against it when I...

No.

Nope.

Stop right there.

Don't even let yourself think about that.

The good news was that Rae lived half a continent away. She headed back to New York with her team the next morning. She wouldn't return for a week. It was probably very good she wasn't around. She was necessary, but she was incredibly distracting. To say the least.

I kept myself busy in her absence by working on Notable Match and daydreaming about what I would do after I sold it and got back together with Victoria. Maybe I'd take her on a vacation. Perhaps Paris? Victoria had always talked about wanting to visit France, although the thought of being in the land of amazing food and not being able to eat anything disagreeable to her sensitive palate was almost too painful. The woman lived off a diet composed almost entirely of things I stopped enjoying around puberty. PB&J sandwiches, chicken nuggets, bagel bites, and Lunchables all featured prominently. None of those things were going to be available in France.

Maybe a tropical vacation would be better, although Victoria also had an enormous dislike of being too warm. Alaska? No, she hated to be cold, too. Japan? Food issues again, plus a serious language barrier. Then I figured it out.

Disneyworld. It was so obvious I could barely believe it had taken me the better part of two days. Victoria loved princesses, she loved shopping, she loved taking pictures, and the food there would be exactly up her alley. It wasn't my ideal vacation—I find the Lifesize cartoon characters incredibly creepy, get nauseated by rides, hate crowds, and generally dislike the blatant commercialism of all things Disney—but I knew she would love it. As long as she was happy, I was sure I could be too.

It was with thoughts of the happiest place on earth on my mind that I found myself sitting in the Lone Star Lounge a few days later in the late afternoon. I was researching 'adult activities' at Disneyworld when a huge, man-shaped shadow darkened my laptop screen.

"Did you have your recurring Mickey nightmare again?" asked Ward, rounding the table to sit next to me. "You really have some deep psychological issues to fear Mickey, you know that, right?"

I hadn't had my recurring Mickey nightmare in years. Until Ward mentioned it, I'd actually forgotten about it. *Thanks for the reminder, dude.* In the dream, which I had over and over during a health scare in college, Mickey chased me around with a knife. It always ended with me jumping off a building to avoid him.

"I'm planning a vacation," I told him, trying to stay focused. The only bad thing about working at the bar on a quiet afternoon was that if Ward didn't have enough to do, he'd go looking for entertainment. His favorite? Teasing me. Luckily, I was very good at turning his crap back on him. We both enjoyed our little talks.

He raised his eyebrows at me. "So, you're going to Disneyworld? By yourself? I'm pretty sure they'd put you on a list if you did that."

I smirked at him. "Not alone."

Ward gave me a genuinely sympathetic look and shook his head. "You're going with Cheryl and her brood? Man, that's not even a vacation. I'm sorry."

My older sister, Cheryl, and her husband, Rob, had seven kids. Seven! And all of them were under the age of eighteen. The kids were all nice and generally well behaved, but with that many, someone was always sick, crying, or fighting. Going to visit them made my real life feel like a vacation. Don't get me wrong. I like kids. Just not that many of them all at once.

"Thank God, no," I told Ward with a smirk. The idea of

going to Disneyworld with all those kids was truly terrifying.

"Who are you going with then?"

"Hopefully Victoria." I smiled.

Ward didn't reciprocate my happy smile. Instead, he went very, very still. I could practically hear the gears turning in his brain.

"You're planning a vacation with *Victoria*? Is she onboard with that?" His question was tentative, as if concerned I might have lost my mind. Little did he know, but I'd never been more mentally healthy in my whole life. Hope does wonders for a guy's mental health.

"Not yet, but she will be." I grinned.

"So...are you two...?" he tried, and then trailed off. He was still looking at me like I was nuts.

I shook my head. "Together again? No. But we will be."

He looked even more confused and concerned. I was excited enough to enlighten him.

"I've got a plan about how to get back with her." I turned the laptop around and showed him the pictures of Rae and me from our 'date.' He looked at them for a moment, then looked at me, then back at the pictures.

"I really don't understand." His eyes were fixed on the computer screen. "That's Emma's friend, Rae."

"Yes. Rae Lewis. She's going to help me get Victoria back."

"Does she know that?" Ward sounded incredibly disapproving. I frowned at him.

"*Yes*. I'm not leading Rae on. We're in on it together. Give me some credit. Rae and I have a whole plan." I was somewhat offended that he thought I might be using Rae. She was tough as nails, fully informed, and would be fairly compensated. I refused to feel guilty.

Ward looked like he'd just eaten something sour. "Let me guess. Is it to make Victoria jealous so she'll take you back?"

"That doesn't sound nearly as sophisticated as it would have if I'd explained it, but yeah. Basically, that's the plan." I sounded defensive. I knew that I did.

Ward stared at me for a moment before letting his eyes wander in silence. He waved Wendy, who was restocking glasses behind the bar, over to our table. She wandered over warily. The young, bubbly blonde seemed worried Ward was angry with her.

"What's up?" she asked, looking confused. She glanced over her shoulder at the bar, just as visibly worried she'd miss a customer.

"You've met my buddy, Lucas, right?" Ward asked Wendy, tilting his head in my direction.

Her chin bobbed up and down, sending her gold curls bouncing around her heart-shaped face. "Yeah, we met a couple of weeks ago. He's in here all the time." Her southern accent was thick as molasses.

"Lucas has a plan to get his ex-girlfriend back. I think he'd benefit from an independent, female opinion. Will you listen to his plan really quick and give him your opinion?"

Her gaze pinged back and forth between Ward and me. "Okay. Sure." She smiled tentatively and relaxed a bit.

I looked at Ward in annoyance and he raised his eyebrows at me. I sighed.

Fine.

The story flowed out of me in a rush. "My girlfriend and I broke up a while back. Call it creative differences, but I know we're meant to get back together. Rather than waiting on the universe to work its magic, I've got a better plan. I've found someone who is willing to pretend to be my girlfriend. Once my ex sees me with someone else, I know that she's going to realize she made a mistake. Then we get back together."

Wendy stared at me. "Hmm," she said. Then, when I didn't say anything else, she frowned. "That's it?"

I frowned right back at her. "What more do I need?"

My plan was simple, elegant, and I knew it would effective. Victoria was nothing if not possessive. She couldn't stand it when other women looked at me. Knowing another woman had me would infuriate her. I was sure of it.

"Why did you two break up again?" she asked, perching lightly on the chair across from me.

"Creative differences." I wasn't going to be more specific than that. Wendy was a sweet girl, but I barely knew her. I wasn't about to lay my heart on the table in front of her for critique.

"How will getting back together with her through jealousy fix those, um, creative differences?" she asked.

I smiled. "She'll realize that they weren't important after all."

She looked unconvinced. "But these creative differences were important enough to her to break things off with you in the first place, weren't they?" Her voice was gentle.

"Obviously yes, but only because she didn't realize what we had." I could hear defensiveness in my voice, and I tried to mitigate it by smiling.

"And seeing you with someone else will make her realize that."

"Exactly."

"Is she the jealous type?" Wendy asked next.

"Yes." Ward and I answered in unison. He was obviously holding back some additional comment he wanted to say about Victoria, either to avoid angering me or prejudicing Wendy. Maybe both.

After another moment when Wendy's blue eyes crawled around my face curiously, she shrugged. "It might work." *Yes!* "But it won't last." *What?*

Ward laughed. His smile was victorious.

"Wait, why won't it last?" I asked Wendy.

She looked at me like I was an idiot. "Because you didn't address the real problem. Clearly, she had some reason to leave you in the first place. Maybe it's her fault. Maybe it's your fault. Probably it's both of y'all's fault. But she was unhappy and wanted to go, and so she went. If she comes back without fixing the issues, it won't last. Once she takes away the source of her jealousy, she'll be unhappy again."

I shook my head at her. She clearly wasn't thinking it through all the way. "But once we're back together we'll have another chance to fix everything. We can talk about it and figure out what went wrong."

"But why didn't you just do that the first time?" She asked.

"I don't know. I guess I didn't listen enough to her complaints."

Ward rolled his eyes. "Dude, you did nothing but listen to her complaints."

I glared at him. "I'm talking to Wendy right now," I snapped. I turned my attention back to the coed in front of me. "Whatever happened the first time around won't happen again. I'm sure of it."

She shrugged, rising. "Okay. Well, I gave you my opinion, Lucas. I think you might get her back, but it won't be the way you want. She'll just end up leaving again if you don't fix whatever drove you apart last time." She paused. "What about the other woman?"

Rae? I shrugged. "What about her?"

"She's helping you for a reason, you know." Wendy's words were slow and gentle, like she was explaining a complex concept to a very small child.

At my side, I felt Ward sit up straight like something

very significant had just been shared. I merely shrugged. "I know that. She's getting something out of it, trust me. I made sure it would be worth her while." I grinned.

Wendy looked at me carefully, as if trying to decide whether to give me unsolicited advice. Her blue eyes were curious, but also guarded. We didn't know each other well. She chose not to push it any further. I could tell this entire conversation was out of her comfort zone.

"Okay. Well, good luck!" She headed back to the bar, clearly neither overly invested in my story nor concerned about my wellbeing. I had a feeling that she thought I was a bit dim and just not worth the trouble. Ward, however, was now looking at me with an expression of urgency and worry.

"Tell me that made a difference," he pleaded.

I smiled my most confident smile. Once everything had worked out the way it should, Ward would see. "I'll think about it."

It made absolutely no difference whatsoever.

11

RAE

My week in New York felt incredibly long. All I could think about was getting back to Austin. I told myself I was just excited about making the deal, but it wasn't only that.

I had to explain the situation to Kate and Emma, who both thought I was batshit crazy. After a long, tense conversation, they both agreed to keep my secret, but neither one of them thought it was a good idea. They also both had strong feelings about Lucas' ex-girlfriend, Victoria. At least according to them, she was pure evil.

Speaking of evil exes, I ran into an ex-boyfriend of my own at the grocery store on Tuesday. In the frozen food section, to be specific. All I wanted were some frozen blueberries for my morning smoothies, and sure enough, they were on that aisle. But so was Ivan.

"Rae? Wow, how great to see you!" he said, hugging me in the sort of awkward side-hug you would only give an ex-girlfriend. His British accent was just as crisp as ever. I was still staring at him like a deer in the headlights when he withdrew.

"Hi Ivan," I eventually managed to stutter, feeling grateful beyond belief that I'd put on real pants instead of wearing my pajama bottoms to the store.

Ivan looked the same as he had the last time I saw him, right down to the sharp suit and the wingtip shoes. We'd broken up about a year and a half ago, after he gave me an ultimatum about my job. We'd both exploded as months of small annoyances boiled over into a screaming fight.

He thought I travelled too much. I thought he needed to be more supportive and less controlling. He wanted to be with someone he could imagine having a future with, and despite the fact that we'd gotten together in an MBA program, he somehow thought I wanted to be a housewife. I wanted to be with someone who could imagine a future where we could both be successful professionals. He made me choose.

I chose.

And now there was a thin band of gold on his left ring finger.

"How have you been?" Ivan asked, treating me to the most cliché of all questions. He smoothed down his already very smooth, dark hair.

I put a big, fake smile on my face. "I'm doing great! Busy as ever. How about you?"

"I'm doing well, too." He paused. "Actually, I could use

some help. What kind of ice cream do you think my wife meant when she said, 'the monkey kind'? Joanne is pregnant, and she sent me over here to get it for her, but I don't know which one that is. I don't want to call her because I just want her to get some rest."

Well, that was obvious. Did he just say that to drive home to me that he's married and expecting a baby now? What a showoff.

I fought down my inner bitchy cynic. That wasn't fair. Ivan was a bit of a jerk, a fact I'd figured out far, far too late but, somewhere, a pregnant woman named Joanne was depending on me. She already had to be married to Ivan and have his baby, so the least I could do was make sure she got the right ice cream. "She means Chunky Monkey. It's a Ben and Jerry's flavor," I told him, pointing to the right section.

Ivan grinned. His teeth were still just as straight and perfect as I remembered. "Thanks! I never would have figured that out."

I smiled back. *You're an Ivy League educated businessman who graduated second in his class. You work for one of the most prestigious venture capital firms in the country, which your own family happens to own a majority stake in. I'm calling bullshit.* "Happy to help. And congratulations by the way."

"Thank you. I see you've found someone too. I saw your pictures from the other night. How's the long-distance thing?"

Thank you, Lucas.

Not having to be honest with Ivan that I couldn't find a guy to date to save my own life was a freakin' miracle. It wasn't like I didn't try. It just seemed like every guy I met in this city was looking for something I wasn't. Eight and a half million people lived on top of each other in this city and I couldn't find one good one to fall in love with me. Plenty of losers who sent me unsolicited dick pics, but no keepers. Just last month I'd gone on several incredibly underwhelming first dates. There would be no second dates.

"It's going good so far," I said, shrugging and gratefully pretending like Lucas and I were real. "Who knows what the future will bring?"

"That's fantastic, Rae. I'm so glad you're happy." His brown eyes weren't warm. I didn't believe him, but given how we'd parted, it wasn't a huge surprise. He probably still thought I should have been grateful to be his smiling, submissive trophy wife.

"I'm glad you're happy too," I told him with matching insincerity.

Although I wanted to be cynical and mean because of the way our relationship had ended, I found myself finally no longer feeling hurt. Ivan had proven to be controlling and petty when it came right down to it, but I was still brokenhearted when our relationship went off the rails. The fact that I had lost my job and my relationship at the same time added insult to injury. Somehow, my position had been mysteriously eliminated the same day Ivan and I broke up. It was nepotism at its finest and turned my whole life upside down.

We made forgettable small talk for a few minutes before going our separate ways again, but the conversation itself stuck with me for several days. Ivan and I were wrong for each other on so many levels, not just because he was an ass who needed a much more traditional partner. Our personalities were similar, and our politics were aligned, but there was always something missing between us. The spark that would make a person bend their own needs and will for someone else's was never there with Ivan and me, and he had a cruel and vindictive streak that always scared me a little bit. Overall, our differences made us less likely to compromise, and that ultimately compromised us.

I tried to live my life without dwelling on the things I couldn't change. Mostly I was good at it. I managed to avoid focusing on *why* my brother, Jarrod, had to have such a difficult time in our world as a trans guy and focus on *how* I could help him. I also managed to avoid focusing on *why* my dad died of cancer when I was eight and focus on *how* I could love and support the family I had left. But when it came to my dismal and unsuccessful love life, it was hard not to focus on whatever it was that must be wrong with me.

The feeling that there was something wrong with me stuck with me all week, until Lucas smiled at me again. Then it vanished like smoke. What could be wrong with me if he smiled at me like that? I basked in the warmth of his smile and let myself pretend, for just a second, that his smile was really for me and not Victoria.

"How was your flight?" he asked, grabbing my roller board and putting it in his trunk. He'd been kind enough to pick me up at the airport this time. I'd flown in the afternoon before Annie and Kyle, so that Lucas and I could have some extra time to 'date.'

"It wasn't bad," I answered, smiling back at him. "To be honest, I'm just glad to be out of New York. This time of year, it's always just cold, wet, and miserable."

Austin was eighty-five degrees and sunny. In October! It was a harvest miracle.

"When does the rest of your team get in?" he asked. He opened the car door for me, and I smiled at his polite gesture.

"Tomorrow morning." When he joined me in the car, I continued, "The due diligence process is going really well so far. I know you've only done this once before, but trust me, this is not how it usually goes. This has been the easiest deal I've ever worked on."

Lucas had sold his first app straight out of college. It had netted him a cool, low seven figures with which to fund his young adulthood. I didn't know his net worth, but unless he was just terrible with money, he was probably still in the black.

Lucas smirked at me. "I'm glad it's been relatively painless for you and your team."

"You haven't made us root through even one vermin

infested basement yet, so yes. It's painless." I smiled at him. "I hope we haven't been too awful to deal with, either."

"I'm not complaining."

A rogue thought killed my smile. "Did you look through the management agreements that I sent you?"

Lucas stopped smiling as well. "I did."

"And?"

"I guess Azure Group really wants to make sure they have a way to get rid of me the moment I think for myself." His voice was more resigned than bitter. I let out the breath I'd been holding.

"That's the general idea, yeah. I'm sorry." I felt weirdly ashamed of how shitty the agreements were. Usually it would be a platitude when I said as much to a client, but in Lucas' case it was true. I was sorry that he'd be losing control over his company. He seemed like he really believed in it.

But Lucas merely shrugged. "It's not your fault. My lawyer told me it would probably be like this." His voice held no recrimination.

I was glad he had a good lawyer. Having to explain to Lucas that I had no control of this part of the negotiation would have been difficult. I was basically just a conduit of information anyway. The truth was that I was more client wrangler than lawyer at this point.

"Well, I hope you're ready to get out and enjoy the sunshine," Lucas said, changing the subject. "You did remember to bring your swimsuit, didn't you?"

He'd texted that I should bring one. Butterflies flapped around wildly in my tummy. Of course, he would want pictures of me in a bikini to really make Victoria jealous. But it would also mean *I'd get to see him in a bathing suit.*

"We're going to Zilker Park," he told me as he eased his sleek Tesla out of the waiting line at the airport. "There's a natural swimming spot there called Barton Springs. Have you ever been there before?"

I shook my head. "No. Even though I lived here for two years, I barely saw anything but the inside of the library."

"You're gonna love it."

12

RAE

I'D NEVER BEEN AS FREAKIN' miserable in my entire life. The water in Barton Springs was deep, clear, and so incredibly, freakishly, nightmarishly cold that my toes cramped up. I scrambled out of the frigid water like a cat that fell into a bathtub and panted on the concrete. Somehow, it felt *even colder* outside the water.

"What the fuck, Lucas?" I cried between gasps. My voice was shrill. He'd challenged me to a race across the pool and stupidly, I agreed. I only made it about ten feet after jumping in.

From the icy cold water, Lucas laughed his ass off. "Cold huh?"

No shit.

"I thought you meant it was a hot spring, not an ice bath!" I was lying flat on my back, staring at the blue autumn sky, and shivering. I turned my head to see a concerned expression had appeared on his handsome face. He quickly swam toward the edge of the pool.

"Oh, no. Not a hot springs. Just a regular springs. It's sixty-eight degrees all year-round." He pulled himself smoothly out of the water, giving me an excellent view of his chiseled abs and pecs, as well as his sturdy shoulders. I ought to be panting from the sight of him, but I was too damn cold to care.

He scooped me up by the shoulders and settled a towel around me, half pulling me into his lap. The towel did next to nothing to warm me, but his body heat helped ease the cold. I sunk guiltily into the feeling of being held, even like this. It had been a long time since someone had held me.

"Shit, Rae. I'm sorry. Don't be mad." His voice came through as a rumble with my ear against his chest. He had a really nice voice, smooth and low. The combination of the voice and his lanky, muscular body was impossible to ignore. Even being plunged into the awful, cold water wasn't enough to distract me from Lucas.

"That was a mean trick," I told him, pouting. In New York we don't go swimming in water that cold. Not ever. At least, not on purpose. If we get accidentally shoved into the Hudson, then sure. But no one would ever consider a dip in sixty-eight-degree water to be a healthy, normal activity.

"I'm sorry," Lucas said. His expression was total contrition and his incredible hazel eyes were wide and innocent. He looked genuinely sorry, but I wasn't about to let him off the hook so easily. He had just tricked me into jumping into frigid water. The fact that other people—children even—were swimming in the pool didn't excuse it. Apparently, people in Texas are completely and totally crazy. Their summer heat must have driven them insane, or maybe it was the politics. These were the people that put jalapeños on a burger. In hindsight I probably should have known.

"I'm gonna get you back for this," I promised him fake-menacingly, leaning in until I was just an inch from his ear. "Somehow, some way, I'll get you back."

I pulled back and stared at him with my meanest, most unpleasant face, but when his eyes went wide when he started to wonder if I was really mad, I couldn't keep it up. I giggled, and he joined in a moment later. Relief was evident in his laugh. He rocked me lightly in his arms and I laughed even more.

When our laughter subsided, we found ourselves wet and almost naked in each other's arms on the side of the pool. The noise around us, a cacophony of children playing, swimmers splashing, and people talking, receded. They all but disappeared. I was only seeing Lucas.

I became hyperaware of everywhere our bodies touched, his arm behind my shoulders, my palm against his bicep, the soft curves of my chest pressed to the muscles of his, and most especially, where my ass rubbed against his lap with only thin, wet fabric to separate us. My nipples were so hard from the cold that they ached. In fact, my entire body had started to ache with an urgent, dull feeling. Not from the cold. For him.

My breath flowed out of me in a rush as I stared into Lucas' incredible hazel eyes. I thought I saw my own shock, and my sudden wanton need, reflected there. Seeing his desire multiplied my own tenfold. My heart hammered against my cold, exposed ribs. Neither one of us seemed to know what to do with our feelings. We were caught up in a moment, and I think it shocked us both. I felt his cock growing long and hard against my backside. It was impossible to ignore, and I didn't want to. I wanted more.

"Look at you two lovebirds." The voice that ruined it was throaty, female, sarcastic, and oddly familiar. Lucas and I both looked up. My mouth dropped open.

"Victoria?" Lucas stuttered.

Lucas' ex-girlfriend Victoria was *Victoria Priestly*. The lead singer of Edelweiss, an indie rock band whose debut single was on heavy rotation on every alternative rock radio station that didn't suck from coast to coast, Victoria Priestly was about to become famous. She was poised right on the edge of stardom.

Lucas' ex was a fucking rock star? That's just not fair.

I wished I didn't know who she was, but I did. I'd actually known about her for almost a year, well before her music got big. Edelweiss played a super trendy club in Brooklyn that I'm still not sure why I was allowed into, but I'd bought the album that night. It was still my go-to jogging music. Her voice sounded like an edgier Adele crossed with a more polished Janis Joplin, low, throaty, and full of wild emotion. She had a voice that was meant for rock and roll and a look that matched. I liked her. Or I had until this moment.

Victoria was quite a bit taller than me. I realized this fact when Lucas and I both scrambled to our feet in a rushed, ungainly tangle of limbs. She was at least three inches taller than me, and I felt small and fragile by comparison. Never had my perfectly respectable, above average height felt so thoroughly inadequate. In fact, almost everything about me felt inadequate by comparison. Having this conversation while we were all wearing swimsuits made it about a thousand times more awkward. At least her tits were a lot smaller than mine. She barely filled out the triangles of her yellow, polka-dotted bikini.

"Hi Victoria," Lucas was saying at my side. He'd wrapped an arm around my waist possessively and pulled me against his erection, presumably to hide it from her. He was smiling confidently and with such cool, total nonchalance that I would never have known it was a moment of a lot of conflicting feelings for him if I couldn't feel his hard cock pressing firmly against the cleft of my ass. "Rae, this is my old friend, Victoria."

"Hello Victoria. It's very nice to meet you," I told her, putting my emotions on lockdown and extending a hand. I bent forward a bit and rubbed my butt against Lucas' cock just a bit to remind him that I was aware of it. My face was a neutral, impenetrable mask. "Lucas has told me so much about you."

"Nice to meet you too, Wren," Victoria said smoothly, shaking my cold, wet hand with her warm, dry one. Her meticulously made-up green eyes lingered on where Lucas' palm sat firmly atop the curve of my hip. They narrowed dangerously.

"Rae," I corrected with a big smile.

She adjusted her view from my midsection to my face. "What?"

"My name. It's Rae, like Rachel. Not Wren."

She smiled a very fake smile. "Oh, *Rae*. I'm so sorry. I'm just horrible with names."

I shrugged. *You're not sorry*, I thought to myself. Dislike for me was practically radiating off the gorgeous woman in waves. The feeling was becoming increasingly mutual.

It certainly didn't help that she was fucking gorgeous. Tall, willowy, with bright orange hair that fell around her perfect face in ringlets, Victoria looked more than a little bit like a wild, fairy princess. Her fey look was accentuated by a variety of tattoos and piercings, a razor thin figure, and elaborate winged eye makeup. I felt decidedly ordinary and, well, fat next to her. At least my black, scalloped bikini was cute, and I filled it out nicely. I may not be super tall and skinny, but I'm not exactly hideous either.

I'd imagined that when I met Victoria I would feel some sort of sympathy for her. Part of me had convinced myself that I was doing some sort of good deed by helping

Lucas and Victoria get back together. But now that I was staring at her, I didn't feel anything positive whatsoever. Actually, I felt possessive of Lucas, which was ridiculous, because he wasn't mine.

I forced those feelings away and tried to focus on the conversation that Lucas and Victoria were having.

"I didn't know you were in town," Lucas said to Victoria, and I could very well have believed that it was true if I didn't *know it to be bullshit*. There's not a chance that Lucas didn't plan this. He was just too damn clever for that. I just wished he had let me in on his plan. A warning would have really been nice.

"I still live here!" Victoria replied with another big, white smile. She laughed lightly. "Although," she added with a dramatic sigh, "with all the traveling we've been doing, it's hard to remember that sometimes. Sometimes I just feel like a gypsy on the road. But I'm here for at least the next month or so while we recuperate from the tour." She paused for a moment. "We're playing the Zilker Hillside Theater tonight." Her eyes searched Lucas' face. "You should come. We could hang out afterward."

Lucas had explained to me that the hillside theater just across the street from the pool was a popular venue in the summers. Which explained why she was here. And why he knew she would be. Damn scheming Lucas. He was lucky he was so damn hot and charming. Otherwise I'd probably be really pissed off. As it was, I could only work up a mild irritation.

"I wish we could," Lucas told her, shaking his head in obviously fake sorrow. His wet hair flew everywhere, and I wanted to push it back. "But we've got date night plans. Reservations, you know."

"Too bad," she replied, pouting. "But we're sold out anyway. I doubt you could find tickets."

Lucas and Victoria proceeded to make meaningless small talk that was a poorly veiled verbal sparring match. She would make a snippy, borderline rude comment, he defused it, and then she pushed harder. Each time, he calmly redirected the conversation, which only worked her up more. It was like watching someone stoke a fire. Sooner or later, she'd ignite. I was pretty sure I didn't want to be around when she exploded.

She was ignoring me entirely, which was fine, since it gave me a better chance to observe her. Everything about her radiated tension and jealousy. Her arms were crossed in front of her chest. Her eyes darted around Lucas' face urgently. Even her toe was tapping restlessly. When her attention did slide to me, her expression was dismissive.

Lucas had to have known that she had a personality that was highly motivated by jealousy, but now that I saw Victoria in action, I could see that it was very, very true. I was slightly afraid of her, truth be told. I'm not one to intimidate easily, but I don't seek out conflict or drama, either. It seemed to me like Victoria thrived off it.

"So, Rae," Victoria asked me. "How long have you and Lucas been together?" Her eyes looked me over like she expected the answer to be "ten minutes ago" and "we met on Craigslist's escort section."

Why she was asking me and not Lucas was a mystery. She clearly didn't mind ignoring me. I decided to be cautious and succinct with my replies. I didn't want to be drawn into any traps, and I'm not the best liar.

"Not super long. A few weeks." I smiled up at him and Lucas pressed his lips to my forehead. As first kisses go it was unimpressive, but it was enough to make Victoria's left eye twitch and her smile freeze on her face.

"*That's just wonderful,*" she said, using the same tone of voice that I would use if I got off the subway to find it was raining and I'd forgotten my umbrella. I smiled like Mona Lisa. Then she struck, "Jason and I have only been together a few weeks too. *Isn't new love fun?* It's the best part."

Lucas had gone still at my side, but a feeling of competitiveness had been growing in me during the entire exchange with Victoria. I wasn't about to let her come out of this conversation with the upper hand. And Jason, whoever the hell he was, didn't seem to be around.

"It really is," I answered her, turning to Lucas and angling his chin down to kiss him. I winked as I went up on my tiptoes. He hadn't been expecting it, but after a heartbeat, he caught on. Then, a heartbeat after my lips brushed his, he took over the kiss.

Lucas' strong, long fingered hands gripped my waist tighter, pulling me flush against him, hip to hip and chest to chest. He kissed me urgently, not going for chaste like our first kiss. Not at all. His tongue sought mine passionately, exploring and claiming every inch of my mouth. He stole my breath, leaving me panting and no longer remotely cold by the time we pulled apart. Instead, my whole body felt warm and feather light. I stared at him in wonder.

Until I turned to see Victoria, that is. All the kinetic energy pinging around in me drained when I got a load of her hateful expression. If looks could kill, hers would be a war crime.

"Well, I need to go get ready for tonight," she said into the pregnant, hostile silence that had descended. I could tell that she was more than ready to leave. "Jason and I will see you around, right?"

Lucas went still but he was still staring down at me. "Yes, I guess so." The fact that she was seeing someone apparently was a surprise to him. He recovered a second later, but continued to stare at me, rather than her. "See you soon." He sounded totally unconcerned.

Victoria traipsed off, presumably to get ready for her gig. Lucas and I stared at one another. There were so many things going on in my head that I had to physically shake it clear. The fact that he was looking at me so intently wasn't helping.

"I think we need to talk," I told him.

13

LUCAS

"Are you mad at me?" I asked Rae as we walked back to the car. She'd said that she thought we needed to talk, but instead of talking, she was totally silent. If my experience with Victoria was any indication, silence meant she was fucking furious. The longer the silence went on, the bigger the eventual explosion would be. Given the sea change that had taken place in my brain at the pool, I was now doubly terrified that Rae would tell me to fuck off forever.

Rae looked over at me in apparent surprise. "Mad? No. I'm just organizing my thoughts."

I didn't trust that response at all. I steeled myself for an outburst, but it never came. By the time we were pulling into the garage at my condo, I was wondering if my life was in danger.

Part of me welcomed death—Victoria was seeing some-one. Not just any someone either. I assumed her Jason was

Jason Kane, lead singer and guitarist of Axial Tilt. Kane was almost obscenely famous. His music was everywhere, and up until this moment, I'd quite enjoyed it. I made a mental note to delete him off every playlist as soon as possible.

The recent success of Edelweiss was probably due in no small part to a recent collaboration between the two groups that had brought Kane and Victoria together. The fact that Victoria was dating *him*, a bona fide rock star who liked to perform shirtless and probably had more groupies at his disposal than I had bad code, was an ego blow. To say the least. So much so that I almost laughed at it. Yet, somehow, I was less upset than I'd thought I'd be. Maybe the pain would hit later.

"Okay," she said as I let the car park itself. "I'm ready to talk now. I really appreciate you waiting." Rae's tone of voice was completely normal. "Sometimes people rush me when I'm thinking, and that *does make me mad*. So, thanks." She smiled.

I blinked. "No problem?" I hadn't meant it to be a question, but it came out that way out of concern and disbelief.

Her smile turned thin. "I have four issues I want to talk about. The first is the fact that you didn't tell me that your Victoria was the lead singer of Edelweiss. She's famous enough that I would have appreciated a heads-up about that."

After a moment, my head bobbed up and down. "I

didn't realize how popular they'd gotten. Sorry. I wasn't trying to keep you in the dark about that. Promise."

She thought about that for a moment. "Okay."

"Okay?" I didn't like that my statements were coming out as questions, but I couldn't seem to stop it from happening. I was becoming a parrot.

"Yeah." She paused. "The second thing is that you knew she might be there. You knew that we might run into her, but you didn't tell me. Why did you do that?"

This was why I thought she'd be the angriest. I resisted the temptation to swallow nervously.

"I wanted your reactions to be genuine." My voice sounded confident, but in reality, I was anything but. I sighed. "Honestly? I thought that Victoria and I would be back together by now and that we'd never have to even have this conversation."

She arched an eyebrow at me. "That's kind of a shitty answer."

I'm kind of a shitty guy. Why do you think Victoria left me in the first place? The insecure thought pinged through me unexpectedly.

"I'm sorry." It was true, I was sorry. Actually, I was pretty ashamed. It had been a shitty thing to do, and I'd done it because I was afraid that she wouldn't want to follow through with her end of the deal when actually faced with Victoria. I underestimated her. Immensely. She'd definitely held her own against Victoria's 'charm.'

Rae was searching my face for something, but I don't

know if she found it. Eventually, she shrugged. "Next time, I'd appreciate a heads-up if you plan out any elaborate set ups."

"I can do that." I was still stunned she wasn't yelling at me. Maybe women were only irrational and volatile in relationships? This pleasant, reasonable conversation we were having was a nice surprise.

"Next is the fact that Victoria is seeing someone. It seems you didn't know that. Are you sure you want to continue with this plan?" she asked me.

Rae was looking at me like she wasn't sure if she wanted me to say yes or no. In truth, I hadn't considered the possibility that Victoria would go and get herself in a relationship with someone else. I'd not factored it into my mental calculus. But it didn't really matter. I wanted Victoria back. Whether or not she was seeing someone else was really irrelevant.

"I don't think it changes anything," I told Rae after a beat. "I still want her." Thinking about her with Jason Kane made me feel vaguely nauseated. "I wasn't expecting her to be in a relationship, but it's new. I'm sure that my plan will still work. For all I know, she started dating Jason Kane just because she was jealous of seeing me with you."

Actually, the more I thought about it, the surer I was that Victoria had done just that. She'd been friends with the guy for months on social media. But until today, I had no idea they were dating. They might have been keeping their relationship a secret to avoid paparazzi attention, but that wasn't really the style of either of them. Rock stars tend to be exhibitionists in a fairly big way.

Rae blinked in confusion. "Jason Kane?" she repeated. "From Axial Tilt?"

The man was a household name and a modern rock legend. His band, Axial Tilt, was ridiculously popular. Despite being roughly the same age as Victoria and me, Jason Kane had more Grammys and number one hits than The Beatles. He was rock and roll royalty.

I winced and nodded. "Yeah." I shook my head in dismay. "I'm fairly certain that's the Jason she's referring to. They've been chummy for a while. I didn't think they were dating though."

"It must be weird to read about your ex in the tabloids," Rae remarked.

My smile was bittersweet. "Yeah. There's nothing quite like watching TMZ to find out who your ex is screwing. It's not fun."

Rae shook her head as if to clear it of Jason Kane and Victoria Priestly. Her expression cleared. Unfortunately, it wasn't that easy for me. "Okay. Well, if you're still committed to the plan, then I guess that brings me to the last thing." She took a deep breath. "Lastly—and this was the thing I needed to think about for so long—but I think we need to set some physical boundaries." Her voice had become unexpectedly soft and vulnerable sounding.

My brain was swimming with thoughts I hadn't figured out how to interpret yet, but that tone worried me. Did she find me repulsive? She kissed me. Had she hated it? I hadn't hated it. Not at all. Not remotely. In fact, despite all my plans about Victoria, I'd do just about anything to do it again. I was having some serious cognitive dissonance.

Something important had happened to me when I gripped Rae's little waist and kissed her to break Victoria's heart. Something broke alright, but it didn't have a thing to do with Victoria. It had to do with me and with Rae. The lie I'd been telling myself, the one where this was purely about Victoria and that the only reason that I was attracted to Rae was that she somewhat resembled Victoria in appearance and temperament was shattered. But I'd deal with that revelation later. I had a more pressing crisis to attend to.

Unfortunately, I didn't know how. So, I just did my stupid parrot thing again: "Physical boundaries?"

"Yes."

"*You kissed me.*" I felt this was a very important detail.

She turned in her seat to face me better. "You're right. I did. And now I'm not sure that was a good idea."

I paused for a moment and examined her face for clues. There were none. "I'm sorry if I made you uncomfortable." The thought that she hadn't enjoyed kissing me made me feel somewhat ill. Oddly, it was even worse than learning about Jason Kane. Apparently, my ego was just really fragile these days.

Unexpectedly, she laughed at my words. "*Uncomfortable?* Did I seem uncomfortable to you?"

I could only reply honestly. "Not really." Rae had

seemed to enjoy our kiss, but maybe she was just a really good actress.

She was smirking at me, but it was short-lived. "I wasn't uncomfortable. I think I was too comfortable, Lucas. I... I just think we should set some boundaries over what we're going to do physically. Are you open to that?"

"Sure." I didn't understand what I'd done, but I didn't want her to be unhappy. "I'm open to whatever you need to feel comfortable. If you don't want to do anything other than hold hands, I'll figure out a way to make it work."

She smiled at me, and it was genuine this time. I could tell when her smiles were real when the corners of her eyes crinkled. Most of her smiles at me so far had been fake, but this one was real. I smiled back at her encouragingly.

"Come on," I told her. "Let's go inside, get some takeout, and make some rules for our fake relationship."

"You know," I told Rae as we drank a couple of beers while we waited for the food to show up, "I really thought you were going to yell at me. I keep waiting for you to start, but you just sit there all normal and calm."

"Yell at you?" She asked, eyes wide. "Why would I do that?"

She looked a bit offended. Her red eyebrows knit together. I backpedaled.

"I, um, I just thought you were really mad at me about what happened at the pool."

"Now you're worried I'm mad at you because you said that," she guessed.

I hung my head. "Guilty."

She sighed. "Do you think I'm crazy?" Her breath slipped out in exasperation. "Why do guys always think that redheads are going to be crazy women?" She did something with her hands that conveyed frustration in a universal language. "We're not crazy! It's just hair!"

I smiled at her. "I think it's just an urban legend that redheads are any crazier than anyone else. I'll try not to jump to conclusions next time."

She returned my smile with a wry little one of her own. "I'm hypersensitive to people thinking I'm crazy or one of those women who complain constantly and for no reason." She sighed. "It's actually sort of a weird thing for me." Her voice had gotten small and hesitant all of a sudden.

I didn't know what that meant, and I was probably supposed to let it drop, but I couldn't. My curiosity wouldn't let me ignore a nugget of Rae trivia. "What kind of a weird thing?"

She shifted in the chair she was settled in and her gaze darted around the room nervously. "You really want to know?"

I nodded. I was finding that I wanted to know everything about Rae. It was an insatiable hunger for information. The more I knew, the more I wanted to know. It couldn't be normal, but I didn't know how to stop it. I'd developed some sort of an addiction to her. Protracted loneliness must be taking its toll on me.

Still, I knew I had no right to my curiosity. "Only if you don't mind sharing," I added carefully. "I don't want to be pushy or make you uncomfortable."

"I don't mind," she said with a little self-deprecating laugh. "It's just a silly story. You know that my dad died when I was a kid. One of the things that he told me, and it's just one of those things that's always stuck with me for some reason, was that 'someone else is happy with less than you have.' I guess I was being a pain in the butt one time. I think I was complaining about wanting some toy. Anyway, he told me that and I've always tried not to complain about stuff unless it's really, really important to me."

I paused. Rae didn't want to appear spoiled, so she didn't complain? It seemed so at odds with her dominant personality. But at the same time, it made perfect sense why she'd internalize a lesson like that from a parent who died. My heart broke for her. I hated the idea that she'd had to go through something so terrible and scary as a young kid as losing a parent. I couldn't imagine losing a parent now, and I was pushing thirty. I found myself wishing I could protect Rae from the pain.

"I don't think you're crazy for complaining when I do something that bothers you," I told Rae. "Also, I complain all the time." She smiled thinly.

"I'll keep that in mind."

I knew it was an inadequate thing to say, but I didn't want her to think that I considered her unbalanced or irrational. I'd been with an irrational partner before. Victoria, although she had many wonderful qualities, was the queen of becoming irrational, especially when challenged or stressed. Sometimes it was completely exhausting. By comparison, Rae was the most even-keeled, rational woman in the world.

"I've never subscribed to the irrational redhead theory," I told Rae, watching her skeptical face for some sign that I had convinced her.

She rolled her eyes at me instead. "Oh, so you believe the whole 'gingers are soulless' thing instead? Because let me tell you, that's not a whole lot better. I used to get teased about that at school." Rae's sense of humor was as dry as the Sahara.

I laughed at her sarcasm. "I'm not even going to touch that one. I'm not even sure *if I have a soul*. But, trust me, I think you're great. And it has nothing to do with your hair color."

"Well alright then," she answered. I wasn't sure if she was completely convinced, but she wasn't frowning anymore. I'd take it.

"Alright," I repeated.

I ordered pizza, which was another food I would have to cut back on when Victoria and I got back together. Rae, however, had no objections to a nice greasy, cheesy slice of heaven. Instead, she had objections to Texans making pizza on principal. Apparently, they had no right.

While I waited for the pizza to arrive, we traded off taking showers. While Rae took her shower, I did my best not to think of her, naked, less than fifty feet from me. Seeing her in that tiny black bikini had tested the limits of my usually excellent self-control. Especially once she'd gotten all soaking wet and it clung to her *just so*. Even the shock of seeing Victoria again wasn't enough to dispel the image of Rae in that bikini, or the feel of her pressed against me, or the taste of her lips...

By the time the pizza arrived, I was so deep in thought about Rae that I nearly jumped out of my skin. Rae wandered out of the bathroom a few moments later.

"I've seen the shit that qualifies for pizza outside of New York," she told me skeptically. "If you serve me ranch dressing with my pizza, I'm so out of here. And I do mean permanently."

If she knew what we put on pizzas in California, she'd have a seizure.

"Oh, ye of little faith," I told her, shaking my head at her. "Trust me, Homeslice is the best pizza in town. It will not disappoint you. And there will be no ranch." I hoped my confidence in the local pizza hotspot was not misplaced.

When the food arrived, I stood back and watched her evaluate it. Rae cracked the lid of the pizza box with a manicured, careful hand and lifted it just enough to smell.

She then removed a piece of pizza and held it in her hand, testing the width and pliability. Finally, she delicately folded the slice and nibbled on the edge.

"Well?" I asked from my position leaning against the fridge.

"It'll do." I thought I detected a grudging respect in her tone, but I wasn't going to risk asking if she liked it.

"Good," I told her, loading myself up a plate and then grabbing a couple of beers from the fridge. "So, now that we've got the food thing worked out, you wanted to talk about boundaries?"

She nodded and accepted the bottle I was offering her. "Yes. I think we need to determine what sorts of public displays of affection are necessary."

Something about the way Rae was talking made me concerned. I took a risk.

"You regret kissing me."

She blinked. "I didn't say that."

Rae might say she wasn't a lawyer yet, but I needed a damn court reporter to argue with her.

"Do you regret kissing me?"

"I—" she paused and hung her head. "No."

I frowned. "But you don't want it to happen again?"

Her face looked as confused as I felt. She shoved her plate away from her in what I interpreted as frustration. "I don't know." I waited while she took a deep breath in and out before continuing. "I think I like you more than I should."

14

RAE

WHEN IN DOUBT, tell the truth. That was what my mom always told me. I doubt she ever had this situation in mind. Lucas looked at me quizzically and I felt my cheeks burning. He didn't reply for a long, long time. His silence was my answer.

"Rae..." Lucas' voice was soft. Sweet. Comforting. I shook my head.

"Don't," I interrupted. "I don't want you to let me down gently, okay?" I sighed. "I know that you want Victoria and not me. I agreed to help you get her back, and I'm going to do it. Let's just agree that we won't kiss anymore. Okay? *It confuses me.*"

Lucas' eyes held secrets he wasn't going to confide. The bright, brilliant hazel I'd so quickly grown accustomed to seeing was suddenly dimmer. He looked like he wanted to tell me something, probably something meant to ease the sting of rejection, but he listened to me. He didn't try to let me down easy. He just nodded.

"Okay, Rae." He was silent for a while more. I waited as patiently as I could. "It confuses me too, if it makes you feel any better. It confuses the hell out of me." The raw honesty in his suddenly gravelly voice, and the heat in his eyes when he looked at me told me it was true.

My lips parted in surprise. Meeting his eyes had become difficult, so I stared straight ahead of me. "It helps a little," I admitted. I stole a glance at him and saw that he was staring at his feet. Apparently, this was a hard conversation for both of us. At least we were being honest. I couldn't stand it when people danced around the truth. It was better just to admit the hard things. Even if it meant not kissing Lucas again when I really, really wanted to. The shower I'd taken in his loft had been as ice cold as Barton Springs, and it still hadn't helped with the constant, aching desire that I was feeling for him.

"I didn't ask you to dye your hair because I didn't like it," Lucas said suddenly. I looked over at him in surprise, both by the change of subject and the subject.

"You didn't?"

Lucas shook his head. "No. Not at all. I actually love that color hair." He sighed. "I asked you to change it because it reminded me of Victoria's hair color when we first met. Obviously, it's not that color anymore. But I just thought it would be too weird. It was a selfish thing to ask. I'm really sorry."

I shrugged. I touched the vibrant strands of my new hair self-consciously. "I'd been wanting to dye my hair for a long time. I like it like this." Every time I saw myself in the mirror, even after a week, I smiled. This was the color hair I wish I had naturally. It was perfect, and everyone said it looked really good. Even my brother liked it, and he was obnoxiously conventional.

"It does look really nice on you." His tone was admiring.

"I'm honestly not angry about the hair thing at all. I swear." He seemed weirdly hung up on it. Hair was just hair. Plus, the dye was temporary. It would fade in six weeks.

"I still feel bad though." He frowned like he'd asked me to pierce my tongue or get a neck tattoo or something else permanent.

"Why?"

His frown deepened. "Victoria and I were together for four years. We got together in college, and for a long time we were happy. But over time, I think I messed up with her. She didn't get what she needed from me and it made her unhappy. I tried, but it just wasn't enough. But even though things weren't perfect, I was still really surprised when she left." He trailed off in memory. I wondered if I was the first person he'd told this story to. It seemed to be costing him a lot to relive it.

"You don't have to tell me this," I told him. "You don't

owe it to me." Like I'd told him before, I didn't want to make him sad.

He shook his head. "After Victoria left, I threw myself into my work. That's paid off, or it's about to." He grinned at me for a second, reminding me why I was in this city in the first place. "But when I saw Victoria a few weeks ago, I realized that I had to get her back. Then when I matched with you, saw you.... When we talked, I realized how smart, beautiful, sophisticated, and pragmatic you are. I thought it was fate. The universe had given me all the tools to get Victoria back. Was it a well-thought-out plan? No. Not at all. It was totally impulsive, and I'm not really an impulsive person. I'm not good at it. So, I didn't think about you, Rae. I didn't think about how all this would make you feel. Like with your hair. I didn't think about that before I said something. I didn't think about you getting confused today at the pool when we kissed. And I didn't think that I would get... so confused, too."

Once he finished, I couldn't say a thing. My heart was in my throat, threatening to escape out my mouth if I opened it. Lucas stared at his mostly uneaten pizza. Then he picked up his beer and took a drink of it before setting it back down self-consciously. "Rae, you're staring," he said. "Say something, please."

I looked away, embarrassed. "I'm not sure what to say, Lucas." I played with my charm bracelet nervously before folding my hands primly in my lap and sitting up straight.

Curiosity got the best of me. "Do you really think that I'm all those nice things?"

Lucas looked confused. "What things?"

I squirmed. "You said I was smart, beautiful, sophisticated, and pragmatic. Do you really think I'm those things?" It hurt my heart just to ask, but I wanted to know. No, I *needed to know*. I needed to know if someone like Lucas could think so highly of me. After so many failed relationships, so many nasty dick pics, so many first dates that never went anywhere, I had to believe it meant something.

Lucas smiled at me. "Yes. Very much. Although it doesn't help me feel less confused to admit it." His tone was melancholy.

In that second, I wanted to be confused. I wanted to be totally and completely befuddled and lost and addled. I wanted Lucas to make it so much worse. I wanted him to get lost at sea with me.

I wanted to feel *anything* that wasn't alone and rejected. I looked at him sitting there, fresh from a shower, looking like everything I could want in the world. Lucas was smart, ambitious, and kind. He was handsome, his body was terrific, and he wanted me. He was also hopelessly in love with someone else. Sitting on Lucas' couch, stone cold sober, I made a fully informed, terrible decision.

"Lucas," I told him. "I really think we should have sex now."

15

LUCAS

I TOLD Rae that I'm not an impulsive person, and I'm not. I usually think through all my decisions very carefully and from as many angles as I can. Something that my friends sometimes interpreted as me psychoanalyzing them was actually my attempt to understand how other people make decisions, so I could use what they do well in my own life.

But I wasn't thinking at all when I leaned over and kissed Rae.

Her mouth was soft against mine, and she yielded instantly when I flicked my tongue against her lips. Like our kiss at the pool, I found myself unable to stop once I got started. Her mouth was perfect. Our tongues danced and wrestled against each other, seeking sensation and finding smooth, hot friction.

"This is just to get our confusion out of our systems,

okay?" Rae whispered in my ear when I finally left her mouth to kiss her long, beautiful neck.

"Mhmm," I mumbled against her skin. Her neck was everything I'd fantasized about and more. She smelled so good. Rationally I knew that she just smelled like the same body wash that I used on a daily basis since she'd just used my shower, but somehow, she didn't. She smelled like Rae, and her smell was unbelievably good.

"It doesn't matter, right?" she asked.

I mumbled something incoherent back against her neck in affirmation. Talking had become too difficult. Besides, I had better things to do with my mouth. Like kiss her.

We shifted on the couch, becoming more horizontal. Beneath me, her body felt soft and pliable. Her little hands wove their soft fingers in my hair, and she spread her legs beneath me.

With the few rational brain cells left in my brain, I knew that this was not the right thing for us to do. It was an objectively bad idea. I knew my heart still belonged to Victoria. But at that moment, my body belonged to Rae. And I'd sell my soul to keep on touching her curvy, perfect body.

Rae sighed softly when I lifted the hem of her shirt and cupped her. Under the soft, lacey bra she was wearing, her skin was as smooth as silk. Her perfect, pink nipples darkened to duskier pink as they grew harder under my fingers. They hardened even more when I dipped my head to kiss them. My eyes slipped closed as I tasted her there for a long time, enjoying the feeling of her arching up beneath me to urge me on.

It had been so long since I'd touched someone like this. Had it ever been like this before? Had I ever felt so overwhelmed by the way a woman's breathing caught when I dragged my teeth along her neck? Or the way she smiled victoriously when she undid the buttons on my shirt and slid her hands up and down my back?

What was she doing to me?

Rae had said that she was confused. I didn't know what fucking planet I was on anymore. I didn't even know my own damn name. All that I knew was that I needed to keep getting her more and more naked. That was clearly the solution to all my problems: Rae, naked. In fact, I was pretty sure that was the answer to all problems.

What should I have for lunch tomorrow? Rae, naked.

How could I find happiness? Rae, naked.

One plus one? Rae, naked.

World hunger? You guessed it: Rae, naked.

She lifted her shirt all the way off and I unsnapped her bra clasp to free her from it. Covered, Rae was beautiful. In a bikini, she was sexy. Topless, she was exquisite.

Her high, full tits swayed slightly with every breath, and her alabaster white skin was so dewy and fair it almost glowed. I was just pale. Rae was as luminous as an angel.

She smiled up at me, pushing my unbuttoned shirt off my shoulders and giggling when I wrestled it all the way off with an effort and a curse. Every second that I wasn't touching her was too long. I could tell that she liked me like that, desperate and overwhelmed by my need for her. I was happy to give her all she could stand. In fact, I had nine thick inches that were more than ready for her.

My rock-hard cock was throbbing against her thigh between us, trapped by the fabric of my jeans. Her clever, searching hand found it and I moaned against her neck. It had been eighteen months since I'd had sex. I nearly came like a teenager when she touched me through the thick denim. At this rate, I wasn't sure I would even get to fuck her. So, I wouldn't waste time.

Rae was conveniently wearing a skirt, and I lifted it up and got my first look at her creamy white thighs and lacey panties. Bright red, just like her new hair. Good god, she was hot.

Peeling them off of her would be nearly impossible on the couch, and I had no intention of stopping. I twisted the fabric in my fist like a caveman and ripped them off of her, kissing away her squeal of protest until she was sighing against me again. I'd get her some new panties. I was, however, gratified and excited to find them soaking wet.

She probably would have liked to pay me back in kind for destroying her clothes, but even in a violent passion there was no way in hell Rae could rip through my jeans with her bare hands. Instead, she flicked the button, wiggled down the zipper, and took me in hand with all the delicacy of a virgin and the flawless technique of an expert.

She smiled up at me eagerly, clearly pleased by what she saw. I arched into her touch gratefully, already so far along that I was seriously worrying about performing.

"You have a condom, right?" she whispered, pumping her fist along my length eagerly. She rubbed the tip against herself, torturing me with her soft, perfect heat. I might be on top, but in that moment, she was definitely in charge.

Her question took a long second to permeate my lust-addled brain, made worse by the way she was teasing me.

You have a condom, right?

Another slow pump of her hot, soft hand. I was panting. So was she.

You have a condom, right?

She rubbed the tip against her sweet, swollen little clit. She ground herself against her sweet spot and arched her back.

"Lucas?" Her voice was a sexy, high, whispered plea.

Fuck. You don't have a condom, you pathetic, game-less, fucking moron. While you've been living like a monk, the ones you had expired.

"I... No. I don't have one," I managed to bite out. She looked up at me like I'd just doused her in cold water for the second time that day. Her hand disappeared.

16

RAE

"I CAN RUN down to the corner store and grab some," Lucas offered, but the spell was broken. The thought of protection, and the mere suggestion of reality had snapped me out of my fantasy where sex meant nothing and had no consequences.

I shook my head and pulled away from him. Sexual frustration made my whole body feel tight and uncomfortable, like my skin was two sizes too small. My shirt was on the floor, and I snatched it and covered myself awkwardly with it. "We shouldn't be doing this. I'm sorry."

Lucas opened his mouth to protest, but no noise came out. After a second, he closed it again. He pulled his pants back on. He must have known that I was right. Eventually he spoke. "I hope you aren't angry with me, Rae." His tone was unexpectedly mild.

I blinked. "I hope you aren't angry at me!" I felt like I'd

led him on, although the fact that he wasn't prepared was his fault. If he'd had condoms we'd be... *don't think about that.* My pulse was still hammering away excitedly, and I told my body firmly to calm down. It didn't listen. My body didn't understand why it was being denied sex and it was starting to get angry at me. I could feel a headache coming on.

Oblivious, Lucas shook his head. "Of course, I'm not angry with you, Rae. This was... this was my fault." His voice was gentle. Guilt was evident on his features. He looked away and put his shirt back on.

I wondered if he felt like he'd been unfaithful to Victoria. The thought of her made me want to be wearing all my clothes. Immediately. This was the opposite of our agreement. Sleeping with Lucas was the opposite of getting him back together with Victoria. *The woman he loved. Not me.*

I looped my bra straps around my shoulders and shrugged back into it, refastening it with hasty fingers behind my back. Then I fumbled with my shirt, dragging it over my head. Finally, when I was covered, I felt brave enough to look at Lucas again. He was staring at his cold pizza with an expressionless face. I wondered what he was thinking but was too afraid to ask.

"I'm sorry, Lucas," I said again. "I should really just go," I told him. "This was all a mistake. We should just forget about it." I paused, waiting for him to reply. When he didn't, I rose. "I'll, um, I'll just get out of your way..."

He blinked as if woken from a trance, stared at me, and

then glanced at his watch. "Rae, don't worry. You don't need to feel bad about any of this. It really wasn't your fault. But look, it's really late. Stay here. You can sleep in my bed. I'll sleep out here."

It was late? How long had we made out? I looked at my phone to find that it was almost two a.m. *Jeez. Time flies when you're having fun and making out with the guy who'll never love you.*

"The hotel my company booked is four blocks away," I said, but the thought of walking that far felt surprisingly difficult. Some New Yorker I was. Four measly blocks?

Lucas frowned, but nodded. "I'll walk you."

"You don't have to do that."

"Yes, I do," his voice was surprisingly firm. "It's the middle of the night."

I had no idea if this part of downtown was dangerous at two a.m. or if he was just too much of a gentleman not to 'walk me home.' Honestly, I was too tired to argue with him. I'd gotten up early, endured a New York airport, sat through a five-hour flight, and then had a full day in Austin. I'd been awake for almost a full twenty hours.

"You wouldn't mind if I slept here? I can sleep on the couch."

"You'll take the bedroom." Lucas' voice was firm and stubborn again.

"Lucas, no. It's your bed."

"I insist."

He seemed determined to make me comfortable and be

chivalrous, and although I found it antiquated and unnecessary, it was also oddly endearing.

"Alright," I told him, "you're clearly not going to let me be a good guest." I pouted.

"I'm just determined to be a good host, Rae," he retorted. The world's smallest smile threatened to break out on his face.

This was the dynamic I was more used to with Lucas. The mild, friendly argument helped me feel more normal. I smiled at him, and although it might have been tired and thin, it was real. He smiled back with thoughts I couldn't decipher swimming behind his eyes.

Why couldn't he have just had some damn condoms?

We got Lucas situated on the couch and said some painfully awkward goodnights, before I shuffled off to the bedroom. I closed the door behind me and leaned heavily against it.

God, what had I been thinking?

Lucas' bed was big and soft, and I flopped down into it guiltily. Although exhausted, I couldn't relax. I glanced at my phone, looking for an escape from feeling restless and confused.

I had a bunch of new group texts from my team.

Annie: Given the news, are you two flying up tomorrow morning or waiting until Monday?

I blinked. What news? These texts were almost four hours old.

Kyle: *I'm about to board now on the last flight out. I figured it would be better to get there ready to launch tomorrow.*
Annie: *I'm on the first flight tomorrow morning. What about you Rae?*
Kyle: *I bet she's already on a flight.*
Annie: *Probably. I'm sure she wants to get this deal done ASAP before the client finds out.*
Kyle: *Poor guy. He's not going to be happy when he learns what we did.*
Annie: *Yeah, I feel bad for him. His algorithms make no sense to me, but only because I haven't figured them out yet. They clearly work, though. It's a shame the public will never see this thing. Notable Match is some next-level shit.*

What the hell were they talking about? I opened my email and scanned.

Right about the time Lucas and I were talking to Victoria at Barton Springs, an internal memo hit my inbox. Azure Group was acquiring one of the major, nationwide dating apps--Datability. Excitement kindled in my tired brain. This could be great! Lucas' app technology could be merged into this company's existing infrastructure.

I opened another email entitled 'Notable Match Post-Acquisition Strategy' from McKenzie.

Dear Michelle, Kyle, and Annie, I'm sure that you three have seen the recent company confidential memo about the acquisition of a competitor of Notable Match, Datability. This does not change our acquisition strategy for Notable Match, however, we are embargoing the public announcement for now. In order to make our purchase yesterday, I had to sweeten the pot. My solution was to show Datability's CEO the details of Stevenson's technology. Datability agreed to the acquisition on the condition that Azure Group not materially modify any technology or algorithms for five years. That means Notable Match will be a containment only acquisition...

Containment. It was the approved Azure Group euphemism for a company we wanted to kill. My stomach clenched, and my headache pounded. This was my least favorite part of my job, and why I specifically didn't work containment deals unless I had to. There was nothing quite as soul crushing as purchasing a company and then turning around and firing everyone that worked for it. Although I didn't have to personally fire anyone, I always knew in the back of my mind that I was working a containment deal. It was just too depressing.

Lucas thought we were acquiring his company to grow it and make it successful. To either take Notable Match and infuse it with enough capital to properly launch it or integrate the technology into another company. Either way, the plan was to create a future for Notable Match. We'd told him all about our plan to do just that. He wasn't selling his company to us so that we could kill it to prevent him from competing against another portfolio company. But now that was exactly what Azure Group wanted to do.

I lay back on Lucas' pillows and stared at his loft ceiling high above my head. I couldn't tell him. I wanted to, but I couldn't. If I told him what we wanted to do with Notable Match it would kill the deal. Not only that, I would also lose my job and be virtually unemployable forever after. But once Azure Group owned his technology there would be nothing to prevent them from immediately liquidating it and locking his precious algorithms in a safe somewhere to rot. I felt like I was in a no-win scenario. No matter what I did, the answer was wrong.

If I thought everything was complicated before, now it was a thousand times worse. Lucas' bed smelled like him. My body smelled like him. I'd almost slept with him, and now I was going to betray him.

It was a very long time before I fell asleep that night.

17

LUCAS

THE NEXT MORNING found me sore, cold, and disoriented. My couch was plenty comfortable for sitting. It was plenty comfortable for sleeping, too, if you're five-foot-two. I'm almost six-foot-two. I spent the whole night trying to figure out if it was better to have the top of my head or the tips of my feet more cramped up against the arm rests. The answer was neither.

When I woke up, Rae was already awake and active. It must be her east coast biological clock. She'd stolen out of the bedroom and started another shower. The fact that there was a woman in my house in the morning was immediately apparent, although I tried not to be offended that she must want to wash me off of her.

From the high heels next to the door, to the prepared pot of coffee, to the soft, feminine singing I could hear beneath the water noises, it all made me smile. God, I'd really missed having company in the mornings. I don't think I'd even realized how lonely I was until Rae stayed the night. The idea of spending another night on my torture couch was somehow a lot more appealing if it meant waking up to Rae.

My two shy little cats, Moxie and Bob, were sitting outside the bathroom door. They'd been invisible all the prior night, hiding from the stranger, but now their curiosity had gotten the better of them. The two roly-poly tabbies typically didn't like company, but if anything stayed in their environment for long enough, they had to claim it. I was willing to bet they slept with her the night before. I envied them.

The sound of the shower (and singing) cut off while I was getting myself a cup of coffee, and Rae emerged from the bathroom a few moments later.

"Hello there, sweet kitties," she whispered. She hadn't realized that I was awake yet and was trying to avoid waking me. "Did you sit there the whole time I was in the shower? I missed you too." They looked at her with interest.

"Yes, they did, although they would have preferred to watch you shower," I answered for Moxie and Bob. Rae jumped a little and looked over at me in obvious embarrassment. Was she embarrassed that she talked to the cats? I did it all the time. Me and those cats had long, drawn out, detailed conversations. I also let them watch me shower.

They were super into it, and I felt cruel denying them such a simple pleasure.

"Good morning," Rae said formally. She'd gotten partially dressed in the bathroom and was wearing a pale pink, knee length slip. Her cute, light dusting of freckles stood out better from her white skin when she wore pink. I tried not to stare at them and failed. She looked younger in the morning without her mascara and her freckles on display. I knew that she was twenty-seven, but she didn't look a day over nineteen. Maybe that was why she always wore makeup and dark clothing. It was to make her look older and more mature.

"Good morning. Coffee?" I extended a second mug.

"Please." She accepted the mug from me carefully, not touching my fingers or meeting my eyes.

She was nervous and jittery this morning. Maybe the coffee wasn't such a good plan. I'd never seen Rae hesitant or unsure for more than a few seconds at a time. Usually she snapped back to bold and teasing within a moment or two. This morning her nervousness was sticking around.

The silence grew thick in my kitchen. I felt like I could have cut it with a knife.

"Did the cats bother you last night?" I asked her, trying to make conversation.

She shook her head. "No. But I like cats. They slept next to me. I woke up and they were just there, chilling. They're very sweet, even though they wouldn't let me pet them."

Moxie and Bob didn't let anyone pet them. Except me

and Victoria. I quashed the thought. The two were winding around my feet now, staring at me and probably wondering where their breakfast was. I grabbed the bag of dry kibbles out from under the sink and they both started meowing excitedly.

"Do you have any pets?" I asked, although I couldn't really imagine it. Rae's job would make having pets difficult.

The moment the bowls hit the ground, both kitties had their faces buried deep in the food. They attacked their breakfasts like they were lions attacking gazelles on the Serengeti. That kibble never had a chance.

She frowned at my question. "I travel far too much. I used to have a dog, but I gave her to my brother when I got my job."

"What kind of dog?" I tried to imagine Rae walking a dog and found myself imagining her with a big, elegant type of dog. An Airedale maybe, or a greyhound. Something with long, sleek legs like her.

"A Bullshit," Rae said, grinning. I gave her a weird look and she explained. "Half French bulldog and half Shih Tzu. A Bullshit. She's the best. Her name is Tootsie."

Not what I expected. I grinned.

"Sounds cute. Would you have pets again if you could?"

"Yes, definitely." She smiled brightly, and I felt victorious for drawing her out of her silence and reserve. "If I could, I'd have lots of pets. I like animals." Rae paused. "I volunteer at the animal shelter when I can. Usually in the kitten room." She admitted this like it was a secret she was reluctantly letting me in on.

"Hanging out in the kitten room? That seems like something you should have to pay to do. That's not volunteering, it's entertainment." My tone was teasing, but I was secretly charmed. The idea of fierce, career-minded Rae playing with gobs of little fluffy kittens to de-stress was absolutely adorable. Every layer I managed to peel off her made me more interested to find the next detail, the next secret.

Even my gentle teasing this morning seemed to be too much. Rae's expression closed up again. "You're right, but maybe they've gotten wise. I haven't been there in a while." She sighed. "I'm too busy these days."

"Do you want to go out and get some breakfast?" I asked, wondering if a change of venue would help bring her out of her shell. There was something strange going on with her this morning. She kept looking at me and then darting her gaze away. I must have really fucked up last night.

"Um, sure," Rae answered, then froze. "Actually, I should probably go. I have work I need to do. You know, due diligence work..." her eyes flitted around onto every surface that wasn't my face.

"Okay." I nodded, but I don't think she saw because she was already headed toward the bedroom, presumably to pack up her things and finish getting ready. She already had one foot out the door.

Rationally, I knew that I shouldn't be worrying whether

Rae still liked me or not. We weren't friends, or lovers, or anything. We were supposed to be business associates and nothing more. Sure, our arrangement was a bit unconventional, but it was based on an exchange of goods and services, not on feelings.

But you don't choose your feelings. My heart had started to have ideas about Rae. Ideas about keeping her. Serious ideas. Ideas that stuck around. My body had ideas about Rae too, obviously, but if it was just that, I could probably ignore it. It was my heart that I was concerned about because I'd thought that Victoria had a monopoly on it and would forever.

"Lucas?" Rae snapped me out of my thoughts. She must have gone in the bedroom and turned right back around.

"Sorry, I was off in la-la land," I told her, trying to smile reassuringly. She just stared at me with a determined look on her face.

"Lucas, there's something really important I need to tell you about Azure Group," she said.

"What—"

Ding-dong!

Someone was at the door? Rae and I exchanged a confused look. I shrugged. It was ten a.m. on a Sunday. I headed to answer it while Rae hid out of sight in the hall and stuck her head around the corner to peek. Who shows up unexpectedly at ten on a Sunday?

18

RAE

"Kyle?" Lucas' surprised voice echoed against the hard walls of the loft. "Hey man, you know it's Sunday today, right?"

I froze. He couldn't mean Kyle Chen, my teammate. Maybe Lucas had a friend named Kyle. It was a common name.

"Hi, Mr. Stevenson." No, that was definitely Kyle Chen. I'd travelled all over the country with the nerdy little guy over the past six months. I knew his voice. "Sorry for showing up unannounced and so early. Can I come in? I have something important to talk to you about."

"Uh, one sec," Lucas said. He came back into view and gave me a 'what the fuck do I do?' look. I shrugged, panicked, and pointed at the bedroom. He nodded, and I went to hide. I darted into the bedroom and left the door cracked so I could listen. "Sorry about that. Come on in," I heard Lucas telling Kyle. "You want some coffee or something?"

"Oh, um, no thanks. I won't be here that long," Kyle said. He sounded profoundly nervous. I could imagine him shifting from foot to foot the way he did when he had to present in meetings. Cliff called it the "Kyle Shuffle" and teased him about it mercilessly.

I mentally flew through the reasons that I could think of that might bring Kyle to Lucas' door this morning. There weren't very many. One, he could have discovered something deeply problematic in the financial records that he'd been reviewing and wanted to discuss it personally with Lucas before telling me and Annie. Two, he could have his own weird side arrangement with Lucas that neither had shared with me. Or, three, he could have an unknown personal reason.

"What's up?" Lucas asked Kyle casually. I could hear in Lucas' voice that he was very curious as to why Kyle would show up here, which contradicted reason two. I didn't really think that was likely either.

"Your app matched me with my coworker, Annie," Kyle said. The first few words had been slow, but he accelerated as he went on until he was speaking so quickly it was almost unintelligible. "I'd been trying to work up the courage to ask her out for months. You see, we travel together a lot for work. Cliff, Rae, Annie, and me. We've been all over the country together. So, I saw Annie all the time. But I was too afraid to ask her out and then your app matched me with her this morning when I picked her up at the airport and it was just like lightning... you know—bam —all of a sudden we just both knew." He finally fell silent.

My jaw had gone slack in disbelief. Annie and Kyle?! I'd never would have thought. They were about as different as two people could be, although they were both mega-nerds in their own respective domains. Annie was zaftig, blonde, and techy. Kyle was short, quiet, and five years her junior.

"I'm, um, I'm happy for you," Lucas told Kyle. He sounded as shocked and confused as I felt. Yeah, it was weird that Kyle and Annie had successfully been matched by Notable Match. Very weird. But it didn't necessitate Kyle running over here immediately afterwards.

"How does your algorithm work?" Kyle asked. He sounded awed.

"You should ask Annie," Lucas replied. He was using that smug, secretive tone of voice that he always had when he spoke about his app.

"She doesn't have any idea how it works," Kyle replied. "She's been all over the code and she said it's totally incomprehensible."

I could almost hear Lucas shrugging. I imagined the look on his face as being a mixture of pride, amusement, and disinterest. "Is that what you came to tell me?" he asked. There was still confusion in his voice, and I shared it. This made no sense.

"No. I mean, partly, but there's something else, too." I heard him sigh heavily. "I really think your technology could help a lot of people. I'm not the sort of person who goes out of their way for no reason." He paused. "I usually avoid all kinds of risks." Another pause. "I really shouldn't tell you this. I might lose my job. But maybe it's worth it." An even longer pause. I was starting to get very nervous. "You know Azure Group owns all types of companies in their portfolio, right?" Oh no. He was going to tell Lucas that Azure Group was going to kill Notable Match. There was only one thing for me to do.

"Good morning, Kyle." I slid out of the bedroom and watched all the blood drain out of his face.

Surprise! It's me, your boss.

"Rae?" Kyle stuttered. Lucas was watching me with wide eyes too. He looked almost as shocked as Kyle. I was still wearing just my slinky, pink silk slip, but I stood up straight and tried to look as confident as I could. I didn't even care that my nipples were probably clearly visible. Well, I cared, but only a little. This was more important.

I know what you were about to do, I told Kyle with my eyes. He clearly knew he'd been caught. I arched an eyebrow at him, and he turned a bright, frightened pink color.

Kyle swallowed hard and his Adam's apple bobbed up and down in his neck. I could see him weighing alternatives in his mind and trying to come up with an explanation for why I was there, dressed like I was, in the morning. He came to the logical conclusion a second later. I could tell by the way he glanced through the bedroom door at the mussed up covers on the bed. His gaze, when it came back to my face, was dumbstruck.

Don't judge me. You're fucking your coworker. At least I'm just almost fucking our client.

I smiled widely at Kyle. "I got your text that you and Annie were flying up early. I was already here. Actually, I was just about to tell Lucas the good news myself!" My voice was convincingly warm and enthusiastic. I usually wasn't a very good liar, but panic was fueling me. In reality my tone was fueled by nervousness and desperation, but it still sounded enthusiastic.

"Good news?" Lucas echoed. He looked incredibly confused. I swallowed my guilt and forced myself to be confident.

Do your job. Keep it together. Just do your job.

"Yes," I said sweetly, coming up close to him and grabbing his hand in faux excitement. "Very good news." He looked at our joined hands in surprise and up at me with a little smile. "Notable Match passed the preliminary due diligence examination. We can now start the final checks and begin our real negotiations!"

Technically this was not a lie at all. I had all the information I needed to move the process forward, although in an ordinary situation I'd wait until the end of the trip to announce that we were moving forward. But time was of the essence. McKenzie wanted this done and done quickly.

"That's great," Lucas said, returning my smile. He still

looked confused, but I could tell that he bought it. My heart twisted painfully in my chest.

I'm sorry, Lucas. I don't want to betray you. It has to be like this.

While I'd been hiding in the bedroom, I'd had a change of heart. As much as I wanted to, telling Lucas the truth would almost certainly destroy my career. I couldn't let Kyle do it either. Lucas and I were just business associates. This relationship we had was fake and the rest was all business. I would do well to remember that. Lucas wasn't going to worry about my feelings when this was over. He was going to be with Victoria.

At Lucas' side, Kyle blinked at me. I could see judgement in his eyes, but also acceptance. He'd been beaten and he knew it. He must have thought I flew down here and fucked Lucas last night to make sure this deal went off perfectly and as quickly as possible. It was a thoroughly Machiavellian way of making sure I took Cliff's spot on a permanent basis and was more or less exactly what was expected in this business, although I'd long believed that I could succeed without doing deals on my back. Still, I'm sure McKenzie would be proud. The feeling didn't comfort me.

I held my head high and smiled at him. *Think whatever you want*, I thought at him. *I'm doing what I have to do. If you know what's good for you, you'll go along with my plan.* After a moment Kyle looked away and nodded. *Good.*

"Y-yeah," Kyle said hesitantly, "that's what I wanted to

tell you Lucas. Congratulations." His voice sounded shocked, but given how strangely he'd behaved since he arrived, I don't think it made Lucas suspicious. He probably just thought Kyle was a strange guy. He wasn't wrong.

The two men shook hands and Kyle made his stunned way toward the door. I walked him out.

"I'll call you in a couple of hours, Kyle," I told him with a final, threatening smile.

"Okay boss," he answered meekly.

The look he gave me as I closed the door was a mixture of fear, disgust, and disbelief. I didn't blame him. That was how I felt about myself.

19

LUCAS

"THAT WAS REALLY WEIRD." I shook my head at the closed
door.

*What a bizarre little dude. I guess staring at spreadsheets all
day has taken its toll on him.*

"Yeah." Rae's response was small. I turned to find her
staring out the window with her arms wrapped around
herself. "Weird."

More than anything, I was shocked that Rae had outed
herself to her coworker. "Why did you do it?"

She smirked at me and then swiftly looked away. "Well,
it wasn't my preference, but if Kyle had told you that you'd
passed due diligence, I would have had to fire him."

I paused. "You really would have fired him?" I had a
hard time imagining it, even though I believed Rae had it in
her. Her take charge personality made her a good leader,
but leadership has its costs.

She looked over at me with a sad, resigned look on her face. "We have these rules for a reason. What if he'd told you before the final decision and then you went out and bought a yacht? But then there was a delay in the deal and you and your company went bankrupt because you'd drained all your resources? How would that be good for Azure Group? He's not authorized to make these announcements. Only I am. So yeah, I would have had to fire him for violating company policy. If I violated company policy, somebody would fire me, too."

This was why I worked for myself. Well, that and I couldn't wake up before nine a.m. unless pharmaceuticals were involved. Rae's argument made sense. I didn't like it, but it did make sense. Rae had to do her job whether I liked it or not. If she didn't follow and enforce the rules, she'd lose her own job. I nodded.

Rae looked unhappy with the situation too. "It's not like I wanted Kyle to see me like this with you."

Her words made me uncomfortable. Was she ashamed of being here with me? Of course, she would be. I'm sure she didn't like her coworkers thinking that she was sleeping with a client.

I keep screwing things up with you, don't I Rae? This is all my fault.

"I'm sorry if I've made your job more difficult," I ventured, watching as she turned and pulled a dress out of her suitcase. She laughed, and it was a small, bitter sound.

"Don't worry about it," Rae said, stepping into the grey tweed dress and pulling it up around her. She'd lost any self-consciousness or timidity she'd shown before. Confident Rae was back, but she was also distant. "Would you mind?" She turned around to display her perfect, round butt. I stared, hypnotized.

"Mind?" I repeated.

"Will you help with the zipper?" she clarified.

"Um, sure. Of course, I will." I stepped forward and obliged, careful not to touch her inappropriately. Somehow the balance of power between us had shifted heavily in her favor. I felt nervous as I drew up the zipper. As soon as I fastened it, she turned. We found ourselves face to face. The moment stretched and became tense. I broke eye contact first. I had no idea what to say to her.

"I really have to go," she told me a moment later. "I'll be super busy these next few days working on the deal paperwork. Annie and Kyle will be here tomorrow to do the remaining investigative work. You probably won't see me until next week." Her voice was distant, like her mind was somewhere else.

"Oh. Alright." I'd been hoping to spend more time with her on this trip. I knew I should be happy since this meant that the due diligence process was moving faster than expected, but I found myself feeling oddly disappointed.

Rae had held up her end of our deal perfectly so far. Yesterday she'd performed incredibly in front of Victoria.

But when I woke up this morning, I wasn't thinking of Victoria. I was thinking about Rae. Last night when we were kissing, I was thinking of Rae. Last night when I'd spent hours fighting down my desire to go knocking on my bedroom door, I was thinking of Rae. Even now, as she was gathering her jacket and slipping on her shoes, all I could do was think of Rae.

"Are you sure you don't want to grab some breakfast before you go?" If I sounded desperate, I didn't care. I wasn't ready for her to disappear.

Say you'll stay with me, Rae? Let's pretend for a little while longer. I need it. Maybe, just maybe, you need it, too.

She shook her head and kissed me on the cheek. It was a decidedly impersonal, formal kiss. "I really can't. I'll bring a dress for the wedding next week. Is there a particular color or style you want me to wear?" Rae was being so incredibly businesslike. It was killing me. The easy, teasing version of Rae was gone.

"No, you can wear whatever you want. I trust you." It hardly mattered what she wore, it seemed Rae had a closet entirely full of sophisticated, dark colored clothing. I'd yet to see her wear anything that wasn't black, dark blue, green, or purple. It all looked incredible against her pale skin. Rae could come to the wedding dressed in a burlap sack and still easily be the most beautiful woman in the room.

Rae, I don't want to be alone.

"Sounds good. I'll text you. Bye Lucas."

Don't go. Would it be so bad if you stayed?

Rae was already gone. Even as she waved goodbye and grabbed her suitcase, I could tell her mind was elsewhere. After she left, I stared at the closed door to my loft and a familiar feeling of loneliness started to creep in. I sat back down on my couch and tried to organize my thoughts. Moxie and Bob, sensing that the visitors were gone, crawled out from underneath it to beg me for attention. At least they still liked me, because all of a sudden, I was pretty sure that Rae no longer did.

THE WEEK WAS ENDLESS. The days crawled by, leaving me in a state of ever-deepening confusion. The more I was alone, the more alone I felt. The more alone I felt, the less I wanted to try to dig myself out of it.

I tried to focus on getting Victoria back. I stalked her online, looking at pictures of her and Kane at various trendy bars and clubs and restaurants. They looked so goddamn happy. In every photo, Victoria was smiling at the camera like she was telling me to fuck off. I was jealous, yes, but it didn't feel like the jealousy I was used to. I didn't know what to make of it.

As usual, I found myself at the Lone Star Lounge halfway through the week. Neither Ward nor Emma was there that afternoon, just Wendy.

"How's your scheme going?" she asked when she delivered my drink.

"Scheme?" I wasn't sure if she was talking about my plan to sell my app or my plan to get Victoria back. The fact that I was now a man with multiple schemes felt a bit worrisome.

"Yeah, with your ex."

"It's all going exactly according to plan," I told her. My voice was confident even if I wasn't.

"That's great. I hope you weren't offended the other day when we talked."

My lips parted in surprise. "Offended?" I thought back to that day. "Why would I be offended?"

She frowned and looked around. Apparently seeing no other tables that needed her, she sat down in the chair across for me. "Because I don't know anything about anything. I shouldn't have given you any advice you didn't ask for. I'm sorry."

I cocked my head to the side, half wondering if she was messing with me. She continued to stare back with guileless blue eyes. Wendy looked genuinely upset and concerned that she'd offended me.

"Wendy, you didn't do anything wrong. I wasn't offended. Ward asked you to give me your opinion. It's not like you just barged into a conversation and started imitating Oprah."

She brightened a bit. "I like Oprah, but I'm really glad you weren't offended." Her expression still seemed to be clouded by something. "I would hate to think that I contributed to you not getting back with your one true love."

My one true love?

Was Wendy really as sweet and innocent as she seemed? She was clearly a small-town girl, and with her curly blonde hair, big blue eyes and deep country accent, she could be Cowgirl Barbie. She wasn't my type at all, but it was no wonder her grandfather, Willie, had set Ward on protection duty.

"Don't worry, Wendy. I promise you didn't."

The cloud finally lifted from Wendy. "I'm so glad," she told me again. She smiled at me happily. "Have you two gotten back together yet?"

"Not yet.

"Did you make her jealous yet?" She looked excited for me, and I found myself warming to the conversation. No one else supported me in this idea. I'd told one of my best friends, Ward, and got nothing but derision and pity. I'd also kept it from my good friend Cole. This was both because he was still in the honeymoon phase with his girlfriend Kate, and because he would almost certainly disapprove. It was nice that Wendy seemed like she really wanted me to succeed. It was also just nice to have someone to talk to. I grinned at her.

"I've made progress," I told her. "I've still got work to do, but I know I'm getting closer to her to admitting she still wants me."

"What's your next step?"

"I'm going to take Rae to a wedding and introduce her to all of the mutual friends Victoria and I shared."

"Rae is your fake girlfriend and Victoria is your soulmate, right?"

Soulmate? I would have laughed but Wendy was looking at me with such seriousness that I couldn't. I guessed this was just how she talked. It was a bit odd but endearing too.

"Um, yes."

"Well, I hope you make Victoria super jealous once you introduce all your friends to your fake girlfriend, Rae. Then she'll come back to you and everything will be right." She nodded her head as if thinking it through. "Good luck, okay? I really hope it all works out just the way you said. I'm so glad I didn't do anything to stop you from getting back together with the love of your life and living happily ever after. Sometimes people have to go to great lengths for love. I'm glad you're willing to do what it takes to win her back."

The love of my life? Happily ever after?

Even after Wendy and I wrapped up our conversation and she went back to work, the words she had used stuck with me. *Soulmate. True love. Love of my life. Happily ever after.*

Wendy was definitely a bit of a doe-eyed innocent, but she clearly *believed in love*. The way she talked about love made me feel insecure and jaded though. Wendy was obviously and totally, one hundred percent sure that I should do whatever it took to win back Victoria if she was my true love. Her conviction was total. I used to be that convinced about it too. But now I wasn't as sure. Why was that? And what did it mean? I went to bed that night worrying about it.

20

RAE

VICTORIA REACHED out to me on Facebook with a friend request. I noticed in the middle of the workday and didn't have a chance to think about it until I got home in the evening. I wasn't expecting to have any contact with her and had no idea what to expect, but I was bored and lonely on a Tuesday, so I accepted. Being friends with her allowed me to look at all her pictures, which I began to peruse with a masochistic interest in her glamorous, musicians' life. Her life looked a lot more exciting than mine. It wasn't fifteen minutes afterward that she messaged me.

Victoria: It was so great to meet you this weekend Rae!
Rae: You're so sweet. It was nice meeting you too.

I hoped that she'd just leave it at that. Although I was curious about her, I had no idea what to say to her. I thought we'd both benefit from just cyberstalking one another from afar, not talking.

Victoria: How are you and Lucas doing?

How are we doing? I paused. What was I supposed to say to that? I tapped out an answer and pressed 'send.'

Rae: We're doing great. Thanks for asking.
Victoria: I'm so glad to hear that. I want you both to be happy.

Something told me that she didn't mean that. Call it a woman's intuition. I could only imagine she was looking through my photos and wondering how her ex-boyfriend had ended up with someone so boring and pedestrian. The majority of my recent posts were work-related. I probably looked like someone with no life whatsoever. At least I didn't have a bunch of photos of my cat or anything embarrassing like that.

Victoria: How's the long-distance thing going? Is it tough?

When I saw the message, I stared at it for a full five minutes and seriously considered not replying. I mean, this was getting inappropriate, right? It was weird, wasn't it? How much did I have to talk to my fake-boyfriend's ex? It seemed like I'd already put in enough effort in being polite to Victoria. Unfortunately, even though I thought it would probably be better to take the high road, my curiosity got the best of me.

Rae: It's going fine so far. I'm in Austin quite a bit.
Victoria: That's good. It's a great city isn't it.
Rae: Yes.
Victoria: Are you going to be moving here soon?
Rae: We're taking things slow.

There. Surely, she would get the message that I didn't want to discuss the details of our 'relationship' any further. She'd initiated each and every one of the messages so far. I'd replied with succinct, short answers. Obviously, I didn't want to chat with her.

Victoria: Look, don't take this the wrong way, and I know it's none of my business, but I don't think Lucas will be able to do long-distance for long. He'll be lonely. If you know what I mean.

Holy hell. Lucas was right about Victoria. She was so transparently jealous and possessive that it was almost sad. I didn't realize that real people behaved this way. It was like something out of one of those bad romantic comedies that were always playing at the nail salon I frequented. Soon she'd be trying to trick me into believing that Lucas was an abusive partner or something. I wasn't nearly that gullible.

Rae: You're right. It's none of your business.

I wasn't the type of person that's foolish enough to engage in some sort of pissing contest with Victoria. Even in the fantasy that Lucas and I had concocted where I pretended to be in love with him, he'd never asked me to pretend to be a moron. Seeing what kind of person she was, however, made me feel a bit bad for him. I couldn't help but think he deserved better than someone like Victoria. She seemed vaguely psycho to me.

Victoria: Ok. Fine. I'll back off. I'm just trying to warn you. No one likes being cheated on.

Whatever Victoria, I thought to myself, *this isn't a bad romcom.* Even if Lucas and I were in a relationship together, that kind of transparent bullshit wouldn't have done anything to dissuade me. There was no female solidarity between us. She had an agenda, and while I was going to ultimately help her to fulfill it, I was not going to make a fool of myself in the process. That wasn't the deal.

After I closed my laptop and paced around my room for a while, I found myself standing with my phone in my hand. I dialed Lucas' number almost without consciously thinking. He answered on the second ring.

"Rae? What's up?" Lucas sounded surprised to hear from me. I looked at the clock. Nine p.m. eastern time. So, ten in Austin. Was that too late to call? Well, it was too late now.

"Hi Lucas, how are you?" I tried to play it cool.

"I'm doing okay. You?" I could hear the sound of music in the background. He was out somewhere. Good. That meant I hadn't woken him up or anything like that.

Maybe Victoria was right, and Lucas was out looking for someone to spend the night with. The thought didn't make me happy. However, even if it was true, it wasn't any of my business. He was a free, single man. If he didn't want to spend every night alone until he and Victoria got back together, that was his choice. I could barely even judge him for it. I definitely wasn't going to let Victoria get into my head and make me paranoid.

"I'm fine. I, uh, I just wanted to call and let you know that Victoria contacted me."

The silence on the other end of the line lasted long enough that I almost wondered if we'd been disconnected.

"What did she say?" He asked eventually. His tone of voice gave nothing away about what was in his mind.

"She basically told me that you were going to cheat on me."

Once again, a long period of silence followed my statement.

"Okay. Sorry. You don't have to talk to her." His neutral tone didn't help me to decipher his feelings.

I didn't know what to make of that response. This was a lot harder when I couldn't see his face. "Do you want me to block her?"

"You don't have to block her."

"Do you *not want me to* block her?

"Either way is fine."

I frowned into the phone and ground my teeth. "Lucas, I don't understand what you want from me here. I know I don't have to do anything. I need you to tell me what *you want*. I don't know how to handle this situation. This whole fake-relationship thing is uncharted territory for me. You have to help me out."

He sighed. "I'm sorry. I'm irritated that she told you that I was the cheater. I've never cheated on anyone *in my life*. She certainly can't say the same." Now that he was being honest, I could hear the anger in his voice. In the background, I heard something hard hitting against something else, like a hand smacking a table.

Why do you want her? What does she have that I don't? I didn't say it. It wouldn't be right. But I was thinking it so loudly I was surprised that Lucas didn't hear.

"I have an idea," I said eventually.

"What's that?" Lucas asked.

"I'll just behave the same way that I would if you and I were really a couple."

"What does that mean?"

"It means I'm just going to ignore her from here on out. I'm sure that will drive her up the wall anyway."

This conversation was a hell of a lot harder than I thought it would be. I didn't want to disparage Victoria in front of Lucas, but I really didn't want a thing to do with her. She was clearly a toxic individual.

Lucas laughed. "You're definitely right about that. She's going to hate being ignored."

"Okay, well, that's what I'm going to do unless you tell me otherwise."

"I'm sorry I'm not good at this, Rae. I don't know what I'm doing either."

"It's fine." I sighed. "We're both just making this up as we go along."

21

RAE

THE AZURE GROUP corporate headquarters occupies the top five floors of a modern steel and glass tower in a part of Manhattan where everyone wears black and looks busy. As I fidgeted with the stiff lapels of my blazer on the long elevator ride up, I found myself missing the unpretentious, casual, laid-back attitude of Austin. I didn't see a single person wearing a suit last week. Just seeing someone taking a fashion risk on pinstripes or navy was uncommon here.

I made my reluctant way to my cubicle on the forty-seventh floor, dodging Stan from Finance. He clearly wanted to ask me out for coffee again, but the answer was no. I'd only be going out of pity if I did. Last time he spent twenty minutes telling me about his huge snake, Dominic (an actual boa constrictor, mind you, not his dick).

Although I didn't have any natural light at my desk, I managed to keep a small garden of succulents alive in a planter there. They didn't mind not being watered when I was away, but I liked to think that they still missed me. I'd just watered them and started up my computer when Annie dropped by.

"Hi Rae," she asked. "Can I talk to you really quickly?" Her voice was hesitant.

"Of course." I tried to sound welcoming instead of Monday-grumpy. "What can I do for you?"

She took a seat in the open cube next to mine. "I'm having a lot of trouble with my report on the algorithms for Notable Match. I know Kyle is already finished with his financial report and you're waiting on me."

Although Annie and Kyle both reported to me in Cliff's absence, their expertise was much more focused than my own and I knew there was no way I could do their jobs. The three of us had always gotten along well, and it was disheartening to me that Kyle had caught me with Lucas. He probably thought I was a scheming slut. Annie's expression, however, held no judgement or recrimination. Perhaps, despite the fact that Kyle and Annie were now an item, he hadn't told her about our awkward interaction at Lucas' loft? Was that even possible?

"What kind of trouble?" I asked.

Annie frowned. Her voice was even weaker than usual, and I had to strain to hear her. "It's embarrassing to even admit it, but his logic is totally incomprehensible to me. It's almost nonsensical. But somehow, despite the fact that I can't figure out how he's doing it, his matchmaking works."

"It's going to get really technical if you try to explain it more than that, won't it?" I'd worked with Annie enough to know that I shouldn't even try to understand what she did most of the time. As long as she created a report that passed muster with our technical team, that was good enough for me.

She nodded ruefully. "It's almost like he used machine learning or something. There's just no way to break down what he did to get his final product. I think the best way I can explain it would be that he wrote a set of instructions, used Google translate to put it in Ukrainian, then translated that into Chinese, and then back into English."

I frowned. I wouldn't put it past Lucas to think it was funny that his creation was incomprehensible from the outside. He obviously liked complex puzzles; his loft was full of them. But I had a feeling that he didn't do this just to make Annie's life difficult, there would be no point. More likely, there was some key that Annie hadn't yet managed to crack.

I thought about Annie's problem for a minute before answering. "As long as you focus on the inputs and reliable outputs of the algorithm that should be good enough," I told her. "While it would be nice to be able to say exactly how he created it, that may just not be possible."

"Are you sure?" Annie had never delivered anything but the most detailed of technical reports, but she was an overachiever. Other technical analysts were not nearly as thorough.

"We've got the algorithms now, don't we?"

"Yes, I have all the code. I just don't know how it works."

"Then yeah, I'm sure." I shrugged. "It's hardly going to matter anyway."

Even an oblique reference to Lucas' technology being locked away and never used made us both frown deeply.

"Did you get matched with Lucas?" Annie asked, and then looked like she regretted it. I guess it was too much to hope that Kyle wouldn't tell her.

I nodded. "Yeah. I did." It wasn't worthwhile to lie to Annie. We were friends, at least as much as we could be in our line of work. Plus, it felt good to have someone to talk to.

"He stares at you every time you two are in the same room," Annie said. "Then he looks away whenever you notice. It's very cute." She smiled at me encouragingly. I couldn't return her smile.

He does? Well, it must just be because I look like Victoria.

Although, I really didn't think that I looked like her at all. Victoria's features were elfin, delicate, and sharp, while mine were softer and more rounded. Victoria's eyes were true green not greenish blue like mine. I had freckles and she didn't. She was much taller than me. My hair was long, and hers was short. She had bangs, and I didn't. We were both natural redheads, but that was about it.

"Its... complicated between us," I told her. I wished I could tell her everything, but I could barely explain it to myself.

Still, her expression was sympathetic. "Yeah, you've got a hard job to do."

I shook my head at her understatement. She didn't know the half of it. "He's going to hate me when he realizes what we're going to do with his app," I said, feeling horrible.

"You're just doing your job," Annie insisted.

"Why doesn't that make me feel any better?"

She smirked. "Because despite what Kyle thinks, you aren't nearly as ruthless as you pretend to be."

I arched an eyebrow at her and tried to look ruthless, but it just made her smirk turn into a disbelieving grin. I found myself fighting a smile as well.

"Fine, but don't tell anyone my secret," I told her. She mimed zipping her lips closed and throwing away the key. "I'm happy for you and Kyle," I added.

Annie's cheeks turned a deep, scarlet red. Her response was whispered. "He's a really sweet, wonderful person. I'm so happy the app put us together. I don't think we ever would have admitted how we felt otherwise."

I shook my head at her in wonder. I still couldn't believe they'd been into each other all this time and I hadn't picked up on the slightest clue. "I guess it was fate."

She returned my smile shyly. "We make our own fate," she asserted a moment later, surprising me. "That's what I'm learning. You never know what will happen, Rae, but you can decide how to deal with it. Like with Kyle and me. I never would have known he liked me, but once we learned the truth, we decided to take a risk and admit how we felt. This deal's not over until the ink is dry. If you're meant to be with Lucas, it will all work out. If Lucas' app was meant to be out in the world, it will be." She seemed completely sure.

I wanted to believe Annie, but looking around at the serious faces of my coworkers and the joyless office, it was hard to be optimistic. This was my world, and it was cutthroat and high stakes. And even if there was some way to make the deal with Notable Match work out, I still had no solution to the real problem. Lucas was in love with someone else.

When I got home to my apartment, it was long past dusk. I'd gone in before dawn, so the entire day had passed by without seeing the sun once. I made myself the only food I had in my pantry—macaroni and cheese—and settled on my couch.

God, it's quiet in here.

At least when I'd had Tootsie, my dog, there had been someone here to greet me when I came home. I adored her and having her around always made me smile. Plus, she hunted the rats. Now it was just silent. I knew she was better off with my brother, though. Jarrod spoiled her rotten and gave her all the love she could stand.

Upstairs, someone turned on water and the ancient pipes made loud banging noises. It sounded like a family of ghosts were having a rave. In between the clanging, I could faintly hear my upstairs neighbor singing offkey.

Great. That's not any better.

I needed to get out of this place. This apartment was expensive, and it still sucked. The only reason I'd chosen this building was that it was close to work.

Feeling increasingly grumpy, I turned on some mindless TV and tried to get out of my head. The first bite of the macaroni tasted pretty good, but by bite number three the fake powdered cheese taste was grossing me out. I stubbornly made myself eat the whole bowl.

Is this really what I want for the rest of my life? The thought had been rustling around in my head for a while before I was willing to acknowledge it. Once I did, however, it demanded an answer. I wished I had one.

22

LUCAS

IN THE DREAM, Mickey held the knife straight ahead of him with his bizarre, four fingered hand. He ran after me relentlessly, laughing that awful high-pitched Mickey laugh the entire time. In the abandoned, empty warehouse there was nowhere for me to hide.

I was smaller in the dream. Actually, it wasn't possible to tell if I was smaller than normal or if Mickey was just gigantic, but it felt like I was small. I was certainly too weak to fight him off. With nowhere to hide and no hope of fighting, my only hope was to run. As always, the dream ended when I leapt off a building to avoid being stabbed in the heart.

My body was drenched in sweat. Moxie and Bob stared at me with matching expressions of confused betrayal on their little furry faces when I suddenly sat up out of sleep with a gasp. My heartbeat was racing like I'd just run a five-minute mile. Damnit. I hadn't had that dream in almost a decade.

At eighteen, I'd been sure of my plans. I'd already aced every standardized test, made perfect grades in high school, and had my pick of the Ivy League. Instead, I chose to go to college at the University of Texas on a football scholarship. I knew where I'd go from there. First, I'd prove myself enough to replace the jerk that beat me out as quarterback. Then, after graduating with honors, I'd be drafted into the NFL. Next, I would play for a record-breaking fifteen years before retiring to a life of leisure and philanthropy. I'd write a bestselling memoir at forty-five before beginning a career in politics. By fifty-five, I'd be president.

It didn't turn out quite like that. I'd made it to the University of Texas on a football scholarship and was on my way to displacing the quarterback, but a routine echocardiogram revealed a serious defect in the right ventricle of my heart. A potentially fatal, extraordinarily rare defect. The kind that kills you before you even know there's a problem. All my dreams ground to a screeching halt.

I was benched from the team immediately, but that was the least of my worries. The heart murmur meant I was subjected to every test known to modern medicine. The poking and prodding went on for weeks, which turned to months, which dragged on into years. All the while I was wondering if I would even survive long enough for a transplant. Although I had no symptoms, I was told that I might drop dead at any moment.

It was during that period of unbearable uncertainty that the Mickey Mouse dreams started. I'd always found that damn cartoon mouse unsettling, but before the nightmares I'd not found him particularly sinister. Certainly not horrifying. The therapist that I saw during that period informed me that the psychotic murderer Mickey was a manifestation of my fears about my health, and I have no doubt that she was right. No eighteen-year-old boy, and yes, I was very much still a boy, should be forced to grapple with his own mortality. I did. And the way my subconscious dealt with it was by making me spend at least one night a week running for my life.

Maybe the most ironic thing about the dream was that I couldn't actually run. As soon as my heart murmur was discovered, I was told that it wasn't possible for me to continue with any strenuous aerobic activity. Instead of being an active, athletic, happy college freshman, I was an invalid. The fact that I lived with my former teammates, Cole and Ward, and both of them were goddamn football stars only drove home how broken I was.

Eventually, around the middle of my junior year, I learned the truth. My doctors were wrong. There was nothing wrong with my heart. There never had been. The murmur that they detected in my heartbeat was completely and utterly harmless.

Knowing that I was for sure going to survive did not

immediately give me a new lease on life. Instead, I became extremely depressed. My grades, which had been flawless, dipped for the first time in my entire life. Murderer Mickey, who I thought should have disappeared along with my diagnosis, appeared even more often. It was then, when I was at my life's nadir, not sure what I was going to do now that I wasn't going to die, that I met Victoria.

The fact that murderer Mickey had returned to me, now, after all these years, made no sense to me. Victoria had banished him in the first place. As I lay in my sweat-soaked bed, panting in the dark, the only explanation I could come up with was that I needed her back to banish him again. Clearly, I needed to recommit myself to winning Victoria back. Rae had been distracting me. My subconscious was warning me that my heart was at risk once again.

23

LUCAS

WARD'S BACHELOR party was about as sedate and dull as any bachelor party could be. I'd been to livelier funerals. Cole wouldn't let me plan anything. He was taking his best man thing extremely seriously. As a result, the party was doomed to lameness before it ever even began. Although the party barge on the lake was cool, a party can only be rightly called a party if there are women present. Otherwise it was just a sausage-fest.

"Are you planning on being a pain in the ass the entire time, Lucas?" Cole asked me, dropping down in the deck chair next to me. "You haven't even gotten in the water. You're just sitting here sulking."

"I'm not sulking. I'm enjoying this lovely evening," I told him, waving a hand at the expansive view in front of us over the deck of the boat.

"You don't look like you're enjoying anything." Cole's

dark eyes narrowed as he took me in. Although I was not the life of the party—that was Ward, even when the party wasn't for him—I knew I was being more reserved than usual. I had a lot on my mind. And I wasn't ready to confess it all to Cole. I wasn't even ready to confess it all to myself.

"I'm really enjoying this beer. I'm working up to jumping in the water," I told him, lifting my bottle as evidence. Cole raised an incredulous eyebrow and shook his head at me. There was a small graveyard of empties accumulating at my side. I'd been working up for a while now.

"What's gotten into you lately?" His eyes examined me with skepticism. "You've been weird for the last few weeks. I mean, weirder than usual. Quiet. You're never quiet. I don't see you at the bar as much either."

I shrugged. "I've been around." I stared out at the calm, blue lake water and the watercolor sunset above. It was pretty, but I was sulking, despite what I'd told Cole. "How're the dealerships?" I asked. "Do you still like your new venture?"

Cole was adapting to life post-NFL. His professional football career probably could have lasted a bit longer, but too many head injuries convinced him that he'd rather have his health. He'd invested most of his money in a number of BMW dealerships in central Texas and was learning how to run them. Predictably, talking about business distracted him.

"I'm ridiculously busy, but that's only the half of it. I

also now know more about women's underthings than I ever wanted to..." he trailed off with a thousand-yard stare.

I smirked. "Does that mean Kate's store is doing well?"

Cole's girlfriend, Kate Williams, was Ward's younger sister. She had recently quit the bar to open her own boutique. I'd not been to see it as it was entirely devoted to women's underwear. The name of Kate's store? Teddy Bare. Because, of course, it was.

Cole grinned proudly despite his trauma. "Yeah, she's doing incredibly well." He shook his head in disbelief. "I'm happy for her, but all those corsets and stuff need unpacking and stocking and somehow I keep getting conned into it. She just bats her big eyes at me and the next thing I know, I'm hanging up fancy panties and putting hang tags on them."

Rae would look good in some fancy lingerie. Something white or maybe baby pink. She never wears light colors. It must be the New Yorker in her. The thought came out of nowhere and I shook my head to dispel it. Why couldn't I stop thinking about her? I didn't even want to think about her, but every time I closed my eyes, I saw her. The fact that we went a full week without seeing one another did nothing to help banish her from my thoughts. If anything, absence was actually making the heart grow fonder. I'd always thought that was a myth.

I arched an eyebrow at Cole before he realized I was lost in a fantasy. "I bet you're a great stock boy." My voice was teasing.

"I'm a *fantastic* stock boy," Cole replied proudly.

Seeing Cole and Kate get together made me happy, but also jealous of their happiness. They were a good match, but it hadn't been easy for them. Between Kate's stubbornness, Ward's over-protective nature, and Cole's tenacity, they were a perfect storm. It all worked out in the end. The two were engaged now, and they had Ward's full support.

"Have you two set a date for the wedding yet?" I asked, keeping my voice low. Cole was keeping his engagement a secret from Ward. Not because he didn't want him to know, but because he and Kate didn't want Emma, Ward's fiancée and Kate's best friend, to feel like her day wouldn't be hers. It was all too much for me.

"I'm hoping for some time in April, but Kate doesn't think she'll have enough time to plan." He shook his head with a bemused expression. "Kate's got *ideas* about this wedding. Big ideas."

"Sounds very expensive." I couldn't imagine how that could be a good investment of money. Flowers last, what, maybe a week? And the bride only wears the dress once.

"I'm sure it will be extremely expensive." Cole didn't look like he cared. I supposed if he had the money, it didn't matter.

"Emma managed to plan her wedding pretty quickly," I argued. How long did it take to plan a wedding? You need some flowers, a dress, a couple of tuxes. I guess food and drink, but Kate's brother owned a bar. That part would be easy. I shrugged. Weddings weren't really my thing.

"Emma's a girlygirl, but she's actually a lot more lowkey than Kate." Cole wasn't wrong. Kate had a flair for the dramatic.

"Well, good luck man."

"Thanks." Cole looked genuinely excited about the prospect of planning a wedding. "I'm looking forward to it."

This is why I didn't hang out with Cole as much anymore. He was too damn happy all the time. He and Ward were both happily in love and it made me feel worse just to see it. And me? What exactly was I even up to? I was sulking and coming up with ill-conceived secret plots to win Victoria back.

"I heard you were spotted with someone new the other day," Cole ventured. "I heard there was even some photographic evidence online of you leaving the house with a woman. Rae Lewis, Emma and Kate's friend." He took a deep breath. "In fact, I heard you were pretending to date her to get Victoria back." I grimaced.

"Do we have to have this conversation?" I was being a real pain-in-the-ass tonight. I knew it was true, but I couldn't seem to avoid it. "I really don't know that I'm up to it."

"You know this is a bad idea."

I shook my head. "I think we should talk about something else."

There was no way in hell that good-natured, honest Cole would approve of my plan to deceive Victoria into jealousy and loving me again. He didn't like Victoria any better than Ward did, either.

If I was being entirely truthful with myself, which wasn't something I was great at doing at the best of times, I was having serious reservations about my plan to win Victoria.

Cole frowned. "Alright. How's your acquisition going? You found a firm that's interested in buying your app, right?"

I nodded. "Yes. They're in the middle of the due diligence investigation right now. A team comes down from New York for three or four days at a time and they look at all my stuff. Hopefully they make an offer soon. Actually, that's how I met Rae. She's on the valuation team."

"Then what?"

I blinked. "What do you mean? Then I have a bunch of money."

Cole raised an eyebrow. "I mean, then what are you going to do with all that money?"

"Oh, I don't know yet. I'd like to go on a vacation. Somewhere relaxing and sunny."

Maybe I'll take Victoria somewhere she's never been before. It could be the start of our second chance.

Cole nodded. "That sounds fun. Kate and I want to go to Hawaii for our honeymoon..."

As I listened to Cole drone on about all the fun things he and Kate wanted to do in Hawaii, I kept trying to picture myself and Victoria in their place. But it wasn't working. Something just didn't feel right.

I took another sip of my beer and tried to find that feeling that I used to have for Victoria, the feeling that my heart would burst, and the entire world would grind to a halt if I couldn't see her, touch her, and love her again. The miserable feeling had been with me for eighteen months, and it had become a weirdly comfortable companion. Now that my cloak of misery had gone missing, I felt raw. I convinced myself that it was Rae's fault, and she was just distracting me. I just needed to be more committed to my plan. Once Victoria and I were back together again, everything would be right.

"So, are you bringing Rae as your date to the wedding?" Cole finally asked.

I nodded. "Yes. I am."

"Great!" He looked unexpectedly happy, despite his obvious disapproval of my plans. "I'm really looking forward to seeing you with Rae. I bet you two will make a nice couple."

24

RAE

IT WAS A NICE WEDDING, as weddings go. I might be a born romantic about almost everything else, and I'm all for marriage, but for some reason I've never been huge on the concept of weddings. They seem expensive and unnecessary to me. Ward and Emma looked happy though, and that's all that mattered.

"I'm going to go grab a drink," I told Lucas as we were sitting at dinner. It was the first thing I'd said to him in hours. We'd barely spoken at all since I'd gotten into town on Saturday afternoon.

He nodded distractedly.

This wasn't going well.

The deal was going to close on Monday. If I could just make it through this weekend, my obligation to Lucas would be over. I would never have to see him again, and I never planned to. But first, I would have to survive this wedding.

I'd already survived the afternoon. Lucas had been adamant from the start about creating visual evidence of our relationship, and it seemed that the approaching Monday deadline had kicked him into overdrive. We took hundreds of posed, cute, couple-type pictures at locations around Austin. I don't mind being photographed, but this afternoon I smiled so much that my cheeks ached. Lucas could put together months of fake dates with the pictures he'd taken.

All the while, Lucas and I hardly spoke a word to each other beyond what was necessary to take the pictures. I knew why I had nothing to say. Every time I so much as looked at Lucas, I was filled with a sick, tight, guilty feeling. Why he wasn't trying to talk to me was a mystery, but I wasn't going to question it. I might be half in love with him, but I'd never been anything other than a means to an end for him.

Perhaps he'd decided that he hated me. If he did, I would deserve it for making out with him and then lying to him. He'd hate me soon, I had no doubt of that. As soon as we acquired and destroyed his company, he'd never want to look at me again. I tried to tell myself that he would at least have the money, but I knew that Lucas wouldn't consider that fair compensation for the destruction of his technology. He chose Azure Group because of our reputation for developing our portfolio companies, not gutting them.

Unfortunately, we did plenty of both, but we only advertised one.

"Excuse me," a voice to my left asked, snapping me out of my thoughts. I turned to see a smiling man rapidly approaching me across the mostly empty dance floor. "I'm Ian. Would you like to dance?"

Fuck no.

I shook my head and forced myself to be polite. I even smiled. "Oh, no thanks. I was just on my way to—"

"Aww, come on, Red," the guy begged, and it was then that I realized he was drunk. Very drunk. As in, he smelled like he'd fallen into a barrel of tequila. His blood was probably flammable.

"Leave her alone, Ian," another man said, grabbing the first by the elbow. "No dancing for you. Water for you. Lots of water." My rescuer gave me an apologetic look and a rueful smile. "Sorry. Forgive my idiot brother. He's had a few too many."

I shrugged. "No worries. It's a party. I appreciate the rescue." I turned to go.

"No problem. Maybe once I get him settled, could I possibly get a dance? I'm Ryan by the way." My rescuer asked. Ryan was more than decent looking, about my age, and smiling. He seemed normal and well mannered. I wasn't super attracted to him—I just wasn't feeling the spark—but he wasn't hideous. Ordinarily I'd say no to the dance, but at least flirt with him for a minute. But this wasn't a normal situation. I had a role to play.

"I'm Rae, but I can't take you up on the invitation. I'm sorry. My boyfriend wouldn't like it." I nodded in Lucas' direction. Ryan followed my gaze. Unexpectedly, he grinned.

"Oh, you're Lucas' new girlfriend? It's great to meet you, Rae." He shook my hand. Ryan must be one of the mutual friends I was here to meet. And convince. Next to us, his drunk brother, Ian, swayed on his feet.

"*She's not.* Vicky's not here." Ian was slurring pretty badly. He blinked around himself in confusion. A few too many? This guy had clearly gone *well beyond that.* He was trashed.

"Sorry," Ryan repeated, looking doubly ashamed that Ian had brought up Victoria. I shrugged, but Ryan was still apologizing. "I need to get him out of here before he embarrasses me. He's clearly already embarrassed himself."

I smiled politely. "See you around." I didn't get four feet before I was stopped again.

"You're not Victoria," Ian slurred at me, using the bizarre speed of drunkenness to dart out of Ryan's grasp and grab my arm. "You're way prettier than her. Not nearly as mean, either. Do you sing?"

"Oh no, I don't sing," I said, trying to buy time until Ryan could recapture Ian.

"You don't sing, and you don't dance? That's no fun."

"I guess I'm not fun." I shrugged. Arguing with a drunk was never productive.

"Why won't you dance with me, Red?" Ian asked again, arching up an eyebrow at me. "I promise I don't bite." Ian was *extremely* good looking, but slurring drunk is never a good look. Ryan was suddenly blocked by a few people wanting to speak with him. I was trapped with the drunk.

Okay, enough of this bullshit. My name isn't Red.

Apparently, I needed to go full New Yorker on this idiot. Not as mean as Victoria? If properly motivated, I had no doubt that I could be way meaner than Victoria ever thought about being. I drew myself up to my full height and put on my patented anti-catcall tone of voice.

"Listen up oxygen thief," I told him, "I can explain it, but I can't understand it for you. *I do not want to dance with you.* Now, you are going to stop touching me right now or I'm going to kick you in the shins so hard your grandchildren will have bruises."

His eyes widened, his hand disappeared, and he quickly followed suit while apologizing profusely. In fact, several other men who had been near me also vanished. When I tried, I was almost too good at sending men running for the hills in fear. I was disturbingly good at being man repellant. It was no wonder I was single.

I shook my head in bemusement and went back to my table. I no longer wanted a drink.

* * *

LUCAS and I happened to be seated at the same table as his

friend Cole and my friend Kate, who had recently become a couple. They were both phenomenally attractive as well as extraordinarily tall. I blinked at them in amazement. They were so perfect together. Like a pair of pretty giants.

"It's really nice to meet you, Rae," Cole told me, shaking my hand awkwardly around Lucas' back. His hand totally swallowed mine up. "It's not every woman who can put up with Lucas."

I smiled sweetly. "Aww. He's not that bad."

Cole smirked. "Sure, he is," he replied. "But luckily for you, you only have to *pretend to like him*." His voice was teasing.

I blinked. It felt very strange to be honest about our relationship, and I didn't even know Cole.

"Oh, um, yes." Feeling exposed and uncomfortable, I smiled politely. Now that my cover had been blown, I had no idea what to say. What do you talk about with the friends of your fake boyfriend? I certainly had no idea. So, I didn't say anything. My food, which had been lovely, no longer interested me either. I pushed the remains of my chicken around my plate to give myself something to do. An awkward silence descended on our table. I was sure Lucas was staring at me, but I couldn't bring myself to look up.

"Do you like being back in New York?" Kate asked after a few minutes. "I imagine Austin seems pretty boring to you compared to New York."

I looked up at her in surprise. While I'd been staring at

my plate full of cold, uneaten chicken, Lucas and Cole had disappeared. It was just Kate and me at the table now. She looked at me curiously, and I felt guilty for being antisocial. Kate and I usually got along really well (I'd met her while living with Emma), but today it felt weird.

"Actually, I miss it here," I told her. "The people are nicer, the weather is prettier, and the food is really good. I grew up in New York, so it's probably less exotic to me than it would be to someone who moved there."

Kate's beautiful face was wistful. She had incredible sapphire blue eyes. "It must have been an exciting place to grow up."

I bit my lip, suddenly transported to my childhood. I was sitting in my third-grade class during 9-11 and feeling the shock waves through the ground. "A bit too exciting sometimes but yeah." I paused. "Growing up in New York makes you feel like you live in the center of the world."

"You really like Austin? When I moved here it was like coming to the big city—I'm from a suburb of Dallas. But I bet Austin seems like a small town to you." She looked skeptical.

I shrugged. "I like it here. It's not too small, you know. I know I just kind of got settled in New York, but I'm not sure it's where I was meant to be." Although it would mean leaving Azure Group, I was becoming increasingly restless there anyway. The idea of destroying Lucas' company had made me seriously reevaluate what I was doing with my life. There had to be something better out there.

"I love New York, but I don't think I could live there," Kate confessed. "I like to see the sky. And there are too many people there for me. Plus, I'm afraid of heights and all the buildings are much too tall."

I grinned at her. "It doesn't seem like it would be a good fit for you. New York definitely has its drawbacks."

"Rats?" She asked, looking around carefully as if one might be attending the wedding as an uninvited guest.

"Are you asking about the rodent or the human variety? Because we have plenty of both. I've dated a whole bunch of the latter."

"Me too. They're a menace." We exchanged a smile. "Have you ever seen pizza rat in New York?" she asked. I laughed.

"I see pizza rat or one of his family members almost every single day." I thought about the rat traps currently sitting on the floor of my apartment and shuddered. "I'm waging a war against one of pizza rat's second cousins and his twenty kids right now in my kitchen."

She shivered dramatically and giggled. "Gross."

"*So gross*," I agreed. "They say there are as many rats as people in New York. There are almost more rats in New York than there are people in Australia."

We both cringed and then giggled.

"Well, when you put it that way, Austin does sound pretty good." Kate smiled. "We do have a lot of bats here though. They're sort of like rats, I guess. But with wings."

I'd heard about the bats during my two years in Austin,

but thankfully had never seen them. "Never mind. Denver, here I come!" I imagined a winged pizza rat awkwardly trying to fly around with his slice of pepperoni. *No thanks.*

Kate shook her head. "No way. Bats are the best. They eat bugs."

"So, what you're saying is that Austin has a lot of *bugs and flying rats?*" I countered with a smirk. "You're really selling it to me here."

She smirked back at me. I sensed a kindred spirit. "You're a tough customer, Rae. I like you, but if you ever want to buy some lingerie, *let me recommend any other store in town but mine.*"

Before long, Kate and I were laughing uproariously and getting along normally again. She was funny. And she knew a surprising and impressive amount of bat trivia. Everything was looking up until I remembered that Lucas was my boyfriend, and this moment of normalcy was fake. My smile fell off my face.

I was really getting sick of all the lies.

25

LUCAS

COLE CORNED me near the bar. "Follow me, dumbass, we need to talk."

I blinked. This was not like him at all. Of my old college trio, Cole was the most even keeled. Reasonable, charismatic, athletic, and smart, Cole lived the life I'd wanted at eighteen. Although I'd wanted to hate him for being healthy and normal, Cole was just too damn likeable to detest. Along with our third friend, Ward, whose nuptials we were now celebrating, we ended up being friends and roommates all throughout college.

"Huh?" I managed, but I was already being dragged out of the room, down the hallway, and into the bar's tiny office. Cole was enormous—even taller than Ward at six-four—so I had little choice but to go along with him.

Cole closed the door to the office and crossed his arms in front of his chest. I was now trapped in the office with him. Unless I wanted to tackle a retired NFL player (and I didn't want to mess up my nicest suit), I was apparently going to have to hear him out.

I sat down behind Ward's desk to give myself some semblance of a power position. "You wanted to talk? Go ahead. Talk." I made sure my voice was as snide as humanly possible.

"You don't have the slightest idea what you're doing, do you?" Cole asked. Since I'd taken the good chair, he had to take the one facing the desk. It was too small for him. It was like an adult sitting in a kindergartener's chair. He looked like he was going to crush it.

"Is this about Victoria?" I had enough doubts of my own without listening to Cole bash my ex-girlfriend. Just like Ward, Cole made no secret of his dislike of her.

He made a dismissive noise. "No. I really don't give a shit about her. This is about you, Lucas." His Arkansas accent was extra strong tonight.

"Cole, I really feel like this is one of those times where you should mind your own fucking business." Maybe if I was a complete asshole, I could avoid this lecture.

Cole rolled his eyes at me. "Maybe, but I'm not gonna'."
Well, I tried.

"Alright. Fine. Well, lay your sage advice on me quickly so I can get back to the party, will you? I don't want to leave Rae alone out there for too long." I drummed my fingers along the worn wooden surface of the desk.

"Worried someone will ask her to dance?" Cole's tone was teasing.

Maybe. I mean no. Of course not. That's ridiculous.

I frowned. "I'm worried Rae might slug a bridesmaid over the bouquet if I leave her unattended," I lied. Despite their vastly dissimilar looks, backgrounds, and interests, Kate and Rae had disturbingly similar personalities and it didn't surprise me that they were friends. Rae wasn't quite as hotheaded as Kate, but she was just as feisty.

"If she's as fierce as she looks, you won't be able to stop her," Cole asserted. "Trust me, I know all about stubborn women." I had to concede that was a possibility.

"Yeah, you might be right."

We both smirked and then lapsed into silence. After a moment I tapped my watch rudely.

Cole looked me square in the eye. "Victoria doesn't love you."

Shit. Don't sugar coat it, buddy.

I blanched, but my tone was ice cold. "Fuck you, Cole."

Cole's expression was mild. "Whatever, I'm right. Apparently, you need someone to tell you the truth, and I'm the unlucky sonofabitch who cares enough about you to do it. She doesn't love you. She maybe loved you once, but she's been banging groupies from coast to coast for the last year and a half. And she was cheating on you before that too. She dumped you so she wouldn't have to feel guilty about it anymore."

I knew Victoria had been cheating off and on for some

time before she left. I'd looked the other way. This wasn't news. What was news was that Cole knew about it. Did everyone know? The thought wasn't pleasant.

"None of that matters," I told him, trying to refocus myself. "We're going to do better the second time around."

"Why do you want Victoria so badly when all she ever did was treat you like shit?"

He didn't understand. Nobody did. Victoria had saved my life. She had given me something to live for after I found out I was going to live.

"It's not rational," I admitted. "I just do." I wasn't going to defend myself to Cole on this. There was nothing to defend.

"You've clearly got a thing for Rae." Cole kept throwing these statements out like they were the truth.

"Why would you even think that?"

"You're not exactly subtle, you know that, right?"

I'm subtle. I'm as fucking subtle as a stalking jungle panther... aren't I?

"Rae's very pretty, sure. I'm not denying that." It wasn't like I could. "But I'm in love with Victoria."

"Rae wants you."

I paused, looking for a snippy comment to cover my shock. I laughed lightly. "I suppose she's not subtle either?"

"Not really, no. Both of you are a lot more obvious than either of you seem to think." He paused. "Plus, Emma and Kate agree with me."

Aha! He was in league with them. That explains everything.

"Did they put you up to this?"

"Actually, Kate thought this was a terrible idea."

I blinked. "Really?" Since when was Kate so damn reasonable? She was usually the queen of overreaction.

"Kate said that you would just double down on your shitty ideas like you always do because you think you're always right. She said that the more I try to convince you, the more stubborn and stupid you'll be. I told her that you were too rational and smart for that. Was I wrong?"

Yeah. Probably. I'm surprised that came from Kate, but it does sound like me.

I didn't answer, I just stared at him. Eventually, perhaps sensing defeat, Cole got up from his tiny chair.

"Hate me if you want, Lucas, but I'm just trying to help you. Don't lose your chance with Rae over someone that doesn't want or deserve you."

I wasn't able to respond, so I just continued to stare at Cole as he turned and left the office. I'd given Cole plenty of advice over the years. Some of it he'd taken, and some of it he'd ignored. I'd like to think that most of it was pretty good.

This was the first time he'd ever—*ever*—given me relationship advice of any kind. Cole wasn't that type. He wouldn't give me unsolicited advice for no reason. That told me that he really, truly believed what he said. For that reason alone, I couldn't just discount what he was telling me.

But if Cole was right, or even half right, it would mean everything I was doing was wrong.

I needed to get back to Rae before it was too late.

26

LUCAS

"No listen. There was a guy following you this way. I came this way because he looked creepy. He was wearing an ugly green tie. Didn't you see him?" My buddy, Ian, was talking to Wendy when I emerged from the office. Ian was on his hands and knees in the hallway.

"I don't see anyone creepy but you," she answered.

"I'm not the creepy guy. I was trying to stop the creepy guy... Will you help me up? I seem to have tripped."

"I'm not coming over there."

"Please?"

"Um, no." Wendy looked unimpressed.

"But you're so pretty. Like an angel. Angels are supposed to be helpful." Ian seemed honestly confused about being on the ground and unable to get up.

"I don't know you. Stay back. You're very drunk," she

said to him, keeping away several feet, probably to give herself room to run.

"I'm not drunk." He slurred. "I haven't had hardly anything to drink tonight." He tried to get up on his feet again and failed.

"I don't believe you."

"No, it's true."

Wendy, who had clearly just been coming back from the bathroom, looked horrified by the scene before her. I wanted to get back to Rae, but there was no way I was leaving Wendy unattended with drunk Ian. He was harmless, but she had no way of knowing that. Although she could easily just walk around him, it was also obvious that she wouldn't.

"You need help," she told him. "You definitely need some help." She looked unsure about what to do. Her eyes flashed around the darkened hallway, looking for someone to assist her.

"Jesus Christ, Ian. You do need help," I added, surprising both Ian and Wendy. She looked at me in obvious relief.

"Hi Lucas. You know this guy?" She asked.

I frowned. "Unfortunately. He's clearly partied a bit too hard. Can you go in the other room and get the tall guy wearing a blue shirt? He's got glasses that look kind of like mine. His name is Ryan. We'll get him home."

"Okay," she replied, carefully stepping around Ian's

hunched over body. She was almost past him when he popped up and grabbed her wrist.

In a movement faster than I could follow, Wendy twisted her wrist and used her leg to spin and then pin Ian by the throat with her stiletto heel. She'd gone from standing and walking to kneeling down on his chest with her shoe against his neck in the blink of an eye. Ian made a strangled, surprised little gurgle.

What the fuck? Wendy? Sweet little Wendy just did that?

I blinked in disbelief, but the scene was unchanged when I opened my eyes. Yeah, she'd just done that. "Holy shit, Wendy!"

Wendy looked up at me like she was surprised to find herself pinning down a drunk. She stood up gracefully and smoothed down her pink skirt, stepping around him carefully and with as much dignity as she could. She left him prone on the ground. Her movements all looked simple enough, but she performed them with such speed and precision that there were clearly years of martial arts training in her past. I never would have guessed.

Wendy was a secret badass.

"Don't touch me," she told him in her soft little southern accent. He gurgled something unintelligible. She took that as an affirmative and walked off. "I'll go get Ryan," she said over her shoulder.

I blinked after her, looking between her and Ian. He was slumped helplessly in a ball. I had the easy job. He probably wouldn't put up much more of a fight.

* * *

Ryan, Wendy, and I loaded Ian into Ryan's car ten minutes later.

"Are you sure one trash bag is going to be enough?" Wendy asked Ryan. "I'm pretty sure he's not going to make it all the way home without throwing up."

"I'm only going a few blocks," Ryan said, shaking his head. "You'll apologize to Ward and Emma for me for leaving early?"

Wendy nodded. "For you, sure. But Ian has to come apologize to them himself."

Ryan smirked. "That's only fair. Thanks for your help."

I waved to him and he drove off. Wendy and I stared at one another.

"You're a secret ninja," I told her. My voice was appropriately awed.

"I'm not a secret ninja." Wendy shook her head. "I just took a few self-defense classes when I was a teenager."

Yeah sure. That's exactly what a secret ninja would say.

"Well, you definitely put the fear of God into Ian."

She smiled sweetly. "I sure hope not. I just didn't want him to touch me."

"I'm not saying it wasn't justified. I'm impressed."

"Really?" Her eyes were wide.

"Really."

"Well, thank you." The woman was actually blushing.

Wendy really was the real deal. She was every bit as

sweet as she seemed. I was comforted by the fact that she had the ability to beat down anyone who crossed her, though. The world wasn't meant for people as innocent and kind as Wendy. I was glad to see that she had a bit of an edge to her.

"How's your plan going?" Wendy asked when we went inside. "Is your ex-girlfriend super jealous yet?"

I shrugged. Now that I'd come to my senses, I was a bit embarrassed. "I'm not sure it was such a good plan after all."

Her eyes went wide and concerned. "Really?"

I nodded. "Don't worry though. I think I know what I need to do."

"Why didn't your plan work?" She bit her bottom lip and looked so concerned for me that I needed to comfort her.

"It did. It just didn't work the way I intended. What I wanted, well, *who I wanted*, changed. I finally realized what was right in front of me."

She smiled at me. "Okay. Well, you look really happy, so that's a good sign. I guess you just needed to figure things out. Good luck!"

If a real, live Disney princess like Wendy can go from zero to ninja, I might need it.

27

RAE

LUCAS CAME BACK to the table to find Cole, Kate, and me giggling and joking together like best friends. Maybe Cole was just being nice to me for his sake, but I couldn't remember the last time I'd made a friend so quickly. Usually I clam up when new people are friendly with me, but something about Cole's good humor was contagious, and I could tell that Kate adored him. We promised to stay in touch before Kate dragged him off to the dance floor. Lucas and I stared awkwardly at each other once they were gone.

"Want to dance, Rae?" Lucas asked the question carefully. He was watching me with a thoughtful expression.

The song that was playing was slow and romantic. I nodded and followed him onto the dance floor. As long as he didn't expect anything particularly fancy from me, I could dance to this.

"Are you happy here with me?" Lucas asked me as we slow danced. He was a good leader. This wasn't nearly as bad as I'd feared.

There was nowhere to look but at him. Being back in his arms, held close to his chest and breathing his air, it all just made me feel deprived. This was all a lie. I aimed for a properly flirtatious fake-girlfriend reply. "Of course, I am. You're my darling boyfriend." I fluttered my eyelashes at him.

He frowned. "That's not what I meant." His voice was soft.

I dropped the act. "What did you mean?"

"I want to know how you're really feeling. I want to know if you're happy."

"Really?" I'm not sure why I felt a bit angry at the question, but I did. "What does it matter how I feel?" I whispered. "This isn't about my feelings."

This whole day had been spent making it look like we were the most perfect, happiest couple ever. We were weaving this elaborate lie for one reason. Victoria. This was all for her benefit. Once she got jealous enough, she'd come back to get Lucas. Then he'd leave me in the dust. If it wasn't for Victoria, Lucas wouldn't even be speaking to me.

"Your feelings matter to me," he said. His voice was a gentle, whispered rumble. I stared into his huge, beautiful hazel eyes and could barely stand it. "I'm sorry if I've been distant today. I never meant to make you uncomfortable."

I shook my head. "Whatever."

"I don't like seeing you unhappy."

I swallowed hard. *Don't let yourself think he really means it. He only wants Victoria. When he kissed you before, he really wanted to be kissing her. When he touched you before, he wanted to be touching her.*

"You don't need to worry about me," I finally told him. "I'm fine." I could tell he didn't buy it.

Besides, if I could be angry at Lucas, I didn't have to feel so damn guilty.

"Rae—" he started.

"No," I interrupted. "Don't. Please. Just let it go." I heard the vulnerability in my voice, and I hated it. Usually I was so good at hiding my real emotions, but Lucas seemed to bring all my feelings to the surface. It was like he could see right through me.

"I can't. What's bothering you? You've been strange all day, too. Except for when you were talking to Kate or posing for a picture, you've barely smiled today."

"I've been strange? We've spoken more in the past twenty seconds than we have all day."

"I know. I'm sorry." He paused, and then swallowed hard. "I've been having second thoughts."

My lips parted in shock. "What?"

The song had ended, and Lucas pulled me outside by the hand. I went along numbly. In the quiet of evening, I stared at him in total disbelief.

"Rae," he told me, "I don't think I can do this anymore."

28

LUCAS

"I don't understand, Lucas," Rae told me. Her green eyes were as big as saucers. They blinked at me confusion. "Are you backing out of our deal? That's why you've been strange today?" She nibbled delicately on her full, red bottom lip.

I swallowed hard. This conversation would make or break everything. I had to tread carefully. An unfamiliar nervousness filled my stomach and, for once, I couldn't muster any confidence at all. "No, I'm not going to back out of anything I promised you."

"Then what do you mean?"

There was bench just outside the door to the Lone Star Lounge and I sat down on it and patted the spot next to me until Rae reluctantly took a seat. She was staring at me uncertainly.

"Have you ever played Blackjack, Rae?" I asked.

She slipped off her high heels and wiggled her toes. I could tell she was glad to be out of them. Out of her purse, she produced a pair of flats. She came prepared. I wasn't surprised.

"I've played Blackjack. But what does that have to do with anything?" Her full lips were painted a deep cherry red for the wedding. At the moment those lips were drawn downward in a frown. Only Rae could look so pretty when she frowned.

I sighed. After my conversation with Cole in which he basically told me I was gigantic asshole with an additional, gigantic asshole for a face, I felt like I needed a better metaphor to talk to Rae. "Just bear with me. You're familiar with the concept of doubling down, right?"

"Yes. Of course. But I hardly need to play Blackjack to know what that is. I watch the news." She smirked, but it faded quickly.

"When you double down in Blackjack, or politics I guess, you're doing increasingly risky things to try and win." I looked at the ground in front of me, wishing this were easy. "I've been doubling down for the past eighteen months. But I'm in too deep. My plan will never work."

Once the words were out of my mouth, I knew they were true. I'd told Cole that I had everything figured out, but it was pure bullshit. I had nothing figured out. The more I thought I did, the deeper the hole I found myself stuck in.

At least now I knew what an idiot I'd been. But it wasn't

my conversation with Cole that had taught me the truth. It was, of all people, Wendy. Her naïve, painfully innocent outlook on love had cut straight through my wounded, snarky cynicism. At the bottom of all my scheming, beneath all the plots and machinations, there was a deeply flawed premise. Victoria didn't love me.

Victoria wasn't coming back. She'd moved on. It was time that I stopped tilting at windmills and did the same.

"What are you talking about, Lucas? I saw how jealous Victoria was at the pool. Of course, it will work." Her voice was firm.

I shook my head. "No, it won't. She doesn't love me. And by doubling down on her, I've put something else at risk. Something I can't afford to lose."

She frowned. "I'm not going to do anything with your stock certificates. I promise." Rae didn't get it. This was not about business.

I reached for her hands. *"I've put you at risk, Rae. I don't want to lose you."*

Her emerald eyes got even bigger. I didn't think they could, but they did. I squeezed her hands before she ran away. She stared at my face, and then at our joined fingers in confusion.

"Lucas?" Her voice had gone soft and vulnerable. She looked afraid. Like she might get hurt. I didn't want to hurt her. That was the last thing I'd do. I swore to myself in that moment that I'd never, ever hurt her.

"Everyone that matters to me has been trying to tell me

this from the beginning," I continued, looking anywhere but at Rae. "Victoria doesn't want to be with me. She doesn't want me back. But while I've been busy trying to create the perfect fake relationship for myself, I've been ignoring the truth. There's real potential between us. I know you feel it too."

I hope you feel it too. Otherwise I'm going to feel like such a fool.

"Lucas, I don't think you realize what you're saying." Her voice was very small. It wasn't like her at all.

"I know exactly what I'm saying, Rae." I squeezed her hands, warming them in my own. It was a bit chilly outside. "I'm saying that I want you."

Before I could stop myself or wait for an answer, I kissed her. She looked like she needed to be kissed, and she tasted like sweet champagne. Her surprised lips parted after a moment and I kissed her with every ounce of my desperation, trying to convey with my body what I wasn't able to properly articulate with my words.

I've never been great at talking about my feelings. I'm pretty good at figuring out how other people are feeling, understanding their motivations, and predicting their actions, but those same skills have never worked on me. Introspection isn't my strong suit, which was probably why I'd needed Cole and Wendy to lay it out for me. But now, for once, I knew what—or rather, who—I wanted. And she was right beside me.

Rae let me kiss her, and after an initial second of reluctance, I felt her passion rising with mine. She surrendered. Rae buried her little fingers into my hair and leaned into me. She let me kiss down the long line of her neck, wrap my arms tight around her waist, and mess up her carefully curled hair. But when I finally pulled away, her face was soft, but pensive. "You're going to regret this," she told me. It sounded like a promise.

I had a promise for her, too. "Never."

"You will." Her voice was surprisingly sad.

"That's a risk I'm willing to take."

"I thought you didn't want to double down anymore?" She was giving me every opportunity to back away from what I was asking for. Little did she know, I couldn't. Once I'd started down this path there was no changing course. I'd used my last energy on this course correction. I was now on a runaway train. This either ended with Rae in my bed tonight or never seeing her again.

"I'm learning to make better wagers. This is a good one."

"No, it isn't." She smiled a sad little smile at me, and there seemed to be something fierce fighting with something vulnerable behind her eyes. "If you want to get out of here, I'll go with you tonight. But first, I have to tell you something that will probably change the way you see me completely. I've been keeping something from you and I just can't do it anymore." She shook her head and looked miserably at the ground.

For a moment, I was speechless. This was not how I expected this to go.

A tear slid down Rae's cheek. I went to brush it away, but she winced out of my grasp. "You're going to hate me in a moment," she said. "I've been lying to you."

29

RAE

MY HEART WAS in my throat. I brushed my tears away with a stubborn hand and sat up straighter. It was time to tell the truth. If I was going to wreck my career and my personal prospects with Lucas in one fell swoop, I could at least do it bravely. I owed myself that much. "Azure Group is going to liquidate Notable Match once they acquire it and get rid of your technology." The moment I said the words, I felt lighter. I'd hated lying. I'd especially hated lying to Lucas.

He frowned and shook his head at me. "What are you talking about? That's not the agreement."

I knew it wasn't the agreement. The agreement was that Azure Group was going to grow it. Everything we'd told him so far supported that idea.

My voice was sad. "They change their agreements whenever it suits them. Paper is just paper to them. It's now in their interest to liquidate it."

Lucas' eyes had gone huge and round. "Well, if that's true, then I just won't sell." I could almost read his thoughts. He was thinking that there were other private equity investors in the world. He could simply find a better one.

"Yes, you will sell." I sighed and looked back down at my feet. "Azure Group already has your code. You gave it to them. Back out now and they'll destroy it anyway." I took a deep breath before continuing. This was the worst part. "You either let them pay you for the pleasure and enjoy being CEO of a shell for five years or fight them and lose. They'll send your case over to our legal department and sue you for everything you're worth. They want Notable Match dead and their pockets are deeper than yours. No matter what you do, Notable Match gets fucked. But you should still sign the deal, because if you don't, you get destroyed for free."

"The NDA—" He started, and I cut him off with a rude noise.

"It won't save you. They've got an army of lawyers. Real ones, not just wannabes with MBA's like me. You'll never prove their litigation is retaliatory. Even if you somehow could get proof, they'd bury you in paperwork. Individuals don't win against multi-billion-dollar corporations. Trust me. I've seen plenty of people try and fail."

Lucas pulled away from me and I could see him running through my logic in his head. I knew it held up. He'd be looking for flaws, loopholes, backdoors, trapdoors, *anything that would save Notable Match.* There was nothing. Eventually he did come up with a question.

"Why?" He asked me. "Why would they even *want* to bury Notable Match? Was this the plan the whole time?"

He must have been wondering if I had been planning on fucking him over since I first laid eyes on him. It hurt my heart to think about it. I'd already betrayed him. He'd never forgive me. The least I could do now was tell the truth. It was late, but it was still better than never.

I shook my head at him. "No. It wasn't the original plan." I could hear the guilt in my voice. "I swear that it wasn't the plan the entire time."

"But why would Azure Group do this?" Lucas asked. It was a very valid question. They had initially been planning to grow it. No business would buy an asset like Notable Match just to destroy it. It made no sense. Unless you considered the bigger picture.

"They acquired a major competitor of yours last week. Datability. I'm sure you've heard of it. Anyway, in order to cinch the deal, our CEO did something pretty fucked up. The deal was predicated on the agreement not to modify their essential operations for five years. She showed them your technology and promised that your algorithms would never see the light of day to convince them to sell to Azure Group. Now that they have Datability, Azure Group won't compete against their own tech."

I swallowed hard. This was a worst case, no-win scenario for Lucas. And that wasn't even the worst thing.

My heart was pounding a mile a minute. I feared I might hyperventilate. It didn't take Lucas a very long time to figure it out.

"You knew."

I nodded. "Yeah, I did." I refused to lie to him anymore. Even though it would probably cost me my entire career, I just couldn't go through with what I'd been asked to do. It wasn't worth it to me.

"For how long?"

"About a week."

Lucas was still staring at me in disbelief. There was no anger, at least not yet. I was sure it was coming though. "Last week—last Sunday—when Kyle came by... he was trying to tell me what Azure Group had planned." My heart twisted. "He came to warn me, and you stopped him. You kept him from telling me the truth."

"Yes. That's right." I was starting to cry again. "I was afraid." My heart was beating so loud and so quickly that I wondered if Lucas was able to hear it. "Telling you this could cost me everything, but I know it will cost you even more. It's okay if you hate me now. I understand."

Lucas was quiet for a long time. I stared down at the ground and waited for him to start yelling at me. It never came. Finally, when I couldn't stand it anymore, I looked at him.

He was staring off into the parking lot. His profile was lit by the lights of the bar, and I marveled at how handsome he was. Lucas's strong jaw was set in a stubborn line.

"I'll figure out a way to save Notable Match," he said eventually. "I have to."

I nodded. If anyone could, it was him. "I'll go now," I told him. "I'm sure you don't want to see me ever again."

I rose, but I didn't make it two steps before Lucas laughed. I turned, completely dumbfounded.

He's laughing? Has he lost his mind?

"Where do you think you're going?" he asked me.

I blinked. "What? I was going to go home." My voice was shaky. Adrenaline shot through me. Was he angry? I didn't believe there was any chance that Lucas would ever harm me, but I had every reason to believe that he was going to yell at me. I didn't like being yelled at.

"There's no way I'm letting you go anywhere without me." He pulled me back toward him and kissed me again. I couldn't believe this reaction.

"Lucas, you should be angry with me."

"Were you supposed to tell me all this?"

I shook my head. "Of course not."

"You could lose your job for telling me, couldn't you?"

"Yes." I paused. "If you tell Azure Group, I'll definitely lose my job."

"You broke the rules for me."

I had no comeback. I had broken the rules for him. "It was the right thing to do."

His grin was almost unbelievable. "You just proved me right," he said to me.

I blinked at him. "What?"

"You just proved me right that I was smart to bet on you."

He drew me closer and wrapped his arms around my waist possessively. I almost couldn't bear to hope, but of course I couldn't entirely resist. Was there a chance he could forgive me?

"You aren't angry with me?"

"Do I seem angry with you?"

I shook my head. "No..." I still wasn't sure I trusted this reaction. "What are you going to do now?"

"I'm going to double down. Hard. I'm going all in." He kissed me again. I got the feeling that his double entendre was intentional, and it set my heart racing. "I'll figure out the rest later."

30

RAE

WHEN WE GOT TO LUCAS' loft, I could barely remember
how we got there. I was pretty sure there had been an Uber
involved, but all I could think about was getting out of my
dress and closer to Lucas. Anticipation was making my
heart pound and I was dizzy with the feeling. As soon as we
were inside, Lucas slammed the door closed and pulled me
back against him.

The time for slow was over. The time for thinking, and
doubting, and second-guessing was over. I was all out of
worry. But I was prepared this time.

"I have condoms in my purse," I told him with my
remaining foresight while he figured out how to unzip my
dress.

Lucas arched an eyebrow at me as he found the tricky
side zipper. "I bought some too. As soon as you left last
time." He finished with the zipper and pushed the dress off

my shoulders. I stepped out of it.

We both smiled. It was pointless to resist this. It was inevitable that we'd end up in bed together. It had been inevitable since Cliff almost swallowed that damn bee.

My dress was quickly abandoned on the ground by the door. Lucas' shirt ended up on the couch. His shoes were near the kitchen. Mine were next to his pants in the hallway. We ended up in the bedroom. Lucas banished the cats and then came back to my arms.

He was just like I'd imagined him being in the thousands of secret fantasies I'd let myself indulge in over the past two weeks. He was as confident and assertive in the bedroom as he was in the boardroom, and sometimes I needed that. Craved it. I needed a partner that would take control. I found myself tossed up on the bed, turned over on my stomach, and stripped out of my panties and bra in an instant. His hands lingered possessively over my breasts, my ass, my waist, and the curves of my hips. I pressed up into his fingers, reveling in being explored like this.

His hands brushed between my thighs and I spread them wide for him. He made a pleased noise in the back of his throat when he felt my heat and wetness. I was ready for him. Beyond ready. Needy. I pushed my pussy down against his fingers eagerly.

"I don't think I can be gentle," he whispered in my ear between kisses. "It's been too long for me."

"Then be a little bit rough. I like it. I'll tell you if it's too much." I turned around and looked at him when I said it, and I saw his pupils dilate excitedly. I'd always had a bit of a thing for submitting in the bedroom. Nothing crazy or anything. No pain or latex bodysuits. The world of kink is expansive, and I'd barely ever toed the edge of it. But when you spend all your time in charge of things at work, being able to let someone else be in charge feels so good. With Lucas, it felt necessary and right.

He flipped me back over, pinning my wrists to the mattress and kissing me hard. His fingers wrapped all the way around each of my wrists.

"Too much?" he asked, testing the pressure against my wrists.

I shook my head. "Not enough."

He grinned, gripped my wrists tighter and together over my head with one hand, and then leaned in to tease my mouth with his. I arched up into him, greedy for connection. Sensation. Anything he could give me to get me out of my own head. His other hand pulled and pinched one nipple and then the other until they couldn't get any harder. When he pulled his mouth away, I was panting. The emptiness between my legs ached.

Lucas seemed as overwhelmed and desperate as me. When he pulled back to unbuckle his pants and roll a condom on, I watched him with hungry eyes. I could never imagine a more attractive partner.

The strong muscles of his arms and shoulders tensed and flexed when I ran my fingers up his sides and back. His skin was soft, and he smelled so damn good, a heady, potent mixture of pine, clean soap, and citrus. I couldn't get enough of it.

My hands stroked down his chest and he shivered against me before turning his attention back between my legs. I worked my legs wider apart as he eased forward, gasping into the first pinch of penetration before relaxing blissfully into the feeling. He wasn't the only one who was out of practice. But just like riding a bicycle, I found the balance and rhythm right away. We breathed and moved together, wide-eyed, open-mouthed and overwhelmed by the newness and pleasure.

After the first few gentle thrusts, Lucas became more demanding. He held me tighter, staring down at me and watching my face carefully for any sign of discomfort or pain. He didn't need to be so careful. I pushed back stroke for stroke, arching my back, lifting my hips, and urging him on.

My mind was finally empty of any thoughts beyond us. Our movements. Our bodies. Every synapse in my brain was alight with the joy of giving and being taken.

Our mouths found each other again, and I was moaning against his lips for more. He gave it to me, driving into me harder and pinning my forearms to the mattress. I could feel my climax coming and I chased it. I came hard around him, gasping his name and staring up at the ceiling with unseeing eyes.

When my mind cleared, Lucas was looking at me fondly but with a mischievous glint in his hazel eyes.

"More," I mouthed. He smiled devilishly and my heart flipflopped in excitement. I wanted so much more. I wanted everything. If he wanted to tie me up and tease me for the rest of the night, I'd eagerly get down on my knees and beg for it.

He pulled away and turned me over once more. I thought I knew what he wanted, but when I tried to go up to my hands and knees, he pressed against the small of my back to keep me prone. His fingers pushed my thighs apart. Being penetrated again from behind, face down, nearly pushed me right back over the edge. My desperate pussy clenched around him and I heard myself making high, whimpering noises.

"Lucas, harder please..." The voice was mine, but it didn't sound like me. It was breathy and high. He nipped at the back of my neck in reply.

In this position he was completely in control. I ground my ass up against him as best I could, and he reached a hand around my thigh to rub leisurely against my clit. It was exquisite torture to be fucked like this, barely able to move but completely pampered and stimulated.

Unexpectedly, he slowed his hand. "I really shouldn't get you off again after you kept the truth from me for a whole week." His voice was deliciously teasing.

I was so close. This teasing made it so much better... and so much worse.

"Lucas please," I whimpered, pushing against him greedily. It wasn't quite enough without his fingers.

"You've been bad," he growled in my ear. "Why should I give you a reward?"

I was beyond saying anything coherent. I was just sensation. Just breathless, helpless need. All I could do was moan and writhe and push mindlessly against his hand.

If he would just move his hand...

"Oh alright," he finally whispered, sliding his fingers back to put pressure on my clit right where I needed it. I could feel his lips drawn up in a smile against my neck. "I can't say no to you when you make such sweet little noises for me."

His breath in my ear told me he was getting close and I came again just before he did, finally collapsing next to me in exhaustion and bliss.

We cuddled for a long time before a question that had been pinging around in my brain finally percolated to the top.

"Hey Lucas?"

"Hmm?" His voice was a calm, happy sound.

"Remember how you still owe me a question from our first fake-date?"

"Yeah." His voice became more cognizant.

"Well, I've thought of a question."

He looked down at me, smiling. "What is it?"

"How do your algorithms work?"

Annie had gone on and on about how incomprehensible his matchmaking algorithms were. I just had to know. Why were they so damn weird?

Lucas' smile wavered. "That's what you want to spend your question on?"

"I'm curious!" It was true, I was curious. I also half-believed that maybe if I understood the algorithms, I would be able to find a way to save Notable Match from Azure Group.

Lucas, however, sighed. "The answer will disappoint you."

"Let me be the judge of that." Sometimes the smallest, weirdest details could be valuable. I'd learned to overturn every rock in my time working in private equity. This time, I hoped to use a detail to kill a deal, not make one.

His voice was soft. "I reverse engineered the algorithms by looking at the similarities between Victoria's record collection and mine. That's why they're so weird. I was working from the solution instead of the question. It was bad math, and it shouldn't have worked. I had to make up a lot of it. But once I had the similarity measures, I found that I could apply them to other people. Again, I wasn't expecting the algorithm to work. I thought I was just messing around, trying to figure out what compatibility features Victoria and I had shared." He shook his head. "I'm still amazed that so simple of a premise yielded so complex a solution. I just took the person I was already in love with and replicated the formula for musical prefer-ence, making up about a quarter of it as I went along."

My heart sank in my chest. It was all becoming clear. Victoria was the key to Notable Match's success. Everything came down to her. Even when I was lying in Lucas' bed, Victoria had to be here with us.

In fact, the reason that Lucas and I were ever matched must be because Victoria and I had *similar taste in music*. He'd said the reason that Victoria and I reminded him of one another wasn't the hair color and was hard to explain. Well, it wasn't the hair color, that was true. But it wasn't hard to explain, either. The truth was that Victoria and I were just alike, but in a completely innocuous way. He just replicated the formula that had worked with Victoria, but this time when he ran the program, he got me. I was approximately 75% as good as her.

"Were you ever planning on telling me that the reason you and I matched was because I like most of the same music as Victoria?"

Lucas shook his head. "No. It sounds really stupid, doesn't it?"

"Stupid? No." That wasn't what I thought at all. "But it's not very flattering to me to know the truth. I'm just a poor substitute for her. Like a bad copy." I stared up at the ceiling unhappily.

Lucas propped himself up on an elbow and nuzzled my ear. "That's the wrong way to look at it, Rae."

I looked over at him. "How do you figure?" My voice sounded bitter.

Lucas laughed. "This is an example of something working when it shouldn't. The idea that musical preference could predict whether or not people like each other is *ridiculous.* I removed all the other variables. Appearance, income, education, age, all of it. I threw out the reliable measurements and kept something completely pointless. Just music. What does it matter what music people like? It shouldn't matter. The alchemy of human attraction *ought to be complicated*, right? And it is. Even my algorithms look complicated. But I'm taking it from a relationship *that didn't even work worth shit.* Victoria and I crashed and burned. She cheated on me like it was going out of style. But somehow, that equation I made which never should have worked, it brought me you. I think that's pretty cool."

When he finally fell silent, all my anger and bitterness was gone. I looked over at him affectionately.

"What if it doesn't last?"

"Which part?" he asked me. His voice was soft.

"The algorithms. What if all the relationships your algorithms make are doomed to failure because you and Victoria didn't work?"

Were Lucas and I already doomed? I feared I knew the answer.

You're not good enough for him, my conscience whispered. *You know he's being screwed by Azure Group and you don't know how to save him.*

He shrugged. Lucas was oblivious to my doubts. "It's still better than nothing." He kissed me on the forehead. "Nobody who makes a dating app gives people a guarantee, do they? Some love is better than no love, isn't it?"

I sighed, feeling a smile break through even though I

wasn't entirely convinced. "I guess you're right." I paused. "I still wish we could make it last forever."

Lucas smiled sadly. "I'll just have to work on that for version 2.0."

31

LUCAS

Rae fell asleep on my chest, curled up around me with a smile on her face. I watched her eyelids twitch in her dream and wondered if anyone had ever been as happy as I was at that moment. I'd had plenty of sex in my life, but before that night I wasn't sure I'd ever felt like this afterwards. Oftentimes I felt vaguely guilty, or dirty. Tonight, I felt nothing but peaceful, happy, and totally content.

Rae's body was everything a man could ever want. The more I touched her, the more I wanted to go on touching her. And she clearly reveled in being touched too, even with my need to feel in control and push her boundaries to feel her trust in me. Maybe more so because of it. We were compatible on a level I'd never dreamed of or thought to ask for.

Victoria had never understood my desire for even the slightest roughness or teasing. She definitely hadn't appreciated it, although she'd tolerated my mild kinks as well as I think she was able. But I hated feeling like she was indulging a revolting predilection of mine. It made me feel like I was disgusting or deviant, even when I rationally knew that I was hardly left of vanilla at all.

With Rae it felt completely clean when I held her down and fucked her like a wild animal. I felt no guilt or shame because she wanted it too, maybe even more than I did. I hadn't ever thought I'd know that feeling. Now that I'd had it, I wasn't sure I'd be satisfied with anything else.

"I really think I might be in love with you, Rae." I knew she was asleep, but I told her anyway, whispering the words into her cute, little ear. "I sure hope you don't mind."

She smiled in her sleep. Maybe she heard me on some level. I liked to think she did.

I gathered her closer to me and snuggled into her naked, soft body. This was good. It felt right. I felt no regret.

"Sweet dreams, Rae. See you in the morning."

I WOKE up in the middle of the night to find myself alone in the bed.

"Rae?" I called out in confusion after a disoriented second. It was still dark. "Where are you?" I reached over and turned on the bedside lamp. Rae wasn't in the bedroom. "Rae?"

Had she slipped out? Run off? Why? Why wouldn't she at

least say goodbye?

My heart squeezed in my chest. Flashbacks to Victoria breaking up with me via text message hit hard and painfully right above my heart. I wondered what I had done wrong with Rae.

"Lucas?" came a voice from the other room. The pitter patter of bare feet on wood floors was easily distinguishable from the sound of cat paws, but I heard those too. Moxie and Bob preceded her into the bedroom like her feline honor guard. "I'm right here," she said, emerging from the living room with a glass of water in her pale hand. "I was just thirsty, and then the cats were thirsty too, so I gave them some water." She perched on the edge of the bed and looked at me excitedly. "Moxie even let me pet her!"

I grinned right back at her. That was a first. The cats took one look at me, decided I was boring and went back in the living room. It was the middle of the night, after all. That was prime cat prowling hour.

"Is that my shirt?" I asked haughtily, although I already knew it was my T-shirt. She'd also located a clean pair of my boxers and was wearing them low around her hips. "Have you been snooping in my drawers at..." I squinted at the alarm clock, "four a.m.?" This was not an acceptable hour for being awake at all.

She smiled at me. "No. I was just cold. Finding clothes is not snooping. It's survivalism. Besides, this is when I would usually be waking up in New York."

"Well, you don't need to wake up so early here," I told

her. I was vaguely put out that my warm, sweet, sleepy, naked Rae was now clothed and wide awake. I opened my arms to her, and she slid back into bed and into them with a smile. I felt instantly better. My blood pressure returned to normal. "Okay, this is good," I grumbled into her sweet-smelling red hair. "No more getting up." I wrapped my arms around her possessively. It would be better if she was naked again, but I'd survive.

"You're really not much of a morning person, are you?" Rae whispered against my neck.

"No." I confessed, running my fingers under her borrowed shirt and up her back until I reached her shoulders. "I'm really not." I pressed down on top of her trapezius muscles, going alongside of her scapula and working toward the spine. She sighed blissfully and flopped over on her tummy for more back rubs. That one time I'd read a textbook about massage had really paid off. For Rae.

"Oh my God, that feels *soooo good,*" she mumbled into the pillow. I pushed my fingertips deeper into the knots I felt around her neck and she sort of melted into my hands. I worked each little bundle of tangled muscle fibers apart with slow, gentle strokes. She made some incomprehensible little pleasure noises.

"This is my plan to keep you in my bed," I whispered in her ear.

"It's working really well," her muffled voice replied. "It's a super good plan. You're a genius."

"So, you'll stay?" I asked.

She nodded and rolled her head over so I could get the other side of her neck. "Uh-huh. Yes. I'm not going anywhere."

"Okay. Good."

I wasn't capable of rising at four in the morning, but that didn't mean I didn't have a daily routine. I got up around ten a.m., puttered around for an hour, went to the gym, took a shower, and then worked until around nine p.m. Then I would putter around, eat dinner, and do some more work before bed. Bed usually happened around two a.m. My routine worked very well for me, although it was a bit unconventional.

I rubbed Rae's neck and shoulders until I couldn't feel any more knots and then descended down her back to rub her lower back and hips. She liked that too. I could tell by the way she wiggled anytime I wasn't in the exact right spot, went too slowly, or paused. I was happy to oblige, and happier to tease her.

"You're awfully demanding for someone getting free back rubs," I whispered sleepily.

"I'll pay you back," she crooned, and then turned to kiss me. "I always pay my debts. That's why I have such excellent credit."

I was perfectly happy to take my payback for the backrub in kisses. She teased my mouth with hers, eagerly erasing any sleepiness with her clever, soft tongue. Soon, despite my aforementioned inability to do anything at this time of the morning, I could think of exactly one activity I was interested in. But when I reached for the hem of my T-shirt, I learned it wasn't the one that she had in mind.

"Sshh," she told me, stilling my hands and scooting down the bed, and my body. She was taking her soft curves away, but then I realized what she was after. "My turn to make you feel good," she purred.

Okay. Yes. That was better than kisses. That was not an invitation I could ever turn down.

She laid little kisses down my torso as she descended, and by the time she reached my cock it was rock hard and ready for her. When she took me in her mouth, it was all I could do not to grab the back of her head and take control, but I resisted. Not only would that be incredibly bad manners, but this was much more fun. I was more than happy to let her be in control of the process. For now.

She took me eagerly, bobbing up and down deeper each time. The hot, wet, heaven of her mouth was enough to drive me crazy. I threw back the covers to get a better look at her. Her big blue eyes glittered hungrily in the lamp light while she sucked and licked me.

Christ. Look at her go. There's nothing hotter than this.

"Rae, fuck. Please don't stop." My voice was a strangled whisper.

Her little tongue darted out now and then to trace where her lips had been, and she let out a low, moan of satisfaction when she looked up and saw how completely she had control of me. I pushed the hair that had fallen into her face away and she gazed up at me, open-mouthed, to gauge my reactions before getting back to work.

Her cheeks went hollow and I arched my hips into her, unable to keep my hands at my sides any longer. I put a heavy hand atop her head and guided her down, down until I thought she couldn't go any deeper. When I felt resistance I stopped, but she didn't. She pushed on until she was almost gagging, and I was almost coming straight down her sweet, little throat.

"Oh god, Rae, do that again," I heard myself saying, and she did. She took me from tip to hilt, struggling in a way that only drove me higher to see her so determined to please me.

That little mouth on her.

I didn't stand any risk of impressing her with my phenomenal stamina. This was going to be almost embarrassingly quick. Finally, unable to keep from taking all the control back from her, I pushed her head down and fucked her face relentlessly, bucking my hips into her and seeing her eyes go glassy and gratefully relaxed when I did. She needed me to take control. She really did enjoy it as much as I did. It was with that comforting, unbelievably sexy surety that I came, faster and harder than I ever had in my life. My vision blinked out for a second from the pleasure. When my sight returned, I saw her swallowing every last drop.

"You're perfect," I told her when she crawled back up my body to lay her head back on my chest. I kissed the top of her head and touched her wet lips with my fingers. She was exhausted. "Perfect," I repeated.

She smiled dreamily at me, clearly ready to go back to sleep now. If this was what getting up at four a.m. got me, I was willing to consider some serious lifestyle changes. We drifted back to sleep together.

* * *

MEEEEEEEOW!

Meeeeeeeow!

As was their custom, Moxie and Bob sang the song of their people just before noon. They did not appreciate getting their breakfast late, so their pleas for food were both louder and more desperate than usual. At my side, Rae was still sleeping soundly. She'd curled up into an adorable ball of covers and pillows. All I could see was a foot and a few strands of bright red hair sticking out. How someone so small could take up so much room in the bed was simply incredible. Do beds come in larger sizes than California King? If I was going to share one with Rae for any length of time, I was going to need to find out.

I was filled with thoughts of the future as I rose to feed Moxie and Bob. They looked at me like I'd personally deprived them of food for at least a week.

"You two need to go on a diet," I told them as they buried their faces in their food bowls and greedily started scarfing down their breakfasts. As always, they ignored me

245

when there were kibbles to be had. But I didn't care. My mind was elsewhere.

Could I convince Rae to move to Austin? I guess it wouldn't be too terrible to move to New York, either. I could finally see *Hamilton*. It wasn't as nice and warm there, but I'd certainly never be bored. Too excited to go back to bed, I made myself a cup of coffee and sat down on the couch. Moxie hopped up on my lap. I scratched her chubby, soft cheeks as she purred like a happy motorboat.

"Do you think you'd like living in New York, Moxie? Do you want to be a big city cat?"

Her amber eyes weren't giving anything away, but she always made her priorities clear. She headbutted my hand for more pets.

"What about you, Bob? Would you like a change of scenery?"

Bob was still eating. He didn't even look up. I doubted he was even listening. As long as there was food, I was fairly certain Bob would be fine no matter where he lived.

The trill of my phone sent Moxie flying off my lap and scrambling for the safety of the void below the couch. I picked it up reluctantly and then nearly dropped it. *Victoria texted me.*

Victoria: *Hey Lucas. Do you want to have lunch?*

My fragile, healing heart, which had been as content and calm as it had ever been, was thrown instantly into turmoil. My fancy, delicious coffee suddenly tasted rancid. Why was she texting me? What did she want?

It had been eighteen months since she'd texted me. The text directly above her lunch invitation was telling me that she'd left her key with the doorman. I swallowed hard and stared at the text. I wasn't entirely sure it was real. It could be a hallucination. I closed my eyes and counted to ten. Opened them. The text was still there.

Shit. You know it's bad when you're hoping you're just crazy.

The entire premise of my decision to act on my feelings and sleep with Rae was that Victoria didn't care. But the moment I let myself believe it and admit defeat, she texts me? And not even to tell me to fuck off, but requesting to see me? Christ. It was like Victoria had some kind of sixth sense about exactly how to fuck over my life. It was uncanny.

"Lucas?" Rae's voice called out to me from the other room. Her tone was sleepy, sweet, and confused. "Where'd you go? Come back to bed. I miss you."

My gaze pinged between the open bedroom door and my palm. Victoria's next text appeared before my disbelieving eyes.

Victoria: I miss you.

It was lucky that I didn't really have a heart defect, because that moment would have killed me if I did.

What the fuck am I supposed to do now?

32

RAE

LUCAS CAME into the bedroom and slid back under the covers with me. I cuddled up to his chest, wrapping my arms and legs around him and feeling completely content for the first time in weeks. I sighed against his skin and rubbed my cheek against him like a cat. He held me loosely and kissed the top of my forehead.

The guilt about Lucas' deal was still there, but as long as he was in my arms, I could push it away. He made me feel safe. When he held me, I felt like everything would turn out right.

"I'm happy," I told him. "Let's not get out of bed today, okay?"

"I need to tell you something, Rae." Lucas' voice was soft.

"I need to tell you something, too." I told him. Now I knew that he was right. There was something between us.

Something special and rare. We were lucky to have found it.

"Let me go first," he said, and something about his tone sent a shockwave of anxiety through me.

I pulled away and looked at him. "What's wrong?" His expression was closed. "Lucas?"

He pushed my hair off my face tenderly. "Victoria texted me. She wants to have lunch today."

It would have hurt less if he'd punched me in the stomach. I felt like I'd had the wind knocked out of me. When I finally took a breath, it burned from how long I'd been holding my breath.

"Oh," I managed. It wasn't a very articulate response, but it was a response. I searched Lucas' handsome face for some hint to how he felt. I didn't know how to interpret what I saw. He was still cuddling with me though, slowly stroking my hair and back with gentle fingers. I took another cautious breath. He wasn't telling me to leave. This wasn't rejection.

Not yet, whispered my traitorous heart. *But he will reject you. He still loves her. And you knew it all along.*

"I was diagnosed with a terminal heart condition when I was a freshman in college," Lucas said unexpectedly. I gasped and covered my mouth with my hand, and his eyes widened. "Misdiagnosed," he clarified. "*I was misdiagnosed.*"

My heart continued to thump against my ribs. That was not an okay thing to spring on me. "Are you—alright?" The sudden change of subject was disconcerting, but I was frightened for Lucas. I laid my now-trembling hand atop his heart. It felt normal to me.

He nodded. "I have a harmless heart murmur. It was unusual though and initially misdiagnosed. I went through a couple of years thinking I was either going to need a transplant or die."

"That's awful."

"It wasn't fun." He sighed. "But eventually I learned that I was okay. The stupid doctors had been wrong all along."

I tried to wrap my mind around thinking I was terminally ill as a teenager. I wouldn't have had the slightest idea how to process something like that then. Hell, I couldn't imagine how I'd deal with it well now.

"I'm so sorry, Lucas. That must have been a terrifying time in your life." I hugged him close to me to impart some comfort. I hated the idea of baby Lucas—okay, twenty-year-old Lucas—being scared like that.

He shrugged into my hug but kept on holding me. "Believe it or not, it was worse when I realized I wasn't going to die. I had no idea what to do with myself. I'd been preparing to die for so long that I didn't know how to live."

I pulled away enough to see his face again. He looked confused.

"That actually makes a lot of sense to me," I told him.

He raised his eyebrows. "I wish it made sense to me. It still doesn't."

It took me a minute to organize my thoughts. Lucas waited patiently, although I could tell he was curious. I eventually worked up the courage to tell him my own sad story. "I told you my dad died of cancer when I was eight. Well, while he was still alive, I met a little girl in the hospital whose dad was also sick. It was through one of those support groups, you know? Her name was Dawn. We ended up becoming friends, both Dawn and I and my dad and her dad. But Dawn's dad got better when my dad got worse. When Dawn's dad's cancer went into remission, he got really depressed. Eventually he said that Dawn and I couldn't be friends anymore. My mom said it was because he felt guilty that my dad wasn't getting better. It seemed really unfair to me that I lost my friend. I didn't understand it then, but I do now."

"I'm so sorry about your dad, Rae." Lucas' voice was quiet.

"Don't worry about it. That was a long time ago." Almost twenty years was a lot of time for me to come to terms with his death. I mostly had. Sometimes I didn't think about my dad for months at a time. Sometimes I thought about him every day. I knew that I'd never fully heal up, but the wound was closed now. It didn't hurt anymore.

"I guess you have a point," Lucas said after a second. "Maybe I didn't know what to feel. It might have been a perverse survivor's guilt."

"You know, it's okay that you were depressed," I told him. "There's no shame in that, even if there was no specific reason. But especially after what you went through thinking you were going to die, I feel like anyone would have been a bit messed up." I brushed his cheeks with my fingertips and he smiled a sad little smile at me.

"It was during that time that I met Victoria," he told me. His expression was distant, like he was looking into the past.

"You don't have to tell me about her if you don't want to," I told him. It might have sounded like I was trying to spare his feelings, but I was really sparing mine. Every time he talked about her, it took a little chunk out of my pride.

"Yes, I do," he said. "I want you to understand."

I swallowed hard. "Okay."

He kissed my forehead again and closed his eyes tight as he told me the rest. I could feel the emotion in his voice. All his confidence and swagger were gone. This was Lucas at his most raw. "When I met her, I thought I'd never feel normal again. I figured that I would just go through the rest of my life like I was fighting through a thick, deep fog. Nothing felt real. *But she was so alive.* She was talented and artistic, and she felt real when everything else in my life felt fake. I was drawn to her like a stupid moth to a flame. I was happy to burn up in her atmosphere, because at least when she was close to me, I felt alive too." He laughed a bitter little laugh. "Victoria wasn't an easy person to be in a relationship with. She could be pretty cruel sometimes. She cheated on me a lot. But when things were good, they were really good. She reminded me that I was alive."

My heart broke a little bit for Lucas when he looked up

at me after falling silent. His hazel eyes were vulnerable. I hardly knew what to say. My insecurity spoke for me.

"Are you still in love with her?" I heard myself asking.

We looked at one another for a long time before he answered. I felt the world hanging in the balance.

"I don't know, Rae. I wish I could tell you that I wasn't, but I really just don't know." I could hear the honesty in his voice, and it just about killed me.

I nodded. This was what I should have expected. It was silly to expect that he'd say he didn't love her. He'd spent the last three weeks spinning a fantastical tale of our fake relationship just to get her back. He was going to sell his app to Azure Group for ten percent below market price just to get her back. Tears pricked at the corners of my eyes and I beat them down with every iota of strength I possessed.

I won't cry in front of him. No matter what, even if I spontaneously combust instead, I still won't cry.

"If you think you might love her, and if you think she still loves you, then you owe it to yourself to fight for her."

His eyes widened. "But—"

I pressed my index finger to his lips and interrupted. "No. There's nothing to say. I'll... I'll just go."

"Rae, I'm not asking you to go." His tone was surprised, and almost wounded. It made me feel worse.

"You can't tell me you still love her and then ask me to stay, either. That's not fair to me at all. Last night you said that you two were finished. But now, *conveniently after we slept together*, you say you still love her? Do you even realize how fucked up that is?" I pulled out of his arms. I was going to have to get out of his bed naked, and hunt around the entire apartment to get my clothes. That was going to be fun and not at all humiliating. I might as well not put it off.

"I'm sorry, Rae." He sounded genuine.

"Yeah, me too, Lucas. *I'm very sorry I believed you.*" I was aiming to hurt him, and I think I succeeded. He flinched.

Lucas swallowed hard before continuing. "I think I might be in love with you, Rae."

My anger flared and burned. "Then I guess you need to figure yourself out *pronto*. Because I don't share."

I swept out of bed, stark naked, and started hunting around for my underwear with as much dignity as I could muster. It wasn't a lot. It's hard to be properly haughty when you're nude. I wriggled into my bra and panties and was already on the way to the living room to find my dress by the time he caught up with me.

"Rae, please don't rush off. I really want to talk about this with you. I feel like you're the only one who can help me to figure it out."

Too bad. Figure it out yourself.

I rolled my eyes as I snatched my dress off the floor and wrestled it onto my body. It was all wrinkled from sitting on the floor all night. I was going to have to walk-of-shame back to my hotel in a cocktail dress. Fantastic. "Why don't you go meet Victoria for lunch? I'm sure she'll help you feel all better."

Probably by sucking his cock with her evil, cheating mouth.

I might be a lot of terrible things, but I'm not a cheater. I never have been, and I never will be.

I was pulling on my high heels before I realized that, once I walked out the door, there was no reason for me to ever see Lucas again. My presence at the closing tomorrow wasn't necessary, and I had no intention of attending. It didn't stop me from leaving.

33

LUCAS

I wasn't even out of bed before she was out the door. Panicking, I dove for my pants and ran out into the hallway shirtless to chase her. She was already getting in the elevator and I sprinted full tilt toward her. Rae's eyes widened, and she repeatedly pressed the button to close the elevator door in my face as I padded urgently down the hallway toward her. I was quicker than the elevator door, but just barely. I blocked the door with a bare foot.

"Rae. Wait. Please don't go." I was panting a bit from my impromptu twenty-yard dash.

"Lucas, this is ridiculous." She shook her head at me angrily. "You need to just let me go. Call Victoria. Or better yet, someone else. Be happy and just forget all about me. It'll be better for us both. Let. Me. Go."

"I can't." I sounded desperate.

"Why?" She sounded exasperated.

"Because I care about you." I searched for the words but couldn't seem to find them. "I know we just met, but there's something between us. I don't want to just go and ruin it."

She looked away, down at her feet. "You're in love with someone else."

I couldn't deny it. And yet. I couldn't let her go, either.

I'm such a fool. What kind of idiot falls in love with two women? Me. Apparently.

"Tell me you feel nothing for me, and I'll step away and let this door close."

Rae sighed and beseeched me with her wide, beautiful eyes. "Lucas... you don't know me at all. Please just let me go."

I shook my head. She shifted uncomfortably on her heels. It was a standoff. Her blue eyes held no compromise, but she looked away first.

"Fine. Lucas, you want me to say it? I'll say it. I feel nothing for you," Rae's voice was more resigned than anything else. "You were nothing but a way for me to get a promotion. When I couldn't get a promotion, I figured at least I'd have a nice night."

"I don't believe you." What we'd shared the night before meant something. It had to. I refused to believe that Rae felt nothing for me.

"I don't give a shit what you believe! You told me that you would let me go if I said it." Rae arched an eyebrow at me. "I said it. Don't be a liar, Lucas."

"But I—"

"Let me go." Rae's voice was angry. "I've got better things to do than ruin my career over someone like you."

"Rae—"

"No." She looked at me with that wild, cunning ferocity that had first attracted me to her. "Look, you want the real truth? Here's the real truth. I'm impressed by you, Lucas. Really. You tricked me into destroying my whole career for you. That's really something. I was *this close* to closing this deal and getting promoted and having all my dreams come true. If you hadn't said that you cared about me, I never would have told you the truth. But you outplayed me. You really are a genius, aren't you? But don't be a liar, Lucas. You said you'd let me go if I told you I feel nothing for you." She paused for a moment. "Well, now that I know the truth about you, I feel less than nothing for you. I won't be used. Let. Me. Go."

Stunned, shirtless, barefoot, and confused, I stepped back to allow the elevator doors to close. I wouldn't keep her if she really wanted to go.

As the gap between the elevator doors closed, Rae's placid exterior cracked. A tear carved its way down her face. "Lucas, just take the money and run. Forget about Notable Match. Stay away from me. Stay away from Victoria. Live your life." She swallowed, and her blue eyes shined with more unshed tears. "Goodbye, Lucas."

I walked back to my loft alone.

34

RAE

I WAS WAITING at the gate in the Austin airport when I realized that I hadn't told Annie and Kyle I was leaving early. I called Annie with trembling fingers.

"Hi Rae. What's up?"

"I've fucked up big time." That wasn't at all what I meant to say, but it just came out my mouth of its own volition.

"Hold on," Annie said. I heard some rustling before she spoke again. "I just went outside so we'd have some privacy. Are you doing okay?"

I'd reached my breaking point. "Not really." I hated that I was having this conversation in an airport, surrounded by strangers. I could feel people looking at me, and I got up and walked to the bathroom. My eyes burned. "I think I fell in love with our client. And now he hates me." A hot tear tore through my carefully applied mascara. I felt it sliding down my face.

"Oh, Rae. It's going to be okay." Annie's voice was comforting. My head was painful and pounding. I locked myself in a bathroom stall and the tears started falling the moment I was alone.

"No. It's not going to be okay at all. I guess I should tell you that I told Lucas what Azure Group is going to do. I don't even know if he'll show up to the closing tomorrow." My voice came out in shuddering gasps.

"Rae, the deal doesn't matter." She paused for a moment. "You fell in love with him? With Lucas? It wasn't just a fling?"

I nodded, although of course she couldn't see it. "Yes. It was all supposed to be a lie, but I'm a bad liar. It didn't stay pretend for very long." Part of me felt like I should have called Emma or Kate for my confession, but I couldn't stand the thought it might get back to Lucas.

You never wanted it to be pretend. You always wanted it to be real.

"What do you mean, Rae? Why was it supposed to be pretend?"

There was no point in lying to Annie now. "Lucas and I had a deal. Not the deal with Azure Group. Our own deal. I was going to pretend to be his girlfriend so he could win his ex-girlfriend back. In exchange, he would make every-thing easy on us and sell for a good price. But then everything spun out of control, and his ex is a rock star and Azure Group is evil and now I'm in love with him, but he still wants his ex."

God, it sounded like a stupid story. I really should have seen this coming.

"Wow," Annie said after a second to digest everything. "Oh Rae, I'm so sorry. I can tell you're really upset."

"It's all my fault," I told her. I was seriously ugly crying now. "I really shouldn't have even considered Lucas' offer. Who pretends to be someone's girlfriend? That's really crazy, right? I just wanted to finally get ahead at Azure Group. I knew that if I made this deal work that Cliff wouldn't be my boss anymore and he's just such a dick and then I was in love with Lucas and he seemed like he was in love with me..." I trailed off, choking back tears. "He's not though. He's not in love with me. He still loves her."

"Oh, no. It's okay, Rae," Annie was saying. "It's all going to be okay."

I swallowed hard and tried to regain my composure. This was not how I expected this call to go with Annie. "I'm sorry to unload all this on you. It's so unprofessional."

I could almost see her shaking her head at me. "We're friends, Rae. You don't have to be professional with me."

"I'm just so embarrassed by all of this," I admitted.

"Remember that time I got food poisoning in Iowa and you came to my hotel room and fed me Gatorade through a straw while I was sitting on the toilet?"

I paused. "Yeah." Poor Annie. She'd eaten some really sketchy Indian food and it did not agree with her at all. We'd ended up in an urgent care facility at three in the morning. Half the restaurant was in there with us. I'd never been so glad to dislike curry.

"*That was unprofessional and embarrassing.*" Her giggle came through the phone and it was just enough to make my lips curl up into a smile. "Look, I'm glad you told me. It's not good to keep things like that bottled up inside."

"I'm so good at keeping things bottled though." It was like my superpower. I was so good at not complaining that I'd really screwed myself over this time.

"Until you boil over and explode."

"Yeah."

"Would you mind if I asked a couple of questions?" Annie's voice was careful. She probably didn't want me to start sobbing again.

"Feel free," I told her. I wasn't exactly surprised that she'd be confused. I hadn't explained the situation very well.

"So, Lucas wanted you to pretend to be his girlfriend to get his ex back?"

"Yes."

"But you two ended up sleeping together instead?"

I sighed. "Right again."

"And you're in love with him?"

"I think so, yes."

If it wasn't love that I was feeling, I didn't know what it was. I'd never felt so turned inside out.

"Is Lucas in love with you?"

I wish.

"He's in love with his ex. He said that he cared about me too, but I don't think he realizes how hung up on her he is. He's clearly still in love with her."

"So, what are you going to do now?"

"I'm going home. I'm about to get on the plane. That was, um, actually the reason that I was calling in the first place." Way back when I wasn't a weeping, emotional mess.

"To tell me you were going home?"

"Yeah. And to ask you to deliver something to Lucas."

"Rae, I think you should consider that Lucas might be as confused as you are." Annie's voice was careful.

"Maybe, but he's better off without me. I kept the truth about Azure Group from him. I told him, but probably much too late. I betrayed him." My heart hurt.

"No, you didn't. You did your job. You two were doing business together."

"I hate my job."

I heard Annie laugh in the background. "I know the feeling."

"I just want to go home and sleep for a week." I pinched the bridge of my nose, but it did nothing to help my headache.

"So, go home and sleep for a week. The world will work itself out."

"Hey Annie?"

"Yeah?"

"You're a really good friend. Thanks for listening to my meltdown."

"What else are friends for?"

* * *

It was raining cats and dogs in New York. My flight was delayed by the bad weather, and we circled high above the clouds for hours. I wished I could just fly up above the tempest that was raging in me. Instead, I was trapped inside the roiling storm.

Rationally, I knew that Lucas would do what he would do. He was a smart man. Hell, he was a genuine, certified genius. If he couldn't figure this situation out, I knew I had no chance of it. The entire problem was out of my hands now. I wished I could put it out of my mind, too, but I couldn't. I couldn't stop thinking about what I'd said to him.

I hadn't pulled any punches in that elevator. Lucas probably thought I was cruel now, and not worth the effort. Maybe I deserved to be hated for everything I'd done. But I thought Victoria did too. It bothered me a lot that I'd all but pushed them back together. He deserved so much more than either of us. He deserved someone good and pure and worthy of him.

If he wanted to, Lucas could easily cost me my job now.

It would be a petty revenge and an unequal one, but I wouldn't blame him one bit if he called up McKenzie and told her every word of what I told him. I could only imagine that he had a few choice words for her, too. The truth was, I really didn't care if I got fired. Besides, they couldn't fire me. I quit.

While the plane was waiting to land, I emailed my letter of resignation to Azure Group. I'd thought that I wanted to be in charge of the acquisitions team, but I clearly wasn't cut out for it. I was too soft. Lucas had given me a gift in a fucked up, perverse way. He'd given me the gift of clarity, and with it, I was going to get the hell out of Azure Group while I still had half a soul to lose. I wouldn't let them turn me into the type of person who fucks over innocent business owners like Lucas for the almighty dollar and feels nothing. At least I felt like shit. That must mean I still had some conscience left.

McKenzie could shove my promotion up her snotty ass. It simply wasn't worth it to me. I told her as much in my rambling resignation letter.

... Nothing about this deal was made in good faith, and I resent that I was made into your pawn. I know that I can't stop you from doing anything, but I can choose not to be a part of your organization anymore. I've shared your plan to scrap the Notable Match code with Stevenson. It was a hard thing to do since I've always been loyal to my employers, but it was the right thing to do and I can't regret it. Please don't take your

anger out on Annie or Kyle, because they were not involved in any way...

I copied Kyle and Annie on the message and hit send with a trembling finger and a generous sip of overpriced airplane gin. It didn't make me feel better to tell McKenzie to go to hell. There was no righteous victory to be found for me anymore. I was complicit in the scheme to rob Lucas of the success he'd earned. His app deserved to be famous.

The one thing I could tell myself was that at least he'd have his money. I'd gone through the final closing documents and upped the purchase price by ten percent—back up to market price. Since the arrangement I'd made with Lucas was now null and void, it seemed only fair. Azure Group had agreed to the initial figure, so they could hardly complain. It made me feel the tiniest bit better to ensure that Lucas would at least be compensated properly.

The closing was at nine a.m. on Monday morning. Given that I'd emailed on a Sunday night, there was really no way for anyone to do a thing. Azure Group had already signed their side of the deal. All that was needed was for Lucas to show up and sign his side to release the funds sitting in escrow. Simultaneously, the source code and backups would be uploaded automatically from Lucas' servers to Azure Group, giving them formal possession of what they already considered their property.

A light tap on my shoulder pulled me out of imaginings of the closing. A flight attendant was at my shoulder. She frowned at me like she'd been attempting to get my attention for some time. "Please put your tray table up, Miss. And power down your laptop as well. We'll finally be landing soon."

I nodded numbly. "Sorry."

We began our descent into the storm.

35

LUCAS

I SPENT the whole day pacing in my apartment. Back and forth. Back and forth. Like a neurotic zoo tiger. Or a crazy person.

I had very little to show for my day of frantic pacing. It brought me little clarity and less peace. The only thing it did manage to bring me was a well-worn path in the carpet and the bored-yet-somehow-still-judgmental gazes of Moxie and Bob. They probably thought I'd lost my mind. They were probably right.

Victoria's texts from this morning were still on my phone, taunting me, but still unanswered. I had no idea what I should say to her, if anything. Did I still have feelings for her? Yes. But maybe I always would. She'd been a powerful force in my life at a time that I needed someone like her. It was another, much more complicated question as to whether we belonged together now.

It wasn't just Victoria that kept me pacing. Rae's words to me the night before echoed through my brain on repeat.

They change their agreements whenever it suits them. It's now in their interest to liquidate it.

She was right. Of course, she was right. Azure Group was many times larger than any ordinary mortal like me. If I thought I was scheming, I was grossly outclassed. Azure Group was filled with people smarter, shrewder, and more scheming than I ever thought about being.

Individuals don't win against multi-billion-dollar corporations.

Rae was right again. Multi-billion-dollar corporations can do basically anything they want to do in our society. I wasn't such a naïve, insulated member of the white, male, ruling class that I didn't notice how big business was screwing over the little guy hard, early, and often. And that was *legal*. They could take an extra-legal approach if it appealed to them. If I seriously pissed Azure Group off, they could just, you know, kill me. They'd almost certainly get away with it, too. They'd make it look like an accident or pay off some cops. The idea that I might be able to challenge them was laughable.

Azure Group already has your code. You gave it to them. Back out now and they'll destroy it anyway. You either let them pay you for the pleasure and enjoy being CEO of a shell for five years or fight them and lose. They'll send your case over to our legal department and sue you for everything you're worth. They want Notable Match dead and their pockets are deeper than yours. No matter what you do, Notable Match gets fucked. But you should still sign the deal, because if you don't, you get destroyed for free.

There was no system created by humans that can't be dismantled and destroyed by smarter, more determined humans. One of my strengths was in knowing when I wasn't the smartest guy in the room. When it came to the law, I knew I wasn't likely to be the smartest guy. Not by a long shot. I'm sure my agreement with them was *thoroughly exploitable*. My algorithms might be incomprehensibly opaque, but my lawyer was one guy and they had an army.

I ran a hand through my hair in frustration for the thousandth time. I probably looked like a mad scientist at this point. I wished that I was a mad scientist. Maybe then I could figure out how to save Notable Match.

Just take the money and run. Forget about Notable Match.

It wasn't bad advice. Rae was practical, as always. The money that was heading my way was well up into the seven digits. I'd be set for many, many decades. But that wasn't what I wanted. What I wanted was to see Notable Match live up to its potential. I believed in the power of technology to bring people together. I believed that Notable Match offered something very different from what was currently available in the marketplace. It wasn't the cure for cancer or anything but putting people together could make them happy. I wanted to make people happy. That mattered to me.

I'd had a happy childhood mostly because my parents

had a happy marriage. Growing up where and when I did, a lot of my friends' parents were divorced. I knew that I was lucky to have the family life that I had. My sister, brother, and I never had to worry about the things my friends with divorced parents did. I never had to be stressed out about celebrating holidays twice, or whether my parents would get into an embarrassing fight at a soccer game. The idea that in some small way I could help people find the same happiness my parents had was valuable not just to me but to society.

My musings were interrupted by a knock on the door. My heart leapt, thinking that maybe Rae had returned. But when I threw the door open, it was Annie, Rae's coworker.

"Hi Annie."

"Hi, Mr. Stevenson," she said, clearly uncomfortable to be calling on me alone. "Rae caught the earlier flight out this afternoon, but she wanted me to drop this off for you."

She handed me an envelope.

"What is it?" Whatever it was, it was light.

Annie shook her head. "She didn't say." She shifted from foot to foot. "Well, I gotta run. Me and Kyle's flight leaves in an hour. Congratulations on your closing."

"Thanks."

I shut the door and ripped into the envelope. Disappointment shot through me. The only things in the envelope were my stock certificates. I threw the envelope on my kitchen table and almost missed the note that accompanied them. I scooped it up to read it eagerly.

Dear Lucas, I know you've probably got a lot on your mind, but maybe having these certificates back will help just a little. I hope you'll believe me that I never wanted to make your life more difficult or hurt you. I didn't want the deal to go down the way it did. I hope you get everything you deserve in life. If Victoria is the person who can make you happy, then I hope you get her too. I wish things could have been different between us. Anyway, I consider our deal to be complete so I'm returning your stock certificates now. All the best, Rae.

I read and re-read the letter until I could recite it from memory. Does it still count as a dear-john letter if it comes from your fake girlfriend? It definitely felt that way to me. I shoved the note away from me on the table, feeling sick to my stomach.

The day was wasted, but even though I had come to no decisive conclusions, a couple of things did become clearer to me during my pacing. Not fighting—simply rolling over and accepting my fate like Moxie and Bob did when I trimmed their claws down, was not an option. It simply wasn't in me. Surrender was not an option when it came to Notable Match, and certainly not an option when it came to Rae. It was time for me to stop pouting in my apartment and *do something about my problems*. Now if only I knew what that something should be, I'd really be off to a good start.

36

LUCAS

I was hungry, it was dark, and I didn't want takeout. That meant I had to go to the grocery store. After a day spent puttering around my apartment like a crazy person, I dressed and ventured out reluctantly. My mind could have spent forever recycling the same problems and fruitless solutions, but my stomach was a lot less patient. The only thing I had in my barren cupboard was cat food, and I wasn't ready to stoop that low.

"Lucas! Lucas, wait for me!"

I froze midstep in the lobby of my building. *I know that voice. I'll always know that voice.* A moment later, a familiar face appeared next to me.

"Victoria, what are you doing here?"

Victoria didn't look her usual, polished self. Not remotely. Her makeup was smeared, and her nose was red.

There was a tissue clutched in her left hand. She'd obviously been crying.

Because of me and Rae? Had she been crying over me?

"Lucas, I'm sorry for ambushing you like this. I just really need to talk to you." Her voice shook, and her green eyes were wide and bloodshot.

I stared at her in disbelief. "Victoria? How long have you been waiting down here?"

"A while." She looked down at her combat-booted feet. She stuffed her hands into the pockets of the fashionable pair of pink denim overalls she was wearing. A stray thought flickered through my mind that Rae wouldn't be caught dead in those overalls. I beat it into submission. Rae was gone.

I wondered vaguely how long Victoria had been waiting in the lobby that she wasn't willing to share. An hour? Two? Since she texted me before Rae left? That was around noon. It was now nearly seven p.m. My mind resisted my attempts to make sense of the situation.

"Why didn't you come upstairs and knock on the door?" I asked her.

It wasn't like she didn't know where I lived. She'd lived there too, not that long ago. We'd picked it out together, during much happier times. She used to love it there.

Victoria's bloodshot green eyes blinked, and then narrowed. "I didn't know if Rae was there with you... I didn't want to interrupt anything, and I wanted to talk to you alone."

274

I didn't know what to say to that. So, I said nothing. Victoria frowned. Jealousy and dislike were clear on her face. I'd realized long ago that Victoria was the jealous type. She didn't even like it when waitresses smiled at me in restaurants (and had gone off on women who hit on me before in fairly spectacular fashion once or twice). But what had once been vaguely charming and cute to me now felt cloying and obnoxious. I wasn't her personal property. She had thrown me away. Rae also wasn't her rival. There was no competition. And it wasn't just because Rae was gone, either.

There was a time when I wouldn't have considered this moment anything less than a total victory. But now, I felt... nothing. I looked at Victoria and felt absolutely fucking nothing. The emptiness in me was painless, but vast. I could imagine a tumbleweed slowly working its way across a huge, empty desert in my heart. It was too desolate on that barren landscape for any emotion to take hold. Certainly not the elation and love I ought to be feeling.

"I got your text," I finally told Victoria. She stared at me like she was waiting for me to say something else, but I didn't know what to say. There was nothing to say. This morning my entire life imploded. I didn't want to use something so seismic as the double wounds of Azure Group and Rae to explain why I hadn't returned her text for a lunch date. Besides, I wasn't sure if returning her text was still something I wanted to do.

"I miss you, Lucas. I... I think that you and I should give

it another shot. I still want you." The words tumbled out of her mouth like she was tripping over them.

God, how many times had I dreamed of her saying that? At least a thousand times. So why did I feel nothing?

The moment stretched. It became awkward. We stared at each other across a gulf of unspoken pain and misplaced expectations. This wasn't how I expected this to be.

The only thing I could think about was the first time she'd cheated on me. Well, it was the first time I *knew that she'd cheated on me*. It probably hadn't been the actual first time. The feeling of shock and pain was palpable, even now. I may not be able to feel new things now that my heart was a lifeless desert, but I could remember them.

Betrayal is a memorable thing. I felt inadequate and small. Stupid and gullible. Transparent and paper thin. The pain lingered on and on, even after we fought, and I forgave her and tried to move on. It felt like someone had tied an incredibly heavy weight to my ankle and I was doomed to drag that pain of knowing she'd strayed around forever. No matter what I did, I couldn't escape it. The idea that she might be causing that pain to someone else made my stomach cramp with physical discomfort.

"Did you break up with Kane?" I asked, arching an eyebrow at her.

Her lips parted. It wasn't what she expected me to say. "I will." Her alto voice was strong and convincing. She probably believed it, too. But I knew better. She always sounded that way when she told me she'd never cheat again.

"Does he know where you are right now?"

Was he waiting in her bed? Or by the phone? Was he worried about her while she was barking up my tree?

She shook her head. "Jason's at a gig. I had to talk to you. Lucas, please, talk to me." She paused. "I can't keep pretending like I'm happy for you and Rae. You're meant to be with me, not her."

"Do you love me, Victoria?" In my new, desert-like state, I could be direct.

"Yes." She raised her chin up and stared me in the eye. "I love you. And I know that you still love me." Her green eyes held no deceit that I could find. She was telling me the truth as she knew it.

I'd loved her. Now that I was a desert, I could view in hindsight what had not been clear to me when I was too lost in the thick of my emotions. I'd loved her. I'd loved her so much it was still not possible to quantify. But it was also past tense. I was no longer in love with Victoria.

I stared down at my feet. "I'm sorry, Victoria. I can't do this." I didn't want to see her face when I said it, but I couldn't resist. I looked up to see disbelief on Victoria's face. She shook her head.

"Why? Because of that girl? Rae?" She sneered.

That girl?

I resisted the impulse to roll my eyes at Victoria or snap at her. She was too vulnerable to make fun of, even though she'd laughed at my pain enough times. I wouldn't stoop to her level. I wasn't a cruel person, and I wouldn't let her turn me into one.

"No Victoria. It's not because of Rae. We aren't together anymore, and trust me, our relationship was never what you thought. *This is because of me.*"

Once upon a time, Victoria and I had been right for each other. Victoria could be vivacious, fun, and creative. Back then, she'd been more empathetic and less narcissistic. She'd healed me when I was in a very dark and desolate place emotionally. I'd given her the structure and pragmatism she needed to grow and reach her potential. Our time together had been good for a long time. It was full of chemical excitement and hormonal overload. We'd been young. The problem was that we grew up. We grew into strangers who had nothing in common. I wanted to make it work, but she'd ultimately had the right idea. Not all love is meant to last. Now, for the first time, I was willing to accept that Victoria and I were done.

Wendy had told me that I needed to fight for true love. Fight for my soulmate. Fight for my happy ending. All of Wendy's advice had been good, but none of it was about Victoria.

But Victoria was still attractive. I couldn't deny it and wouldn't ever try. Even now, with her mascara smeared underneath her eyes like war paint and her skin blotchy and red from crying, she was prettier than *most women* on their best day. Most women, however, weren't Rae.

When I first met Rae, all I could think about was how

much I wished she were Victoria. Now that I was finally face to face with Victoria again, and she was swearing that she still loved me, all I could think about was how much I wished she were Rae.

You're the biggest fucking moron that has ever walked the earth, my heart whispered. *You let Rae walk away from you. And for what?*

"Where's Kane's gig tonight?" I asked her.

She frowned. "Houston. Why? Lucas, we need to talk. We were meant to be together." She put a hand on my arm. "Let me convince you. You know that I can convince you." Her voice had turned into that throaty purr that always turned me on. It did nothing for me now.

I shook my head at her. "No. I don't want to be convinced. Look, I gotta go," I told Victoria. "I'm sorry you waited so long for nothing."

My words had more meanings than one. She'd waited too long to decide she wanted me. In the meantime, I'd fallen out of love with her. I was in love with someone else. Someone who really was right for me. It was time for me to take some action. I might not be able to save my company, but there was a chance that I could make Rae mine. And if it worked, I'd have Victoria to thank for it.

37

LUCAS

IT BROUGHT me no joy to press send on the text twenty minutes later, but it was necessary.

Lucas: Hey man, you don't know me but I'm Victoria's ex, Lucas. I thought you should know that she just tried to cheat on you with me.

Jason: What? How'd you get this number? Is this a prank?

Lucas: Ryan Conroe gave me your number.

Jason: Nobody has this number. I barely know Ryan. He doesn't have it.

Lucas: Yeah, he does. He got it from Ian Conroe and Ian got it from your manager.

Jason: What's my manager's name?

Lucas: Fuck if I know. Dude. I'm just trying to help you. Take it or leave it.

Jason: So... this isn't a prank?

Lucas: I'm afraid not. Sorry.

Jason: This had better not be Vic.

Lucas: I have no idea who that is. I'm Lucas Stevenson.

Jason: Wait, you're Lucas? Victoria's ex Lucas Stevenson? The genius app guy?

Lucas: Uh, yes. Victoria's ex. That's me.

Jason: ... Fuck.

Lucas: I'm sorry to tell you like this.

Jason: Fuck.

Lucas: I'll leave you alone. I just thought you'd want to know.

Jason: Did you fuck her?

Lucas: No. Definitely not. We're done.

Jason: She came onto you.

Lucas: Yeah. I think it was a jealousy thing more than anything, if it helps.

Jason: Um, not really, no. It doesn't help.

Lucas: I know the feeling. She cheated on me too when we were together. A lot.

Jason: Ok. Shit. I wondered why she was being so weird.

Lucas: Yeah.

Jason: God dammit. Well, thanks man. She clearly didn't deserve you. LOL. Didn't deserve me either. At least this means I can go out clubbing tonight!

Lucas: You're taking this surprisingly well. I'm glad. I was kind of worried you'd freak out on me and threaten me or something.

Jason: Threaten you over Victoria? No way. What can I say? I bounce back. Musicians have to deal well with rejection. Victoria

and I weren't exactly soulmates anyway. I'll be fine... well, after
I dump her spoiled, cheating ass.
Lucas: Glad to hear it. Be safe man. Love your music. Axial Tilt
is amazing.
Jason: Thanks! That means a lot. And I owe you one. You ever
need a favor, call me. I'm good for it. You have my word.
Lucas: No way. You don't owe me anything. But, um, a bit of
unsolicited advice? Get an STD test. I may not be the first.
Jason: Good call. On it. Thanks again.

Jason Kane sounded like a chill guy. I was glad he was gonna be okay. Ratting out Victoria was the right thing to do, even if it did come with just the slightest thrill of vindication. I had no doubt that Victoria would be okay too. She was probably picking someone new up to soothe her ego as I texted with her boyfriend. Victoria really just needed to meet someone that was as insane as she was. Or maybe she just needed to be polyamorous and was trying to fit a square peg in a round hole? I didn't really care much. That was all her problem.

Besides, I had problems of my own. At least I knew what to do now. I was sitting on the plane to New York, about to take off, before I remembered something very important. I whipped out my phone and started tapping surreptitiously and hoping that the flight attendants wouldn't see what I was doing.

Lucas: Cole, you up?

Cole: Seriously? We've been over this. You aren't my type.

Lucas: Yeah right. I'm everyone's type.

Cole: Oh, are we talking about blood donations or something? I was talking about how ugly you are. Is there an actual reason you're texting at 11 p.m.?

Lucas: I gotta go out of town for a couple of days. Can you feed Moxie and Bob until I get home?

Cole: No. Sorry. Ordinarily I'd say yes, but Kate and I are going to visit her mom tomorrow in Plano at the alpaca ranch.

Lucas: Shit. Ward and Emma are on their honeymoon.

Cole: LOL This is what happens when you only have two friends.

Lucas: I have more than two friends.

Cole: Name one.

Lucas: Ryan.

Cole: Fine. Get him to feed the cats.

Lucas: He's in Dallas this week.

Cole: Ok so you have three friends. You're a sad man.

Lucas: Ian's my friend too.

Cole: Ian's an actual idiot. Like, a certified idiot. Did you see how drunk he got at the wedding? That shit was disgraceful.

Lucas: He's got poor impulse control, you know that. He's still my friend. That's four.

Cole: Ian only counts as half a friend. Three and a half.

Lucas: This is fun but do you have Wendy's number?

Cole: Seriously? You're gonna make poor little Wendy feed your cats?

*Lucas: No. I'm going to politely ask Wendy if she will please,
kindly feed my cats.*

*Cole: No way man. Wendy's too nice. You can't ask her for a
favor like that. She'll feel obligated to say yes. But she's allergic
to cats too.*

Lucas: She's allergic to everything. I'll pay her.

Cole: Her allergies are no joke.

Lucas: I'll pay her and buy her a gas mask too.

Cole: Kate says I can't give you her number.

*Lucas: WTF. It takes five minutes to feed the cats. In and out. If
she's really slow.*

Cole: Kate says no.

Lucas: Come on. Don't be whipped. What's her number?

Cole: This is Kate texting now. Leave Wendy alone.

Goddamn it. I ran through my list of contacts and cringed. Cole was right. I only had two real friends that I could trust and depend on. Ryan travelled too much, and I didn't really trust Ian. Ian was the type of guy who would go to my apartment and release a bunch of live mice, so the cats could hunt them, or simply forget to feed them entirely and have a kegger in my apartment. The guy had a lot of growing up to do.

This was a real problem. If the cats weren't fed on time they definitely wouldn't die, but they would certainly poop in my shoes to express their displeasure. They were vengeful little creatures, but I loved them. I thought I was going to need to pay my lawyer to feed the cats until I remembered something. I knew a world-famous rock star that owed me a favor. I hoped that Jason Kane liked cats.

I hadn't packed any luggage for my impromptu trip, and when I got off the plane in New York, it was three a.m. and fucking freezing. Rae hadn't been kidding about the shitty weather. I called an Uber and ended up spending the night in an IHOP on the corner across the street from the building that housed Azure Group.

Rae had blocked my number, and I didn't know where she lived, so ambushing her at work was my only way of getting in touch with her. Was it a creepy stalker-ish thing to do? Hell yes, it was. But I had a plan. So, although I was exhausted, I ordered myself some subpar buttermilk pancakes, drank the stale-ass coffee, and settled in for a good, long wait.

At least I had plenty of time to rehearse what I would say to Rae.

38

RAE

DESPITE BEING NEWLY UNEMPLOYED, I woke up Monday morning and got ready to go into the office. I had a little family of cactuses that needed to be retrieved from my cubicle. I wasn't going to let them die just because I quit. They hadn't done anything wrong. Those cactuses were my one personal item at my desk, and they represented my humanity in the face of Azure Group's oppressive corporate evil. They were my totems. They had to be rescued.

It was a thin reason for going to the office where I was no longer employed, but I'd not been unemployed since I was fifteen years old and honestly didn't know what else to do. The alternative was sitting around in my apartment and agonizing over whether or not Lucas would show up to his closing, whether he had ever cared about me, and whether or not I'd ever see him again. I was fairly certain that the answer to the last two questions were no. I just wasn't ready to confront them yet.

I was right about to leave the house for the office when a knock at my door made me pause. Who on earth would be here at six a.m.? I stared through the peephole warily.

"Annie?" I threw the door open and stared at her in disbelief. "You know where I live?"

Annie hugged me, and I hugged her back with more excitement than I thought I had in me. I was really, really glad to see her. I wasn't sure if I'd get the chance to say goodbye. I was afraid to text her because I only had her corporate cell phone number, not her personal one. I didn't want to get her in trouble for continuing to talk to me or put her in an awkward position by making her decide not to reply. Next to her on the ground, she had my cactuses in a banker's box.

"I've got mad hacker skills," she said simply. "I just looked it up in your HR file."

I smirked. That figured. I'd always suspected that Annie's skill set was a lot more useful than Kyle's. Azure Group paid him more, of course. That company could go to hell.

"Thank you for bringing my cactuses. I was just on the way to go pick them up." They were going to love getting some natural light. I already knew what window I'd put them in.

"No problem. I stopped by early this morning and I thought you might want them."

"Come on in," I said, beckoning her inside. "Do you want some coffee? I've still got some in the pot. It's hazelnut flavored."

She shook her head. "I have to go into work in a minute," she replied. "But I wanted to come by first and tell you about the plan." Annie looked excited.

I felt my eyebrows climb up my forehead. "The plan? What plan? There's a plan?"

She nodded seriously. She raised a finger to pause me, took out her corporate cell phone from her purse and put it in my microwave. My eyebrows were probably threatening my hairline they were so far up my face. Was Annie secretly Edward Snowden or something? Was Azure Group listening in?

"It's just a precaution," she told me. "Do you still have yours?"

I shook my head. "I dropped my phone and laptop in the mailbox right after I quit. I wanted a clean break." I might have also given them both a good once-over with a powerful magnet just to be sure they would never work again, too.

"Good. That's good," she said. I half wondered if Annie was going to go all double-oh-seven and scan my kitchen for bugs, but she didn't.

"Why is that good?" I was beginning to get seriously confused. This was not the Annie I knew. She looked determined, and not just in an ordinary way. This was a whole different level of determination. Her voice was usually soft, but today it was strong and decisive. She was even standing up straighter. "I'm so confused."

"We don't want them to be able to track your movements with the phone," Annie told me. "They probably aren't tracking me or anything, but I figured it was smart to shield the phone anyway."

"We? Who is 'we'?"

"Kyle and I think we know how to save Notable Match. But we need your help."

My jaw went slack. "We can't save it. It's too late." Annie's presence in my apartment would seem to suggest otherwise, however. My inner optimist perked up her ears.

"No, it isn't. It's only six thirty a.m. east coast time. The deal won't be signed until at least nine-thirty a.m. That means we still have several hours before Azure Group will own it." She paused to evaluate my reaction.

"Okay. I'm listening."

If they thought they knew how to save Notable Match, I was definitely listening. I was fucking all ears.

Annie smirked. "Alright, so the plan goes like this. We know that Azure Group wants to purchase Notable Match so that they can contain the technology, right?"

"Right."

"The algorithms themselves are really the only valuable part of the company. But the algorithms are entirely incomprehensible. They were beyond bizarre. There's no way that Azure Group could ever reverse engineer them."

289

"What do the algorithms have to do with anything?" I asked.

Annie frowned at my interjection. "Well, for one, Azure Group has them. If we're going to save them, we need to steal them back. Otherwise they could potentially use them against Lucas somehow."

I blinked. "Well, okay. But we can steal them all we want and that won't save Notable Match. Because if Lucas tries to pull out of the deal now, that will just trigger the typical Azure Group overreaction. McKenzie personally promised the Datability people that she'd kill Notable Match. We both know how this will go. They'll get Legal involved and just bully Lucas into selling by burying him in expensive, endless litigation."

"You'd be right, except that's where you come in."

"Okay. I clearly shouldn't have interrupted. Explain it your way."

Annie's smirk turned into a quick grin. "Thank you. So, while Kyle and I are going in and wiping all the data that Azure Group has on Lucas' technology—and it's definitely a two-person job—you are going to march into McKenzie's Monday morning board meeting and lay down the terms of your sexual harassment lawsuit that will be the lynch pin that prevents Azure Group from bullying Lucas or retaliating against us. As a side bonus, you'll be providing a distraction that will help Kyle and me do the stealing."

I laughed. "I don't have a sexual harassment lawsuit." I

shook my head and smirked, thinking of Cliff. "God knows I should, but I don't."

Annie smirked. "Actually, you do." She pulled out a file folder from her briefcase and handed it to me. It was thick and heavy. Thousands of pages.

I lifted the cover to see one of the many, many emails that Cliff and other managers had sent to me that were inappropriate. This particular one was fairly mild. It was about a blouse that I'd worn to a client meeting that was slightly tighter than my usual loose-fitting, boring, button down silk blouse. In the email, Cliff was suggesting that I purchase more blouses in that style for future client meetings or consider unbuttoning my blouses so that more cleavage was on display. A particular paragraph in the email was highlighted: *You have a unique set of assets that can be used to influence key client impressions. Double D's if I'm not mistaken. They won't stay perky and jiggly forever. You might as well put them to good use.*

"Cliff really is a huge pig," I said with a shake of my head. He stared at my tits all the time. At this point I was just used to it.

"Keep going," Annie encouraged. "It gets better." She was quivering with excitement.

I thumbed through the emails that Annie had somehow gotten her hands on. They weren't all to me or from Cliff. Some of them were to Annie or other women we worked with. Some of them were to Kyle and other men and women of color. We'd all been harassed during our time at Azure Group. Much of it was old fashioned sexual harassment or racism, but not all of it. There was a wealth of employment related lawsuit fodder in the folder. It was diverse, too. There was even some highly inappropriate weight-related bullshit that someone sent to Annie.

I kept flipping through pages, occasionally looking up in wonder at Annie. There even a conversation between Cliff and a client about whether Annie or I would be more likely to sleep with the client as a 'bonus' (apparently the client preferred Annie but Cliff thought I was more likely to put out). It was horrifying stuff, especially when presented all together. Practically every one of our senior managers had put something in writing that was illegal, immoral, or just plain old gross. Azure Group was rotten from the inside out.

It was absolutely revolting, but simultaneously fascinating. Like watching a train wreck. Just reading through all the years' worth of bullshit that we'd each been sent filled me with anger. Bizarrely, even though I knew that it was crap that I'd received so many inappropriate messages from my coworkers and superiors, it was the messages to Annie and Kyle and others that really made me angry. I guess I'd always figured that I could just 'take it,' but I couldn't stomach the idea that by not speaking out, the perpetrators just got away with what they were doing, and then they did it to others.

"This could work," I heard myself saying. "I think it could really work."

Annie grinned. "So, are you in?"

"Are you kidding? Of course, I'm in. I think we might be able to do more than just save Notable Match. We might be able to save Azure Group from itself."

39

LUCAS

I GOT the call at seven in the morning, which meant it was six in the morning in Texas. I stared at the unknown number before picking it up. It must be important. It was probably my lawyer or something.

"So, I don't think that you have any cats," came the voice of Jason Kane through the tinny speakers of my cell phone. "This is a really weird prank. Like, really weird."

I couldn't stop my bark of laughter. "What?"

"I'm at your place right now and there are no cats. I looked all over. Bedroom? No cats. Bathroom? No cats. Kitchen? No cats. Living room? No cats. There are only four rooms and I checked them all. The only logical conclusion is that there no cats here."

"Dude, I definitely have cats. Two cats. Moxie and Bob. They're probably just hiding." I took another bitter sip of my terrible diner coffee and winced. "Did you look under the couch?"

I heard shuffling through the line and the distinctive noise of someone holding the phone directly against their face. "Oh. *There they are.*" In another, crooning baby voice that was clearly not meant for me, I heard, "Hey dudes. Have you been hiding from me? Don't hide from me. Oooh, you're so *fluffy and pretty*. Aww, come here. I'm nice!" Then a sigh. Then, Jason was back. "Okay. I'm really glad I found them. They hate me, but at least now I know they're okay. I was getting worried."

"Um... how long have you been in my apartment looking for the cats?"

"Not that long." The reply was defensive.

I smirked. "Half an hour?" I took a wild guess.

Silence.

"An hour?" I tried.

"Probably a little bit longer than that. I thought maybe they'd slipped out the door and I maybe panicked." He sighed. It was a strangely defeated sound.

It's not every day a world-famous rock star spent his early morning looking desperately for my cats.

"Don't worry, you couldn't pay those cats to go outside. But you're one hell of a morning person, Kane."

"It's morning?" There was shuffling through the line again. "Oh crap. It's really late. The sun is coming up."

I blinked in surprise. "Early actually. What time did you think it was?"

"Um, I don't know. Maybe like two a.m.? Maybe three?"

"So, you haven't slept at all since last night?"

"Not since my gig. No. I came back from Houston, got my shit from Victoria's place and told her to eat dirt, we had a nice screaming fight, and then I came here to feed the cats."

"Do you want to crash at my apartment for a bit before driving?" I was honestly a bit concerned about the guy. At least I'd caught a few hours rest on the plane. He might not be safe on the roads. The last thing I needed was to be responsible for his death.

"Would that be okay?" He sounded incredibly relieved and tired. The poor guy had been up for a very long time.

"Dude, you did me a big favor by feeding the cats. Of course, you can stay for a while." Then I paused. "No crazy rock star parties though. You gotta promise me."

Kane laughed. "I think I'd have a hard time getting all my hard-drinking, hard-partying friends over here at six a.m. on a Monday. I usually can't get them awake before three p.m., and that's on a good day. I pinky swear that I will not trash your place." He paused. "It might scare the cats."

I laughed as well. "Fair enough. Oh, there's a fresh toothbrush under the sink in the bathroom and cold brew coffee in the fridge."

"Thanks." There was another pause on the line. "You're a decent guy, Stevenson. I'm glad you told me about Victoria. I'd rather have you as a friend than her as a girlfriend any day."

"Same."

I wondered vaguely what Victoria was up to at the moment, and how exactly Kane had dumped her after our conversation, but I squashed the thought. It really didn't matter.

"Do you think the cats will come out from under the couch if I stay really still?" He paused. "I feel like they don't like me." His voice sounded inexplicably wounded. I could sympathize. I hated it when cats didn't like me too.

"Once you're asleep they'll probably come out and sniff you a whole bunch. And don't take it personally that they're hiding, they're very picky with new people at first. Once they get used to you, they'll be all over you." I shook my head. He was going to have more cats than he could stand on him.

"Really?" He sounded incredibly excited about the prospect of having them crawling all over him as he slept. "What's the big fluffy one named?" Kane asked.

"Oh, he's Bob. The smaller one is his mom, Moxie." I'd found them in an alleyway downtown. There had probably been more kittens at one point, but the others hadn't made it. Just Bob. He'd been so tiny and sad, and his mom had been scrawny and exhausted looking. They'd cost a fortune in vet bills to get healthy, but they were worth every penny.

I heard the rustling again that told me Kane was looking under my couch. "Bob, your dad said you should be nice to me. You want to come take a nap with me? I'm gonna go take a nap."

I smirked at my coffee and pancakes. Jason Kane was kind of a trip. He didn't sound drunk or high though. Just weird. I could deal with weird. Hell, I was weird. Apparently, Victoria had a type, just like I did.

Okay, let's not ever think about that again.

I shook my head to dispel that disturbing thought. "Talk to you later, Kane. Call me if you need anything."

"Thanks man. I promise I'll be gone by the time you get home and it'll be like I was never here."

"No worries. I'll probably be gone a few days. Feel free to stay."

I knew it was risky to let a guy who'd been known to trash hotel rooms stay in my home and take care of my cats, but I was getting the feeling that the rumors about Jason Kane were a bit overblown. The man loved cats, for goodness sake. How bad could he be?

40

LUCAS

"Excuse me, sir, but you can't loiter in this building." The security guard looked me up and down dismissively.

"I'm sorry, what?" I replied tiredly, feeling profiled because of my jeans, T-shirt, sneakers, and generally unshaven and scruffy appearance. I probably looked homeless or something. There were plenty of people just standing or sitting in the lobby area of the huge office building. But I was the only one who looked like he'd overnighted in an IHOP after a long flight. I was also the only man not wearing a suit and tie.

"You're loitering, sir. I'm afraid that I'm going to have to ask you to leave the premises. Immediately." Every word was enunciated carefully like he was concerned I might not understand English properly. He looked at me like I was a particularly large, ugly cockroach, and he pointed at the revolving doors as if I was too stupid to know they were the way to exit the building.

I frowned at the older, potbellied man. "I am not *loitering*. I have urgent business here. I'm waiting on a meeting with someone from Azure Group." I prayed that would be enough to deter him from hassling me further. I was not aware that loitering was an actual thing that someone could get in trouble for. It definitely wasn't a thing that anyone ever got in trouble for in Austin. The rules were clearly different here in New York.

He looked down at my Converse shoes and then up at my face with a disbelieving expression. He pushed his bifocals up the bridge of his nose. Behind them, his eyes were narrowed. "I see. Do you have an appointment? You can go upstairs and wait in their reception area. But I'm sorry, you can't wait here."

People had begun to pick up on our contentious conversation and were now giving me a wide berth. Ordinarily I'd be somewhat self-conscious to be stared at by so many strangers. Today, I was just plain annoyed.

"Why exactly can't I wait here for my appointment?" I asked grumpily. After spending countless hours in the goddamn IHOP, I was entirely out of patience. It was also cold and rainy outside. This was bullshit. "I'm going to need you to spell it out for me."

"Don't make me call the police to remove you," the security guard said. He had the tired-while-simultaneously-dismissive tone that I usually associated with grade school teachers and government employees. I'd been a problem child all throughout my school experience. I was too smart, so I had free time. That free time was spent primarily getting into trouble. Clearly, nothing had changed.

"You really think I'm lying about having business here? Why would I do that? I just got off a damn plane, I'm exhausted, and I'm honestly in no mood. I'm *so sorry* I forgot to bring my best suit. Do you have a dress code here? I didn't get the memo. Perhaps you should post a sign."

The security guard seemed honestly surprised that I wasn't just tottering off the premises obediently like a good little transient. Unfortunately, it only made him more obstinate and angrier. He put his hands on his hips. "I'm not here to argue with you. Leave now or I call the police." He'd raised his voice considerably. The guy was legit yelling at me. Everyone in the lobby was staring at us now.

"Dude. Are you serious?" I asked with a laugh. I could barely believe this was happening. People were looking at me like I was some kind of dangerous, T-shirt wearing criminal. "I'm an app developer from the west coast. This is how we dress. I don't wear suits unless it's to a funeral or a wedding."

"This is your final warning." The guy didn't even have a taser. He was also way smaller and older than me. What was he gonna do? Lecture me to death? No. He had to call the real cops if he wanted me gone.

"Whatever man. You want to call the police? Call 'em

up," I told him belligerently. "I'm not going to be cowed by some rude, judgmental rent-a-cop who left his chill on the subway this morning." I rolled my eyes at him.

The security guard bristled at being called a rent-a-cop but didn't seem to know how to react to actually being challenged. He turned a bright, angry red color and drew himself up to his full height (I'd estimate him at about five-foot-seven). His eyes blinked repeatedly, and his pudgy hands gathered into pudgy fists.

"Listen up you little—"

"Little?" I looked down at him in amusement. He sputtered.

"Lucas? What are you doing here?"

Both the security guard and I spun around to the owner of the voice. Rae stared at me from the door in obvious disbelief. Her tall, stiletto heels clickety-clacked over the marble floor as she trotted across the lobby. My heart lifted and twisted when I saw her. This had to work. She was wearing the same pretty blue dress she'd worn on our first date. She was so incredibly, heartbreakingly beautiful.

The guard noticed Rae's beauty too. He puffed up importantly and cleared his throat. "Is this man stalking you, ma'am? I was just about to call the police to have him removed from the building."

Rae blinked. "What? Oh, no." She looked between the security guard and me in total confusion. "What's going on here?"

I sighed. "This guy's being a complete and total dick. He thinks I'm loitering and wants to throw me out. I was just waiting for you. Can you tell him to back off?"

Rae looked like she was fighting a smile. I was glad to amuse her. Maybe it would put her in a good mood for what I had to tell her.

"He's an Azure Group client," she explained to the security guard, showing him her employee badge. "I promise he's got every right to be here, even if he doesn't look it. I'll take him upstairs with me."

"Ma'am?" He shook his head as if trying to dislodge something from his ears that had caused him to mishear her.

"Don't worry. I know you were just doing your job," she said diplomatically. She grabbed me and started pulling me away. The joy of being touched by her zapped through me like a static shock. I'd missed her fiercely. Only twenty-four hours away from her had been much too long.

"I told you so," I said to the security guard in my most obnoxious tone over my shoulder. He was still red faced, but now I think it was in confused embarrassment. I winked at him. "See you around."

"Don't antagonize the poor guy," Rae said, grabbing me more firmly by the elbow and propelling me toward the elevator banks with surprising speed. "I didn't expect you to be here," she continued as we walked. Now that we were away from the rent-a-cop, her blue eyes were wide, almost panicked. Her words were barely more than a whisper. "This could really mess up the plan."

I drew her to a stop and grabbed both her soft little hands in mine. "Rae, I need to talk to you." I'd been rehearsing my speech to her for hours. I hadn't expected to require a rescue directly before delivering it, but now that I had her attention, I wasn't going to waste time. The people swirling around us and staring at the underdressed man meant nothing. I was just focused on Rae.

But she was looking at her watch. "Lucas... there's no time. We gotta go. You'll just have to tag along." She pulled out of my grasp and then pushed us both past the main elevators to one around the corner that said 'Azure Group Executives Only' above the panel. She swiped her badge against a card reader and the doors opened. Rae exhaled in obvious relief.

"Tag along?" I was now thoroughly confused. "Rae, we need to talk. I've got some really important things to tell you."

The doors closed behind us, and the elevator started to rise. Did we have to have all our important conversations in an elevator? It seemed so. I turned to face her.

"Rae I—"

"Later," she said, leaning up to silence me with a swift kiss on the lips. Stunned didn't begin to explain what I was now feeling. She kissed me? I was now unable to speak, which was apparently what she wanted. Rae smiled at me and it crinkled the corners of her eyes, so I knew it was real.

"We'll talk soon. But first I've got to destroy someone real quick."

I was speechless, and the ding of the opening doors kept me from asking any questions. I'd never been to the Azure Group offices before, so I stared around myself with interest when the doors opened to reveal what was quite possibly the fanciest office that I'd ever seen.

The walls were covered with what looked like mahogany paneling, and the floors were inlaid marble. Above our heads, expensive-looking gold chandeliers lit everything in a warm, soft glow. As before, Rae grabbed my elbow to drag me forward. She seemed nervous.

"This is where you work every day?" I should have really been asking her about that kiss, or how she thought we were about to save Notable Match, but damn. This was one nice office. I'd never seen an office with crystal chandeliers before.

Rae chuckled. "No. I worked in the joyless cube farm one floor below. This is the executive wing. I was only ever allowed up here for meetings."

"Worked?"

She nodded. "Yes, I quit. Fuck this place."

"Then what—"

"I'll explain soon." Rae drew us to a halt in front of what was clearly a board room. She looked down at her watch again. "Are you ready?" she asked me.

I frowned. "I honestly have no idea what's going on."

"Well, then just try to look confident."

I raised an eyebrow at her in confusion and she nodded approvingly.

"Yeah, just like that," she said.

She pushed the doors open wide and strode into the room.

41

RAE

THE EXECUTIVE TEAM stared at me with a universal mixture of confusion and annoyance. 'Who the hell are you?' their beady eyes asked me. I ignored them all. There was only one person I was really here to talk to. At the head of the table, the woman I wanted stood up in anger. Her pink skirt suit made her look sweet and grandmotherly. I knew better. She was a traitorous shark. Right now, she was giving off some serious Dolores Umbridge vibes. She cleared her throat primly.

"Miss Lewis--" began McKenzie, but I cut her off. Should I be appreciative that she knew who I was and what I looked like? I so wasn't.

"*I'm terribly sorry* to interrupt the Monday morning meeting, but I'm afraid you've got a bit of a situation. Azure Group is about to be sued in an enormously expensive and embarrassing class action employment lawsuit. I thought you might appreciate a quick heads-up."

That shut her up. Her pink-painted lips parted in surprise. I knew her shock would only last a moment, so I pressed on. I stalked forward into the room like I owned it, Lucas following along behind me. Every eye in the room was trained on me and I stood up straighter. My mom would hate it if I had bad posture during my big moment.

"In this folder I have copies of thousands of emails sent between employees that demonstrate a pervasive culture of sexism, racism, ageism and every other ism that's illegal in the state of New York," I told the men and women around the table. "I know you probably don't believe me on that, so go ahead and pull out your phones and check your email. You've got a message from me, Rae Lewis. I've shared them with you to peruse at your leisure."

"You can't just barge in here and threaten—" McKenzie started to say.

"Um, sure, I can. I'm doing it right now," I told her with a shrug. "Want to hear a few excerpts of the evidence that I have? *It's really quite fascinating.*"

She'd turned as pink as her outfit. "No, I do not. Miss Lewis--"

I interrupted again. "Are you sure? I think the board might like to hear it." My heart was pounding with fear, but I was doing my best Lucas Stevenson impression. I'd told him to project confidence, but he was always confident. He was naturally confident. Me? Not so much. I was faking it. I could hardly contain my fear, but I was unwilling to fail. My voice was coming out smoothly.

I could do this. Annie and Kyle were depending on me.

I would do this. Don't faint. Don't run away crying. Keep it together.

McKenzie laughed a mirthless laugh that was more like a little bark. "Miss Lewis, your behavior is as pathetic as it is appalling. Please leave before you embarrass yourself any further." Her carefully made-up face folded into an expression of displeasure that I was surprised her botox and fillers would allow.

I frowned right back at her. "It's not nearly as appalling as the evidence I have against Azure Group, and against you. Did you know that over four hundred complaints about employee civil rights have been ignored over the past five years alone? And that you, personally, have prioritized retaining the highly-valued perpetrators over the lesser-valued victims? Or that Paul here—" I pointed at Paul, Azure Group's head accountant, "has been regularly banging his secretary on this very table during business hours? And that you, McKenzie, knew about it? And that I have the video proof?"

Everyone looked at Paul, who was bright red and shaking his balding head. Most of the board knew better than to trust him. A few even pulled their hands back from the table in disgust. If I were them, I'd definitely wash my hands. Paul and Stacey had really been rolling all over the place. I had to shake my head to banish the image.

"Besides," I continued, "this isn't even about threatening you. I don't really want to sue you or embarrass Azure Group. I'm just here to make a deal."

McKenzie's expression, as well as the expressions of everyone else at the table, had turned dismissive. "I'm uninterested in your idle threats. There will be no deals and no discussions. You don't work here anymore. Get out before I call Security. Nothing that you stole from this company is even admissible in court."

"I know you've already texted Security," I told her. "But if you don't re-text them that it was a false alarm, just know that my huge employment lawsuit won't be a lawsuit. It'll be a *viral news story* that will make 'Me Too' look as relevant as the Harlem Shake. If you give me any trouble, I'll just publish the email proof I have. Our competitors are very interested in making sure this information gets *extremely wide exposure*. I can't imagine your shareholders would like that much."

She blanched. I'd just been guessing that she was good enough at hidden texting to do so under the table. Clearly, I'd been right. Either that or she really, really didn't want what I had hitting the news. As I'd been talking, a few of the executives had taken my advice and checked their email. They'd turned pale behind their phones.

McKenzie saw their frozen expressions and paused. "What do you want?" she bit out.

I smiled. "Do you know this man?" I asked, pointing at Lucas. He'd been leaning casually against the wall and watching me threaten the board in silence. At mention of him, Lucas smiled and waved.

McKenzie blinked. "No. Should I?" She looked at him warily.

"He's Lucas Stevenson. The app developer whose company, Notable Match, you wanted me to purchase for 'containment'."

"He's the one who helped you hack Azure Group," she guessed, and I shook my head.

I rolled my eyes at her. "No. I don't need any outside help. I've got all the help I need *inside this organization*. Lucas just happened to be here, and I brought him along as an impartial observer."

He nodded. "It's completely true. I have no idea what's happening. It's really entertaining though," Lucas told the assembled members of the board. They looked at him with varying degrees of concern. The fact that he was a relatively unknown witness was a real bonus for me. It helped put them all on edge and prevented them from doing anything too unseemly.

I pushed on. "In exchange for me not releasing all the damning information that I have on Azure Group, I have a modest proposition. Would you like to hear it?"

"Can I stop you?" McKenzie asked sarcastically. When the man on her right leaned over and whispered something to her, she stilled. She stared at him for a moment and then sighed. "Fine. Ugh. Tell us," she amended with a roll of her eyes.

I grinned. "It's extremely simple. All I want is for you to leave me and mine alone. That means that you will not retaliate in any way against me, Annie Washington, Kyle Chen, or any of the victims that appear in this correspondence. Next, you will take action against all the perpetrators of harassment in accordance with Azure Group's policies and the law. All *fifty-nine of them*."

McKenzie looked like she'd swallowed a toad. She cleared her throat uncomfortably. "I can't just fire half the company's senior staff. Even if I wanted to do that, I couldn't. It would be chaos if we decimated our workforce. We'd be totally hamstrung."

I smiled even wider. "I understand. In that case, I have a second option that I hope the board will find more palatable."

"You just want money, don't you?" McKenzie interrupted to sneer. "How much do you want?" She looked at me like I was a filthy gold-digger.

"No," I told her. "I don't want your stupid money. I want you gone forever. Let me rephrase that. I want you to resign. You, Carla McKenzie, are the primary enabler of Azure Group's polluted culture. Someone with much better values and attention to state and federal labor laws should take your place as leader of this organization. If you leave, I'll go away forever as well."

There, my trump card was on the table. McKenzie was

the root cause of the culture at Azure Group. It was because of her tone at the top that people thought their power entitled them to do whatever they wanted. It was also because of her personal agreement with Datability that Lucas' company was in danger. Getting rid of her wouldn't necessarily fix everything and make it perfect, but it was a hell of a start.

McKenzie blinked. The silence in the room was unbelievably thick. Twelve pairs of eyes around the table looked at me and then turned to one another.

McKenzie might be a shark, but the board members were piranhas. I'd banked on this. They needed to turn on their master and devour her. It didn't take long before they smelled the blood. Eventually one gained the courage to take a bite.

"We can't allow this story to hit the news," Richard Prince said. He was part of the legal team. "There's no containing something like this once it's out there."

In the wake of his words there were nods and expressions of general agreement around the table.

"We also can't possibly address each of the issues in these emails," said Donella Antonelli, the director of human resources. She shook her heavy curls in frustration. "It would start a class action lawsuit, not avoid one. I've been saying for years that we were going down the wrong road. This moment was inevitable."

Her statement was also met with agreement.

More and more of the board members began speaking

up about the unfeasibility and disruptiveness of my initial offer. No one said a word about the second option. They just continued to gab on about how impossible it would be to do anything else. I let it go on for about five minutes. I was beginning to wonder if anyone would ever challenge McKenzie directly. McKenzie snapped before the board did.

"Fine," McKenzie finally said, slamming her fists down on the table. "I'll leave. But I want the full golden parachute." Her expression held no defeat, only resignation and anger. I'd expect nothing less. I was convinced that she had no conscience.

I shrugged. "I don't care how much it costs to get rid of you. I just want you gone." I turned my attention away from her and smiled at the board members. "I believe your CEO has just tendered her resignation, does the board accept?"

They looked around at one another. No one looked particularly disappointed. They were all little sharks in the making, I was sure of it. But none of them were McKenzie. And they now knew that I had shit on them, so maybe they'd watch their backs.

It was Donatella who finally answered. "We accept your terms, Miss Lewis. Now, will you please, for the love of God, leave?" I nodded, and Donatella looked at McKenzie and shook her head. "I'm sorry, Carly."

McKenzie's reply was venomous. "Like fuck you are Donna. You've never been happier. You're finally rid of me."

"God, McKenzie, can't you be gracious for once in your life?" Donna challenged.

I had no intention of staying for the bloody fallout. I had a feeling a lot of people would want to share their true feelings for their former boss. "Thanks for your time." I told the room. "I'll see myself out." I looked over at Lucas and smiled. "Ready to get out of here?"

42

LUCAS

I'D NEVER BEEN as turned on in my entire twenty-eight years of life. Rae had just wrapped the board of directors of a multibillion-dollar company around her little finger like it was nothing. I'd never thought that I had a fetish of any type before, but apparently, I did. I had a serious, lusty fetish for watching a beautiful woman stick it to the man (or in this case, woman).

Outside the board room, Rae sighed and smiled at me in satisfied victory. I extended a hand to her and she took it. We walked back to the executive elevator together. Just as we were waiting for the doors to close, my favorite New York rent-a-cop turned a corner with four buddies in matching outfits. I made double "finger guns" at him cheerfully.

"We were just leaving," I called out. "I think the guys

you want went that way." I used my finger guns to point down the hall.

"*You*. Stop!" He barked.

Haha. No.

I pushed the close button. "Bye-bye."

He was nowhere near fast enough to stop us, but he waddled toward us anyway. I waved at him as the doors met.

"You really know how to make friends, don't you?" Rae said as the elevator dropped. Her tone was dry, but she was fighting a losing battle with a smile.

"What can I say," I told her, "I just have a lot of natural charm. I think you made some friends just now too, although I confess that I have no clue what just happened."

Rae's smile won. "I definitely made some new enemies. I won't be listing McKenzie as a reference on my job applications."

"She looked like she wanted to shoot blood out of her eyes like those weird, desert lizards."

Rae snickered at the thought. "Gross. I think she'd rather shoot lasers." She paused. "I see you decided not to attend the closing," she said.

"I don't think I want to sell to Azure Group after all."

"Yeah, I'm not sure that Azure Group is the right partner for you."

"I know who the right partner for me is."

Rae's grin faded. She swallowed hard. The doors to the

executive elevator opened on the lobby. "Come on. We need to meet Annie and Kyle."

I WAS NOW BACK in the IHOP. I didn't even like IHOP. Ellen, the waitress that had put up with me for five hours the night before, stared at me without an ounce of recognition. Apparently, I wasn't worth the investment in brain cells.

Gotta love New York. Where nobody gives a shit about you unless you're loitering.

"Coffee?" she offered Rae and me. Her face was impassive.

We both nodded. Across from us in the battered pleather booth, Kyle and Annie were vibrating with excitement. As soon as Ellen was out of earshot, Annie started talking.

"We got it. Nobody even guessed what we were doing. They didn't even look at us sideways when we started messing with the system. All the data was removed from the servers." She and Rae high fived and then Rae and Kyle high fived. "How did your part go?"

"It was pretty epic when I wasn't about to wet my pants with fear. McKenzie resigned," Rae said triumphantly. "We did it."

Did what, exactly? And why?

"Can someone please explain what's going on?" I asked. "I'm really, really confused."

Rae grinned at me. "We just saved Notable Match."

I blinked. "What?"

Why? How?

Rae took a deep breath before explaining. "McKenzie, our now-former CEO, was the one that promised Datability that she'd make Notable Match disappear. While I was up there blackmailing her into resigning, Kyle and Annie went to the server control room and wiped all the data on Notable Match. They can't threaten you now. You're free."

My jaw dropped open. *All of that had been for me?*

"What about your jobs?" I heard myself asking. I stared at three matching smiles in confusion.

Then Kyle made a face. "Did you see the shit in Rae's file? I can't believe I made it six weeks working someplace like that."

"We quit," Annie said, holding Kyle's hand. "We'll find something else that isn't so soul-crushingly evil. I think I'm finished with being used by a company that doesn't value me as a human being."

"Dude, I worked there for so long, I'm lucky I even have a twisted piece of conscience left," Rae said. She shook her head.

"I knew you couldn't go through with the deal," Annie said. "I never doubted you."

The deal for Notable Match? I never thought Rae wouldn't go through with it. She had no obligation to protect me whatsoever. This was a business deal.

"I doubted me," Rae admitted. "That was all really scary."

"When I saw your message to McKenzie, that was what inspired me to go through all the email servers looking for leverage over Azure Group," Annie told Rae. "I wouldn't have done it if you hadn't rage quit and written that email."

Rae had inspired this entire plot? Somehow, I wasn't surprised. Her ability to lead people was truly impressive. She knew how to command a board room, too. The funniest thing about it was that she didn't necessarily seem to know how powerful she was.

"I definitely don't deserve the credit here. You do, Annie," Rae replied. "But I'm just so incredibly glad it worked out." Her smile was big, white and relieved.

"You three put your careers on the line for me?" I was still having trouble wrapping my mind around it.

How could I be worthy of such a thing? And from strangers?

"Notable Match deserves to be seen," Kyle answered. "I don't know how you managed to figure out the secret behind those algorithms, but they work."

Rae and I exchanged a silent glance. "It's less exciting than you think," I told him after a second. "I wish I could tell you it was magic, but it isn't."

"I don't need to know," Kyle replied, looking at Annie adoringly. "I have all the magic that I need now."

Annie glanced at her phone. "Speaking of which, we have an appointment at the Court House with a justice of the peace." She grinned. "We're eloping!"

Rae and I congratulated them, and they dashed off in the direction of the subway. As far as I knew, this was the first match made by my app that had resulted in a marriage. It cut through my confusion and disbelief with a feeling of pride. Kyle and Annie seemed well and truly in love. They'd also done me an incredible favor. I made a mental note to send them a really nice panini press or something. It wouldn't pay them back for what they did for me, but nothing would. At least they could make some nice paninis.

"Wow," Rae said, shaking her head and watching her friends and former coworkers rush off to get married. "That was one hell of a morning." She laughed a little bit into her coffee. "I can't believe we pulled that off. I can't believe you're here. I can't believe Annie and Kyle are about to go get married..." she trailed off, staring at her hands. I could see that she was a bit overwhelmed.

I knew the feeling.

"You were amazing in that board room," I told her. Visions of her telling her former bosses to go fuck themselves played before my eyes, more vivid and erotic than any pornography. Rae was truly flawless.

"I was shaking in my boots." Her blue eyes were shining, but I hoped that the unshed tears were from joy.

"It didn't show." She'd seemed about as frightened as Wonder Woman.

"Of course not. I was doing my amazing Lucas Stevenson impression." She winked at me.

"Can I do my speech now?" I asked her, hoping that I really seemed that confident to her. I was the one shaking in my boots now. "I had this whole long speech planned and you totally stole my thunder by saving Notable Match." I sat up straight and looked her in the eye, trying to project something other than vulnerability and fear.

She smirked, but it was short-lived. "I don't know if I want to hear your victory speech, Lucas. I can't stand the thought of you with Victoria. I'm sorry, but it's true. I do want you to be happy, but I can't pretend to be happy for you."

I sat back in shock. "What?"

Is that what she thought I came here for? To tell her that I was back with Victoria and that my harebrained plan had worked after all?

Her lips parted in surprise. "You aren't here to tell me you're back together with Victoria?"

"No." I shook my head at her. "Rae, I admit I didn't do well with our last conversation. It was bad, and I owe you an explanation. But as far as Azure Group goes, none of what they wanted to do was your fault. You were just trying to do your job." I tried to grab her hand, but she pulled away.

"So were the guards at Auschwitz." She pouted and looked out the window.

The return of her dark sense of humor was a good sign but also proof that she still felt guilty. I shook my head at her. "Rae, it isn't your fault that you worked for someone

322

dishonest. You just went way above and beyond any expectation I ever had for protecting Notable Match. If I'm being honest, I don't even care about Notable Match enough to ask you to do something like that, and I care about it a lot."

"It was the right thing to do." She paused. "Plus, the culture there really does need an overhaul. The sexual harassment there was off the charts. I could tell you stories that would make your skin crawl."

I didn't doubt it. Still...

"You really thought I flew up here to tell you I was back with Victoria?" My heart squeezed.

She honestly thought I didn't want her? How could I not want her?

"I admit that I thought you'd probably send me an email or something rather than coming up in person, but yeah."

Her eyes were fixed on her coffee. I laughed. She said what she said because of Victoria. I knew that from the start. It was time to get to the point.

"Rae, I talked to Victoria."

She looked up at me in surprise. Her big blue eyes blinked, and she said nothing. Her gaze went back to the coffee cup. I took that as a cue to keep talking.

"I told her to go to hell," I continued. "It was exactly like I'd planned it up until then. She showed up in the lobby of my building. She'd been lurking down there for God knows how long, crying and waiting for me to come down by myself. She told me that she loved me and that she wanted me back. She said that she couldn't stand seeing me with you and that she wanted to give our relationship another try." I shook my head. "It was just like in my dreams. But when the time came, I realized that I didn't love her anymore."

Rae took a deep, shaking breath. The hands gripping her coffee cup flew to her face and then down to be clasped demurely in her lap. It was like she didn't know what to do with them and they had a mind of their own. "But—"

I cut her off. "But nothing. I don't love Victoria. She's cruel, and she didn't love me nearly as much as she hated the idea of me being happy without her. It took me eighteen months to come to terms with it, but now that I'm able to admit it, I'm free. I don't love Victoria Priestly anymore. I love you, Rae. I love you."

An IHOP is not the most romantic place in the world at the best of times. This particular one was even less so than usual. Ellen took the moment I was confessing my love to drop off the check. She coughed a smoker's cough before slapping it down on the table.

"Since your friends took off without paying, I put their food on your check." She looked from one of us to the other in bland disinterest. "Take your time."

I shoved a fifty-dollar bill at her and she left. Rae was continuing to stare at me, wide eyed and silent. The moments passed by quietly, ticking my tension up a little bit at a time. By the time that Ellen returned with my change and laid it on the table, I was about ready to explode.

"You two have a great day," Ellen said insincerely. I honestly don't think that she had the slightest idea what she was interrupting, but I got the feeling that she wouldn't care either way.

"Rae, please say something," I begged. "I know my speech isn't as good as what you just did for me, but it's all true. I love you."

"You really told Victoria to go to hell?" she stuttered.

I smiled. "Not in so many words, but yes." I just wasn't mean enough to say something like that to Victoria, although she might deserve it, but I knew she got the message. "I even called the guy she's dating and told him that she tried to cheat on him."

Rae smirked. "That's pretty cold, Lucas."

"Nobody has ever accused me of being too nice." I frowned. "Look, when you've been cheated on as many times as I have—"

She interrupted with a girlish giggle. "I didn't mean that in a bad way. I would have done the exact same thing. I completely approve." Her smile gave me hope.

"So, does that mean you will take me back?"

"As your fake girlfriend?" Her smile was lopsided. My heart leapt at her gentle teasing tone. Rae's wry personality was adorable to me. I loved that she took no nonsense out of me or anyone else.

"No. No more fakeness. No more lies. I want you as my

real girlfriend this time." I smiled back at her hopefully. "What do you say?"

Her answer was a kiss. I leaned into her, wrapping my arms around her waist and crushing her into me. Rae was beautiful, fierce, brilliant, and mine. I was never going to let her go.

EPILOGUE

LUCAS

Two weeks later...

"I told you so," Cole said, wearing the shit-eatingest of all shit-eating grins.

"Yeah whatever," I replied with a dismissive hand wave.

"I also told you so," Ward chimed in, delivering the beer pitcher to our table. "And technically, I was the one who told him so first," he added to Cole. Cole rolled his eyes.

"Anyway, regardless of who told me what first, we're together now," I told them as I filled up my glass and added an orange slice to the rim. "Rae's up in New York today just packing up her apartment. I'm going to fly up there on Tuesday and we're going to rent a truck and drive everything back. She's going to help me run Notable Match. We'll be scrambling for funding for a bit, but we'll be keeping expenses low by living together."

I smiled my most cost-effective smile. It had only been a

couple of days without her and I was desperately missing having her in my bed, even if she did hog the covers. I was looking forward to sharing showers with her too. To save on our water bills. Obviously.

"Already shacking up, too?" Cole teased, his smile growing even wider. "I'm so proud of you. Look at you rebounding from Victoria like a total pro. Sure, it took basically forever, but you still did it. Late is better than never. I knew you had it in you."

"You're proud of me?" I smirked at him. "For living in sin? Aren't you Arkansas boys supposed to be virtuous and God-fearing?"

"I'm plenty virtuous and God-fearing," Cole replied seriously over the edge of his beer. "Like my mom does with Kate and me, I simply assume you'll be sleeping in separate rooms until marriage."

Something told me that Cole's mom's charming cognitive dissonance might actually be sufficient for that. She was super nice, super southern, and super weird. Cole's entire family was a bit weird, actually. It helped explain him.

"Okay, whatever you want to believe, dude," I told him. "We're sleeping in separate beds like in old timey TV shows."

Ward and Cole, both from good, old-fashioned, southern families, nodded appreciatively as if this were a remote possibility. I rolled my eyes. I'm from California.

Rae is from New York. We don't even pretend to subscribe to that nonsense.

"So, she's really going to move down here?" Ward asked me. "She likes you that much?"

"I know, it's incredible," I admitted. "She's going to help me run Notable Match. We're going to try and make it successful from the ground up. It's going to be a lot of work. The first step is getting more beta testers. I need more friends to rope into testing."

"You only have two friends," Ward retorted. "Cole told me about you cat-care emergency while Emma and I were in Cabo."

I smiled. "I'll have you know that I figured that out no problem. Because, despite what you and Cole think, I have more than two friends."

Both of them shook their heads at me. Cole spoke first. "Actually, I acknowledged that you have three and a half friends."

Ward looked confused. "How can there be a half-friend? Is that someone who's only nice to Lucas half the time? Like Kate?"

I laughed, and Cole frowned at Ward. "Kate's really nice to Lucas."

"Kate's not *really nice* to anyone," Ward replied and then paused. "Except you."

I thought about making an off-color comment about why exactly Kate had an incentive to be really nice to Cole but thought better of it. Ward was her brother, after all. That situation was a constant minefield of familial discomfort without me wading into it on purpose. I could only imagine what it would be like when they had children. At least for now Ward could fool himself into believing that Cole and his sister were doing the whole separate bed thing.

"Actually, I was counting Ian as the half-friend," Cole corrected. "He's in rehab now though, so I really shouldn't have been joking about him. The guy has a serious problem." He shook his head. "I hope he's doing okay."

We all paused to appreciate the gravity of Ian's situation by staring at our respective beers in silence. I, for one, was glad he'd gone to rehab. His drinking had gotten seriously out of control, and the wedding had been the straw that broke the camel's back. Ryan had staged an intervention with their family. At least Ian was man enough to admit that he had a problem and do something about it before he or someone else got seriously hurt. Hopefully he would be able to win over his addiction. The fact that one of his friends owned a bar that the rest of his friends constantly hung out at could be a real issue for him, long term.

"Poor Ian," I said, shaking my head as I thought about him. "I owe him one, actually. He was the one who helped me figure out the cat issue you were talking about."

"Wait, you seriously let Ian feed your cats?" Cole asked. "I honestly did not expect that."

I shook my head. "No. I didn't let Ian feed my cats," I said defensively. I loved my cats too much for that. "But he helped me get Jason Kane's phone number. He was the one who fed my cats."

Both Cole and Ward went still. I laughed at their frozen expressions of disbelief.

"Bullshit," Ward said after a moment. His voice was beyond incredulous. "I'm calling bullshit. You did not get a rock star to come feed your cats for you. You might be smart, but you don't have that kind of power."

"Power? No. That has nothing to do with it. We're friends."

"I am also calling bullshit," Cole said this time, shaking his head at me dismissively. "Definite, pure, undiluted bullshit."

I smiled at the both of them. "Okay. Sure. Well, he's supposed to be dropping off the key tonight, so we'll just see about that."

The two of them exchanged a glance between themselves that clearly said 'Lucas is fucking with us.' While it wasn't beyond the realm of possibility that I might be, this time I actually wasn't.

EPILOGUE

RAE

"I REALLY APPRECIATE THE OFFER, but I'm not interested in a role with your firm at this time."

"Are you sure you won't reconsider, Ms. Lewis? We could make it worth your while."

I shook my head at the phone. "It's honestly not about the money. This is a very generous offer, and I'm truly gratified that you would think of me. But I've decided to leave New York and take on some new challenges."

"Well, if you change your mind, let us know. It was a pleasure speaking with you today. I'll reach out to Annie Washington as you suggested. I'm excited to speak with her."

"Fantastic. I know she'll be interested in your organization. Have a great day."

Once I hung up the phone, I stared at it in total disbelief for at least five full minutes. This was the third call today. I could barely get any packing done because I kept getting interrupted by people offering me jobs!

I had fully expected to be totally unemployable after the way I had departed Azure Group. Usually whistle-blowers are not well liked in any industry. But something strange had happened when I ousted McKenzie. All of a sudden, other people started coming forward at Azure Group against management for their misdeeds. Although McKenzie was gone, word got around that the bad behavior was no longer going to be accepted, and it shook loose the avalanche of allegations that her departure was meant to stem. Oops.

Azure Group's stock price abruptly went bottoms up and the company was now being acquired by a larger, less horrifically corrupt competitor. But instead of putting an end to the chaos, the acquisition of Azure Group spread the news throughout the industry that harassment was no longer being ignored. Women and men at all levels of the industry started talking. And once started, they refused to shut up again.

It shook the industry to its foundations. Private equity was the ultimate boys club, but it was impossible to put the genie back in the bottle. Loads of senior executives were 'retiring early' to 'spend more time with their family' and 'focus on their health.' A lot of senior HR executives were 'seeking new opportunities' after they were shown to be total tools. A few C-suite types were even 'seeking treat-ment' at various mental health facilities for their 'sex addictions' that they claimed produced their appalling behavior. It was beautiful, sweet, long-overdue justice.

Watching the industry reel and reckon with what ought to be a thoroughly twentieth century problem was both gratifying and sad. It was wonderful that men and women now felt more comfortable complaining about what ought to be simply unacceptable. It was also sad that it had taken this long for the industry to realize that it needed to root out some terrible practices that had festered and grown for far too long. The strangest thing about it all was that people seemed to think that I was the hero behind it.

Annie, Kyle and I had done exactly one interview with a local magazine to tell our side of the story and it had blown up overnight. We became something of minor celebrities over the course of a single weekend. The funny thing about all this sudden publicity is that it was me *complaining* that made everything possible. I went my whole life carrying around this complex about complaining, and now that I finally got the guts to complain about something big, I was getting more accolades than I'd ever dreamed of. Out of all this chaos, I was getting requests for interviews, book deals, speaking engagements, and jobs.

But the only job I wanted was as co-CEO of Notable Match. Lucas and I were going into business together. Maybe it was a really, really bad idea. After all, we had only just met. Our 'real' relationship was even more new. If I were giving advice to any friend in my situation, I would tell her to stay in New York and accept one of the many high-paying, interesting-sounding jobs that had recently been offered to her. I would tell my friend not to get in over her head for a guy she barely knew. I'd tell her to listen to what her head was saying, because hearts lie. One thing I'd had to recognize about myself over the past couple of weeks, however, was that I needed to think with my heart a little bit more.

Or maybe I just needed to listen to Annie more. She seemed to have her shit figured out. I texted her about the most recent recruitment call as I boxed my shoe collection for the trip south.

Rae: I just turned down another one, but I told them to call you instead. Your voicemail and inbox are going to be trashed when you get back.
Annie: What was this one?
Rae: RAINN. It's an anti-sexual violence organization. It sounded really interesting.
Annie: Cool. I've always wanted to do NGO work. I don't know how I'd be qualified to do anything but mop their floors, but I'm happy to learn! I can't believe all of this is happening!
Rae: It's truly bizarre.
Annie: At least we're not unemployable freaks. That was kind of what I thought would happen.
Rae: I was sure that was what would happen.
Annie: You're such a sunny optimist.
Rae: I'm practical.
Annie: That's what Kyle says when I tell him he's crazy for

drinking beer in the shower, watching television on the toilet,
eating cereal for dinner or any of the other weird bachelor habits
he's picked up. He just says he's practical.

Rae: Is it bad to drink a beer in the shower? I mean, it's weird,
but that actually sounds kind of nice. I don't know how practical
it is though.

Annie: He claims its multitasking.

Rae: I could see that. But the watching tv on the toilet thing?
That's not practical. It's gross.

Annie: Welcome to the realities of relationship bliss. Soon this
will be your life too!

Rae: I sincerely doubt Lucas watches tv on the toilet. He doesn't
even own a tv.

Annie: You know what I mean.

Rae: I'm actually looking forward to living with Lucas.

Annie: I know you are. You two are so sweet it's going to give me
a cavity from looking at you.

Rae: Says you. I saw those honeymoon photos. You and Kyle
were absolutely adorable.

Annie: Yeah. We're not too shabby.

Rae: And so modest too!

I finished piling my work stiletto collection into the box and moved onto my suit collection with mixed emotions. It would be strange to leave New York for Austin not two years after moving back here. I'd really thought that I was moving home to stay. Now I was going to totally change my life, my career, and my relationship status all at once.

Suddenly, I realized the glaring error I was making. This was all wrong. Incredibly, completely, and totally wrong. Like a lightbulb going off in my brain, the realization struck: there was no way I would need so many business suits in Austin.

I started a new box, this one for donations. In my new life, I was going to dress in jeans and T-shirts. And shorts! I could wear shorts for most of the year. No more dry-clean only blazers. No more uncomfortable wool trousers. No more pussy bow blouses that deemphasized my chest. No more hosiery, except maybe in the bedroom. Lucas liked sexy thigh-highs. Those could stay.

EPILOGUE

JASON

The Lone Star Lounge was busy on a Friday night, but I had no trouble locating Lucas Stevenson. He was sitting at a table with several people, and right next to my ex-girlfriend, Wendy.

I suddenly found myself unable to breathe.

Wendy was here? In Austin?

I wondered if Wendy had her EpiPen handy, because my airway felt like it was closing up. When I did get a breath, it burned in my deprived lungs. But not as much as the sight of Wendy burned in my deprived eyes. I could barely believe that she was real.

The last time I saw Wendy, she'd been crying.

"It doesn't have to be this way," she'd told me back then. "I don't care about where you're from. I only care about where you're going."

I'd used her words in one of my first hit singles.

She was still so incredibly beautiful. Her face was heart-shaped, with wide eyes, high cheekbones, and a full, pink mouth. Gold ringlets hung loose around her face, cascading over her shoulders and down her back in loose bundles. She had the golden blonde hair that girls on Instagram would kill for, complete with natural highlights of platinum and white. Nobody real had ever looked so much like an angel, and no one mortal had ever been closer to behaving like one.

Which begged the question of what the fuck she was doing in this bar.

Had Lucas Stevenson brought her here? I guess I'm gonna' have to kill him.

I started to stalk forward angrily, but I caught myself again before I made it two feet. No, he was dating some woman named Rae. Victoria had bitched about her endlessly and she'd even shown me pictures. They were sitting a normal distance apart from each other at the table too, more like acquaintances than lovers. That was good. I didn't want to hate Lucas. He really did seem like a solid guy and had let me crash at his place for two days after Victoria and I crashed and burned. We'd talked a few times since then and really got along.

It was really nice to have a normal, real friend for once. The music business tends to throw a lot of phonies at you. Guys that want to be your friend because they want something. Lucas was a bit of an odd duck, as well as being a huge nerd, but he certainly wasn't phony. The guy was as genuine as they came.

As my adrenaline faded, my rational side decided to show up. Wendy had every right to be in a bar. We were the same age, which meant she now had no reason not to drink a beer on a Friday night. Wendy also had a good reason to be in Austin; her grandparents lived here. In fact, I was fairly certain they owned a bar here. *Maybe this bar.* That would make sense. And finally, Wendy had every right to do whatever she fucking wanted because she wasn't mine.

I never deserved her. I knew it then and I know it now. She's so much better than me in every way that matters.

With a massive effort, I made myself man up and walk over to Lucas instead of being a gigantic pussy and slinking away before anyone saw me. To my surprise and relief, Wendy got up and walked away before I made it over to the table. She didn't even see me.

Maybe she won't notice I'm here? Do I want that? Do I want to leave without speaking to her?

"Hey Lucas, here are your keys." It wasn't the politest of all openings, but I was distracted, to say the least.

She's going to be back any second. What will I say to her when I see her? What could I possibly say that won't sound stupid?

Lucas smiled at me. "Hey man. Thanks. I really appreciate you feeding Bob and Moxie while I was gone."

"No problem. They're great cats. I really enjoyed hanging out with them."

Lucas pointed to the empty chair next to Wendy's vacant seat. "You wanna join us for a drink real quick? These are my friends, Cole, Kate, Ward, and Emma." Lucas' friends stared at me in total surprise and disbelief. Each one of them was wearing a look that said, 'holy shit that guy is famous, I thought he only existed on TV.' It was a look I was used to seeing, but it still made me uncomfortable.

Despite the awkwardness of being the mythical celebrity version of Jason Kane while I wanted to be the ordinary human version of Jason Kane, I would have said yes. Lucas' friends were probably cool. However, I didn't get the chance. Behind me, I heard a familiar voice gasp in surprise. I turned around. Wendy was two feet in front of me, carrying a pitcher of beer with both tiny white hands. Now that I was closer, I noticed that her fingernails were painted a bright red and that she was wearing some light, tasteful makeup on her face.

I guess she's allowed to wear nail polish and makeup now. It looks nice on her.

"Jason?" She blinked her enormous blue eyes several times, maybe to make sure I was really standing there. "What are you doing here?"

I'm not sure. I seem to have forgotten everything about myself, including who I am and how I got here. I have amnesia. Who am I again?

Behind me, one of the two gigantic dudes that Lucas had introduced to me as friends was mumbling. "Does everyone know the freakin' rock star but me?" Something about those two seemed really, really familiar to me, but I couldn't quite put my finger on it. Maybe I'd met them before? Or seen them somewhere? I wasn't sure. I also didn't have the brain cells to figure it out.

Eventually, the guy's words managed to percolate through my thick skull into my brain. Rock star. Yeah. That was what I was. Except to Wendy.

To Wendy, I was just Jason. Not Jason the rock star, but Jason the high school dropout. Jason the menace. Jason the kid who grew pot and then dealt it behind the gym when he wasn't smoking it all himself. Jason the kid that lived in a run-down shotgun shack with two neglectful parents in the middle of a literal junkyard. Jason who could barely read and write because his dyslexia was so bad and untreated, but his teachers all just thought he was an inbred moron. Jason who learned how to play the guitar because he wanted to write a song about his pretty girl-friend. Jason, who knew that girl was way out of his league from the first time he laid eyes on her in second grade. Jason, the guy that no one ever saw any value in except for Wendy.

Wendy was still looking at me the same way now. Like I could hang the moon if I wanted to. Like I could move mountains. Wendy had always believed in me when no one else ever did. In fact, before I met her, I was as convinced of my own worthlessness as everyone else in our town. Her big blue eyes held all the softness and hope they ever had.

It was like I was being transported back ten years and right back to where I came from.

"Hi Wendy," I said, and the accent that I'd tried so hard —*so fucking hard*—to get rid of slipped right out. "What's a nice girl like you doing in a place like this?"

The pitcher that Wendy was carrying slipped from her grasp. We both reached for it, but it was too late. It still seemed to fall in slow motion, and hit the floor with an audible, heavy, plastic *kerplunk*. The beer exploded outward in a wide arc, dousing both of our feet and a large patch of the floor in ice cold beer.

I wasn't noticing. I certainly wasn't minding. I'd been doused with beer more times than I could count. It had been a regular occurrence during the beginning of my music career. There are plenty of places where throwing a beer at someone is a totally socially acceptable form of feedback. I'd played at most of them.

But it wasn't my familiarity with the situation that had me lost. It was the unfamiliarity of touching Wendy. As we'd both reached forward for the pitcher, our fingertips had found one another's. My hands grasped hers and held them. I stared at the sight of her tiny hands in my callused ones.

So small and perfect. I remember these hands. I remember these hands touching me.

An electrical shock shot through me, painful and wonderful. It burned old synapses back open and old feelings stretched and started to stir deep within the buried memories that I'd locked them in. Like zombies, the feelings rose from the grave and started to advance across my consciousness, filling me with elation, guilt, gratitude, sadness, loss, joy, and lust. Love above all. All the hormone-crazed, helpless feelings that eighteen-year-old Jason had felt for Wendy Paxton were alive in me again.

She pulled her fingers from mine with a little squeak of surprise. Her already huge eyes had gotten even bigger. They surely couldn't get any wider. There was a slim ring of white all the way around the dilated, pale blue iris.

"You shouldn't be here, Jason." Her voice was a breathy, reedy whisper. She was still looking at me like she was seeing a ghost. I knew that feeling.

"This isn't the first time you've told me that exact thing," I told her, remembering with a smile. "It probably won't be the last, either."

THANK you so much for reading 'Lie With Me'! Keep your sweet and sexy binge going with the next book in the Lone Star Lovers series, available now!

'*Run Away With Me*' features Jason and Wendy plus Emma, Kate and other Lone Star Lovers characters. It's full of second chance drama, hilarious situations, and buried secrets. Turn the page for an exclusive teaser!

SPECIAL TEASER: RUN AWAY WITH ME

Prologue - Jason

"What did I do wrong?" I asked Ms. May. My eyes felt hot and they were stinging, but I wouldn't cry in front of her.

"You didn't do anything wrong Jason. You aren't in trouble." She shook her head at me and continued to walk me down the hall.

It sure felt like I was in trouble. I wished I could be better. I tried really hard in class, but it was never enough.

"I don't wanna' to go back to Mrs. Thompson's class. I wanna' be a third grader. How long do I have to stay there?"

"I'm not sure Jason. Everybody learns at their own pace," Ms. May told me as we walked through the hallway to Mrs. Thompson's room. She was smiling and walking quickly like she was excited. I tried to keep up. "We just want to see if this is going to be a better fit for you until you get all your letters straight and your phonics down." Ms. May wasn't always so nice to me. I knew she was only being nice because she was happy that I wasn't going to be in her class anymore. "Don't worry," she added as we got to the door, "you can still play with all your friends at recess."

What friends? All the kids say I'm stupid and my family is trash. I kept the thought to myself, even though it was true. Grownups always got angry when you pointed out when they were making things up. Especially teachers, and they made up more things than all the other grownups combined.

"Here's your new student," Ms. May said to Mrs. Thompson. Ms. May was happy; Mrs. Thompson was not. She was frowning so big that her bushy eyebrows made one long, dark line across her forehead. It looked like one of those furry caterpillars. My mom said those kinds of caterpillars were poisonous. Maybe Mrs. Thompson was poisonous. I bet she was. Ms. May took one look at Mrs. Thompson, patted me on the arm, spun, and disappeared out the door.

"Welcome back to second grade, Jason," Mrs. Thompson said to me. "What are we going to do with you?"

I knew that she didn't really want me to answer her, so I just stood there and shrugged. Mrs. Thompson hated me, and I hated her back even more. All summer long I'd been excited to have a different teacher. I thought maybe it would be different this year. But it wasn't. Even though I tried really hard, Ms. May thought I was so dumb she put me back with Mrs. Thompson.

I wondered if I'd be in second grade forever. Mrs. Thompson looked like she wondered that too.

"Let's put you in with the giraffe group reading circle," Mrs. Thompson told me, drawing me over to a familiar corner of the room. "You remember the giraffe group from last year, don't you?" She was using the fake-nice voice that adults used all the time on me. They thought I was too dumb to know the difference between real nice and fake nice.

I didn't roll my eyes at her, but I wanted to. "Yes ma'am."

The giraffe group was the stupid group. Mrs. Thompson used animal names, but it wasn't hard to figure out her plan. She'd divided up the class into four groups. The lions were the smartest, the elephants were the second best, then the zebras, and last, the giraffes.

I didn't know any of the kids in the classroom. They all looked smaller than me, though. That made sense. They were all seven and I was almost ten. At least that was good. Maybe they would leave me alone.

"Bobby, Wendy, Brett, Samantha, this is Jason. He's going to join your group, ok?"

"Is he in our class now?" one of the girls asked.

"Yes," said Mrs. Thompson. She still sounded angry. The girl didn't ask any other questions.

"Does that mean one of us gets to be a zebra instead?" a boy asked hopefully.

Mrs. Thompson blinked. "Oh yes. You have too many now, don't you? Ok Brett, you can go join the zebras."

Brett looked happy. The other giraffe kids watched him go. They looked jealous. Once he was gone they stared at me, but I didn't look at them. I just sat down on the carpet. The giraffe kids had been taking turns reading a book that I already knew from memory, but I didn't join in when it was my turn to read. I didn't even look up. I just stared down at the ground in front of me. After a second, the other giraffes started reading again, ignoring me.

Good.

I was learning that it was better if other kids were afraid of me or ignored me. I would be lonely, but at least they wouldn't tease me. A tap on my shoulder almost started me. I shifted my gaze from my dirty sneakers to a pair of clean, pink shoes with lacey bobby socks. One of the giraffe girls didn't get the message. The others kept reading, ignoring us both.

"Hi, I'm Wendy Paxton," she said. "Your name is Jason?" She said her 's' like it was a 'th'. It sounded really funny and made my name sound like 'Jathon'. I looked up at her in surprise.

My grandma had a Christmas decoration that she'd bought from the Hallmark store in downtown Lubbock. It was her favorite. She said it was really expensive and I wasn't ever allowed to touch it. It was this little blonde angel with curly yellow hair and giant blue eyes, putting the star on a Christmas tree. Wendy Paxton looked just like that Christmas angel doll. She was the prettiest girl I'd ever seen. Except that she was missing both of her two front teeth.

I nodded at her. My mouth wasn't working. My heart had started to beat really loud and hard. Wendy smiled at me with her toothless smile and that just made it worse. I felt dizzy like that one time I held my breath too long. All girls were *supposed* to be gross. Even I knew girls had cooties.

Maybe this is what cooties feel like. It was kind of a weird feeling, but it wasn't exactly painful. I liked it. I felt light like a balloon and I wanted to laugh and smile. I wondered why everybody said cooties were so bad. I was pretty sure that I liked having cooties. A lot.

"It's ok if you don't like this story," she said. "We can read a different one. But we have to read or else we'll be giraffes forever. Giraffes are the stupid group, just so you know. But don't let Mrs. Thompson know that you know. It makes her mad." Wendy frowned.

I knew I shouldn't talk to her. That she would only figure out I was dumb and poor and then not like me, but I couldn't stop my mouth. I also couldn't stop looking at her.

"It's not that. The story is ok." I wanted to keep from telling her the truth, but I couldn't. "All the letters look the same to me."

She blinked. Her eyes were a real bright blue. I'd only seen that eye color one time before when I found a pregnant Siamese cat under a car. My mom made us take her to

349

the pound because she said we didn't need more cats, but not before I named her. I named her Sky because of her eyes. I wished I could have kept her. She was a nice cat.

"I can teach you," Wendy told me. She smiled big again. The gap between her teeth was funny looking, but one of her grown-up teeth was coming in on the right. It was a little, white stub. She would be even prettier when she had all her teeth. "If you want."

"You won't be able to help me," I said. My voice was sad. I wished I could be quiet, but I couldn't. It was like she was using her cootie magic on me to make me talk.

"I can try. But only if you want." She looked down at her book. "Maybe I'll be a teacher one day. My dad says I should be."

"You're too pretty and nice. You shouldn't be a teacher." My mouth was out of control. I felt my cheeks turning red. It was true though. There were no pretty or nice teachers at our school. They were all mean, grumpy, and old.

Her cheeks turned pink. "That's a nice thing to say." She looked around to check that the teacher was on the other side of the classroom. "I don't really want to be a teacher, you know. I wanna' be a princess."

I nodded. That made way more sense. She looked much more like a princess than a teacher. I wasn't sure how someone got a job as a princess, but I bet Wendy could do it. She was so pretty. Just like the Christmas doll.

"Do you really not want my help with the letters?" Wendy asked, looking back at her book. Her smile was gone. "It took me a real long time to learn, too. That's why I'm a giraffe and not a lion. Maybe if I help you learn, Mrs. Thompson will like us, and we can both at least be zebras."

I worried that she would think I didn't like her if I said no, even though I didn't think I could learn. I'd never be a zebra. I knew I was gonna' be a giraffe all year, for the second time. "You don't have to help me," I told her. "But you can if you want."

She smiled like she'd won a prize. I felt like I'd won something too.

Ten years later...

The good thing about living in a junkyard is that when you need a part for your car, you don't have to drive to the junkyard. You can just walk out the door into your regular yard. Which happens to be full of junk.

Woof! Woof! Woof!

The other good thing about living in a junkyard is the company. Most of it walks on four legs and not two. Butch —possibly the world's most terrifying-looking-but-ulti-mately-harmless pit bull—gazed up at me adoringly from his one intact eye. Butch was followed by his cowardly brother, Spike, and ancient mother, Snoopy, along with Mario and Luigi, a pair of grizzled tortoise shell cats. The cats had somehow convinced themselves they were also junkyard pit bulls and were living their best life protecting it. I'd arranged for a friend to take care of my little pack, but I'd miss them dearly. They were all the family I had left.

"Hey guys, wanna' help me find a new solenoid? It's the last thing I need. Y'all wanna' go on one last adventure with me?"

The dogs drooled and wagged their tails excitedly. The cats slow blinked, purred, and twined around my ankles. I interpreted all that as an enthusiastic yes.

"Great! Come on then." I started off toward a recently wrecked SUV.

"Can I tag along too? Or do you not even want to say goodbye?" The voice behind me was soft and feminine. It was also full of pain.

Shit.

Wendy was wearing her red and white cheerleading outfit. She was the head cheerleader this year and ought to be at practice. Apparently, my plan to slink off before she knew about it hadn't worked. I'd always been so transparent to her.

"Wendy, I—"

"You were really going to sneak off without saying anything else to me, weren't you?" Her big, blue eyes started to fill up with tears. One escaped down her pale cheek. It physically hurt me to see her cry. I'd been in many much less painful fistfights.

I didn't know what to say. Before I could even come up with something, I was reaching for her helplessly. She melted against me, her soft curves and skimpy clothing setting my heart racing. I loved that goddamn cheerleading uniform. I especially loved putting her on all fours, peeling that tiny skirt up and then...

"Wendy, I've got to go," I whispered into her soft, sweet smelling hair. Her hairspray had glitter in it. It was going to be all over my face and chest, but I didn't care.

"Don't leave me. Please Jason. Don't go." She held onto my shoulders like her heart was breaking. I'd never hated myself more than I did at that moment. Which was really saying something because I had self-loathing to spare.

We'd been around and around on this in the past few months. The truth was that this was the best thing for us both. I was twenty years old and already a failure of a human being. Wendy was seventeen and full of hope and potential.

My life was going nowhere. I couldn't find a job in this godforsaken town. I was a borderline illiterate high school dropout with no skills and a questionable work ethic. I spent an enormous amount of time smoking pot and playing the guitar, which was resulting in me getting pretty good at the guitar, but also a reputation for being a useless drug addicted freak. Even the McDonald's and the Walmart told me fuck off. Unless I wanted to live the rest of my life here in the junkyard, I had to go.

Wendy needed me gone, too. She had a future that looked a lot better when I wasn't in it. Wendy was a Paxton, part of the richest and most respected family in town. If our town had royalty, it would be the Paxton family. Her family wanted her to go to college and make something of herself. They hated me with a fiery passion, but they had grudgingly tolerated me while Wendy was in high school. Now that she was going to graduate, they'd begun to make their disapproval more apparent. I knew they were right to hate me. Wendy deserved so much more than me.

"We can go together," Wendy pleaded. "I'll go with you tonight. We can run away forever if that's what you want."

I'd never understood what she saw in me. From the moment we met, Wendy had acted like I was worthy of her attention and affection. It wasn't just me that was baffled by it, either. The whole town expressed disbelief and confusion (politely to her and rudely to me, naturally). Wendy was popular, beautiful, kind, and lovely. I was stupid, poor, and lazy. I wasn't even athletic in the traditional sense. The only reason I had any muscles at all was because I did a lot of lifting of heavy shit in the junkyard and a lot of running away from the local cops.

"You have to stay here," I told her. "You have to graduate from high school, go to college, and have a good, normal life. A real life. You know I can't give you what you deserve."

"I don't want what I deserve," Wendy insisted. "*I want better than that*. I want you."

She didn't know how ridiculous that statement even was. In the movies, the guy from the wrong side of the tracks and the rich girl from the nice family can get together and live happily ever after. But this wasn't a feel-good movie. This was my shitty life. I had to leave Wendy behind for her own good before I rubbed off on her any more than I already had.

I'd already thoroughly corrupted her. I'd had my hand up her skirt since she was fourteen, sixty-nine'd with her at fifteen, fucked her pussy at sixteen, fucked her ass at seventeen, and gotten her drunk and high about a thousand times. We'd fucked every way I could come up with (and I was surprisingly creative and tremendously depraved). But the final straw, the thing that made me finally wake up, was that I'd nearly gotten her pregnant.

The condom broke during one of our more aerobic sessions and we'd both spent the next three weeks terrified out of our minds. I'd never been so happy for Wendy to get her goddamn period. It ended up being nothing, but for the first time in my life, I realized that being with me could have real consequences for Wendy. Bad consequences. Consequences that could wreck her life forever.

If Wendy had my baby, she'd be stuck with me for life. Her family, who clung to the belief she was a virtuous little virgin, would disown her. The town would shun her. She'd end up dropping out of school, marrying me, living in the junkyard, working some horrible, minimum wage job, and raising the next generation of failure on welfare. I couldn't let that happen to her. I wouldn't let that happen to her.

She was also just too damn delicate to survive a life of poverty. Wendy had been born with dangerous allergies. Peanuts and penicillin were the two that were the two worst, but she also had sensitivities to cats, wool, pollen, dust, and a thousand other daily things. She'd been to the hospital dozens of times in her life. Without good, consistent medical care and a controlled, clean environment—things I'd never be able to afford for her—she could literally die.

I had to go.

"I'm sorry Wendy," I told her. "I wish I could stay."

For once in my life, I was going to do the right thing. I was going to get the hell out of her way before she got stuck with me (and/or my hell spawn) forever. It was out of character, but I thought I could do it. After all these years, maybe the tiniest sliver of Wendy's goodness had finally rubbed off on me.

"Once you go, you'll forget about me." Wendy's voice sounded hopeless, but she had never been more wrong. She was burned into every cell of my body. Her name was literally burned, well inked actually, into my left bicep forever.

Wendy had been my first and only love. My only friend. She was only girl I'd ever kissed, touched, or loved. We lost our virginity to each other and the thought of ever sharing sex with someone else felt cheap and pointless by comparison. I didn't even see other women. It was like they didn't exist. The idea that I could ever forget her was ridiculous.

"I'm hoping you forget about me," I told her.

"Why would you hope something so awful?"

"It's for your own good."

"I think you need to stop pretending that you're doing

this for me." The uncharacteristic bitterness in her voice made my blood run cold.

Wendy pulled away from me. Her blue eyes had hardened the way they sometimes did when she was really angry. It took a lot to make Wendy mad. She was the kindest, most generous, and most empathetic person I knew. But even her patience and understanding had limits. I'd run afoul of them plenty of times over the years, like when I dropped out of school, or refused to take the GED test. This time, however, her anger had reached a completely different level.

I needed to convince her that me leaving was a positive thing. I'd failed to persuade her that it was in her interest, even though that was true. That left me with only my selfishness. I could use that.

"You're right Wendy." I tried to match her bitter tone. "I want to go. I hate this town. I hate the racist, judgmental, holier-than-thou people here. I hate the ignorant, backward assholes that look down on anything even remotely different. I hate that nothing here ever changes. It doesn't get better or worse. It just stays the same, generation after generation. My family has lived right here on these ten acres of trash for a hundred years. An entire fucking century of poverty. I have to get out."

The truth was more complicated than just that, but Lord knows I wasn't a complicated guy. I wasn't smart enough for all that. I'd just make it simple, instead. And in doing so, I'd convince Wendy she wanted me gone.

Wendy blinked. "I knew this wasn't all about me."

It was at least ninety-nine percent about her but if the one percent was what would convince her...

"Why would I want to stay, Wendy? I can never belong here. You've got options, but I don't. All I have is this." I waved a hand at the sprawling junkyard around us: ten acres of twisted metal, bloodied carpet, and broken glass. Behind us stood the peeling white shotgun shack my mom raised me in.

Mom had died a year earlier when her liver finally gave out. She wasn't eligible for a transplant because she wouldn't quit drinking long enough to even go to the doctor. She said that liquor was cheaper than chemo and it didn't hurt as much. I didn't blame her anymore—not for her addiction, and not for giving up completely when she learned about the cancer. Life had dealt her one blow too many. She was barely fifty years old.

My mom was my last living relative, aside from a much older half-sister my mom had given up for adoption well before I was even a thought. She lived in Kansas and pretended like we didn't exist. I couldn't blame her for that either. I wouldn't want to be related to me if I could help it. My grandma died when I was twelve. My dad might actually still be alive, but I didn't count him as kin. That neglectful, violent asshole could burn in hell as soon as the meth finally killed him. I didn't care if he was still breathing; Satan would get him soon enough. Personally, I couldn't wait.

"You've got me," Wendy sniffled, bringing me back to the conversation. "We can go together."

"You know that wouldn't work. I'm not good enough for you. Look at where you are. This is where I'm from." I'd never understood why she wasn't repulsed by me, though, up until that moment, I'd been grateful for it.

"It doesn't have to be this way," she told me. "I don't care about where you're from. I only care about where you're going."

There was no way to salvage the conversation. I turned away. "I'm sorry Wendy. My mind is made up."

Find out what happens when jaded rock star Jason and sweet small town girl Wendy find each other again at the Lone Star Lounge!

HOW TO GET YOUR FREE EXTENDED EPILOGUES!

IF YOU'RE LOOKING for more **free** bonus content, including exclusive extended epilogues and check-ins with your favorite characters go to www.taylorholloway.com/email.html to sign up for My Mailing List! If you're already a subscriber check the last newsletter you received, the link is always at the bottom of the email.

XOXO
Taylor

ALSO BY TAYLOR HOLLOWAY

FOR FANS OF EXCITING, ROMANTIC MYSTERIES FULL OF TWISTS AND TURNS, CHECK OUT MY SCIONS OF SIN SERIES!